HAPPY HOUR MURDERS

FREDERICK WYSOCKI

ISBN: 978-0-9913756-1-5

This book is dedicated to Denise Wysocki

*Novels by **Frederick Wysocki***

***The Start-up**: A Frank Moretti Thriller (2014)*
***A Timely Revenge**: An Anthony Rizzo Novel (2014)*
***Blood Rivals**: A Frank Moretti Thriller (2015)*
***No Time For Fools**: A Frank Moretti Thriller (2015)*
***The Arabian Client:** A Naomi Dolphin Thriller (2016)*
***The Reluctant Spy:** A Frank Moretti Thriller (2017)*
***Happy Hour Murders** (2017)*

*If you would like to be informed about forthcoming books by Frederick Wysocki, please visit his web site at **www.frederick-wysocki.com/contact***

1

MONDAY - GLENWOOD, ARIZONA

W*hat's that?*

Salvatore Cabella slid his right hand under his pillow and cradled the grip of his sleeping companion.

It's there.

Lying still, all he could hear was the lazy swoosh of the ceiling fan.

As he felt himself drifting back into the fog of sleep he loosened the grip on his Ruger.

Moments later he heard it again.

It sounds like a cop car.

This time he willed his eyes open.

Salvatore whipped the Ruger into the air, finger poised next to the trigger.

In one swift motion with his left hand, Salvatore threw off his bed sheet and swung his feet to the floor.

No carpet, just large ceramic tiles and they were cold in the morning. He ignored the sensation and closed his eyes to focus on what exactly had woken him.

The noise increased in volume.

It's some kind of weird electronic thing.

His grey cells kicked in as the last of the sleep evaporated from his brain.

It must be those damned coyotes.

He smirked to himself.

They're probably celebrating that they've caught and killed a rabbit.

Exhaling, he lowered his gun hand to his side.

Good for them.

With his left hand, Salvatore rubbed his face and eyes then looked at the bedside clock.

2:38.

What gives me the strength to muster through is knowing the wait will soon be over.

Salvatore dropped into bed and closed his eyes.

He'd just drifted off when he heard a car door slam.

There's no mistaking that sound.

Two more car doors slammed.

Who's coming home at this hour?

He'd opened his bedroom window to take advantage of the cool March nighttime temperatures the Arizona desert offered.

Voices.

Instinctively Salvatore knew they were coming from the empty house next door to him. The one whose floor plan he'd asked about.

They're finally here.

He pried one eye open and peered at the bedside clock.

3:03.

Don't they know the normal bedtime around here is eight o'clock? That's when they roll up the sidewalks.

Salvatore took a deep breath and willed himself out of bed one more time. He liked sleeping butt naked. This time he grabbed his underwear and a golf shirt off the floor.

Semi dressed, he went into his den with its white wood plantation shuttered windows. He knew better than to turn on a light. With care, he put his fingers between the slats of one window's shutters to open it ever so slightly.

He squinted.

It was another clear night in March. This one had an almost full moon. He could see a black full-size SUV and a male moving about in the driveway. He was obviously the driver; his door was wide open.

Each garage in the community had a keypad to open the doors. The driver punched in a code and the garage door opened as a soft light bathed the SUV.

The SUV inched into the garage.

Perhaps they're only empty nester snowbirds coming back for the warmer weather.

Salvatore smirked at his attempt at humor.

The garage door closed dousing the light on the concrete driveway.

Salvatore's eyes moved left as the lights went on throughout his side of the house.

I think Barbara said that something like forty percent of the homes here in the Graceful Waters Resort are owned by snowbirds. They're only here for a few months a year.

Placing his palm flat against the shutter's blades, Salvatore pushed until the blades were flat.

They've arrived right on time.

Treading barefoot back to his bedroom, he dropped his

underwear and pulled off his shirt before he sat on the side of the bed.

He glanced at his night table and saw his recently purchased thriller novel waiting for him. He considered whether he was tired enough to fall asleep or if he should read for a while.

I'm too tired.

I need my beauty sleep, even if it doesn't work.

Salvatore plopped onto the mattress, lifting his feet back under the covers. He put his hand under the ergonomic pillow and carefully placed his weapon back in its nest.

Closing his eyes, he thought about why he was living in the retirement community.

Oops. I almost forgot. They market this as an active adult community for those fifty-five or better.

Or better?

Have to remember that.

His mind wandered.

Barbara said that the property owner was only too happy to have me pay cash up front to rent this two-bedroom house for twelve months... Now that they're here, I'll be gone soon enough.

At 6:30 AM, the alarm clock radio jarred him awake.

Salvatore was still wired from the arrival in the middle of the night.

The people next door are finally here.

The waiting's over but there's no rush. This morning I just need to keep to my normal routine.

Salvatore went into the kitchen and flipped on the coffee maker. It could make ten cups but he limited himself to two. He preferred it hot, strong and black.

As he listened to the water gurgle, then the steam hiss, he recalled how he had arrived on location.

I've been a desert rat on the upper edge of the Sonoran desert of Arizona for almost a month now.

Taking his first sip of coffee, Salvatore shivered remembering the frigid morning in Chicago in February where this trip had started.

2

THREE WEEKS EARLIER

Heading south, he'd imagined having to live out in the middle of nowhere.

His preconceptions were based on the little he could recall from watching a few black and white westerns as a child.

What was that show? Oh ya, Death Valley Days.

But I can't turn around. I've got a job to do.

At a roadside restaurant, he tried to telephone Sonia back on the island of St Kitts.

Still no answer; they have her for sure.

When he'd arrived in Glenwood, Arizona, he'd immediately driven into the Graceful Waters Resort. And he immediately appreciated why people came to spend their winters in the desert.

While Chicago had been cold and white, this place was warm and bright.

Where he'd expected to find an arid empty desert, there were over three thousand newer, one story, upscale houses surrounding an opulent green golf course. Instead of a sand pit, he'd found a lush oasis. Even the boulevard dividers had mowed grass. Tall palm trees gave it a tropical feel.

In an effort to be eco-friendly, the home sites had no grass unless it was artificial. The land around each home was landscaped with trees, cacti and flowering bushes. Various sizes and colors of crushed rock covered the dirt between the plantings.

It's very clean and modern looking.

It didn't take him long to locate the Budget Inn hotel he'd been told to check into.

As promised, he was handed an envelope when he checked in at the front desk.

In the privacy of his room, he unfolded the single sheet of paper and it's cryptic information.

The specifics; now I can focus on the job.

The next day, he returned to the Graceful Waters Resort's gated guardhouse. This time he was given directions to the sales office. As he drove past the large water fountain, golf course and adjoining streams, he saw several For Sale signs. Most of them had a picture of an attractive woman wearing a large brimmed hat. He wrote down the number and telephoned her.

They agreed to meet at the Graceful Waters Resort clubhouse. It was large, modern and impressive.

As he drove up Salvatore saw people playing tennis, pickle ball, bocce and golf. Riding bicycles seemed popular.

Inside the clubhouse, he saw card players along with newspaper readers and coffee drinkers. The clubhouse was busy and had a good vibe about it.

Through the floor to ceiling glass, he could see a huge outdoor pool.

He diverted his attention to the inside.

As he wandered, he found it odd that everyone smiled and nodded to him as he passed by.

I must look like someone that lives in here.

A man walked by and said hello. Not sure what to say, he returned the verbal greeting.

What kind of kool-aid do they drink in here? I'm going to have to switch off my natural wariness to pretend that I belong here.

Then he saw the lady in her wide hat.

It turned out that his real estate agent, Barbara Goldberg, specialized in the active adult community.

He commented on the hat she was wearing.

"Oh, it's my trademark, Mister Cabella."

"Please call me Salvatore. You look very nice in a hat."

I've worn hats a few times myself, but always as a part of a disguise.

Once he started his house hunt with Barbara, he noticed she also liked to wear cute sundresses that displayed her still shapely legs. He kept that observation to himself.

I don't want her to think I'm hitting on her.

On the first day, she'd shown him the developer's newer homes in a model home park while waxing on about the modern wonders of solar energy and electronic locks. "You can control your house's energy usage and security right from your iPhone, can you believe it?"

"I don't have an iPhone, just a basic cell phone."

Salvatore explained his needs. "The new model homes are great but they aren't what I'm looking for just yet. I'm moving here from Chicago and before I purchase, I want to rent for a year. I want to make sure I like it in here and that it's a good fit for me."

With as much sincerity as she could muster, Barbara went

along with his wish. "If you're not sure about a community, then renting may be a smart thing to do. That way you'll find out how wonderful it is here and when you're ready, I'll be able to show you everything on the market."

He could sense her disappointment.

Barbara really wants to sell me something.

"Perfect, now are there any rentals available on the golf course? Maybe on one of the later holes so I won't get hit with golfers going by too early in the morning."

"Are you an avid golfer, Salvatore?"

"No, I'm just used to looking at green grass and trees. Mind you, at this time of year they're all covered with snow back home in Chicago."

"You'll fit right in as we have many mid westerners here." Barbara plastered a grin on her face as bright as the sunflowers on her dress.

"I have several golf course homes to show you but I wouldn't be doing my job if I didn't tell you that we're expecting the market to rise very soon and by tying yourself into a long term lease you could end up paying much more in a years time. Perhaps you should consider going with a shorter two or three month rental."

"Please just show me what's available today, on the golf course and for a longer term rental."

"As you wish."

As they toured, Salvatore paid close attention to each home's floor plan and made sketches in a small black notebook.

Barbara was continually trying to qualify and bond with him. "Will your wife be moving here as well?"

Salvatore grinned at her. "I'm not married."

"When would you like to take possession and move in?"

"Immediately."

When she'd shown him the Spanish style home with two bedrooms and a den on the sixteenth hole of the golf course and how quiet the street was, he'd immediately said he was interested. "I like this floor plan. Now, you said the one next door is also empty."

"But I'm afraid that it's not available to rent or buy."

"I understand, but how is it different from this floor plan?"

"Although the street side elevation may appear different, it's basically the same in the front half of the house. The difference is in the rear. In particular, this one is available for rent and has a covered patio area that extends across the entire width of the house. The one next door does not."

"So with this one, if I want to go outside and have a cigar without getting in the sun or the rain, I can."

Barbara had hesitated but only for a heartbeat. "Basically, yes. The lease however does forbid smoking of any kind indoors."

"I fully understand that. And I'll take it."

Barbara seemed surprised. "Great... Let's go to my office and I'll write it up for you."

Once he'd signed the offer and paid in cash for one year's rent up front, Barbara finally asked him why he was moving.

"I'm a former librarian turned author of a crime thriller. I'm looking for a little peace and quiet while I write my next novel."

"Then you'll love it here."

Salvatore Cabella was on track and feeling confident. Within three days, he'd found and closed on the exact long-term home rental he'd been told to rent.

He checked out of the Budget Inn and moved into the Graceful Waters Resort.

It turned out that his real estate agent lived on the same

street and just two doors away from him. Barbara also made it plain to Salvatore that she was a lonely widow.

To his pleasant surprise, the one level home came completely furnished and even included the plates, glasses and silverware. "All you'll need to do is unpack your suitcases."

"Perfect."

The home was furnished as a rental. All the furniture was faux leather and veneer covered particleboard. *Since I won't be here long, this'll work.*

In fact, a large faded green duffel bag was all he'd brought with him.

For his role as Salvatore, his needs were basic. His character had no pretensions, and he was counting on not spending much time in Arizona.

3

MONDAY

A t 7AM Salvatore walked to his sliding patio door and stepped outside. Straight ahead of him was the empty sixteenth fairway.

Mondays seemed to be the quietest day of the week. Seeing no one yet playing on the course or any maintenance men grooming it, he looked up at the horizon.

The scattered morning clouds were allowing a glorious sunrise.

I hope they haven't hurt Sonia.

She must be scared out of her mind.

Salvatore turned to see that Marvin and Joan's kitchen lights were on.

Marvin's up early again, I hope Joan's feeling better.

Glancing to his right again, he couldn't see any signs of life in the house next to him.

Salvatore looked more closely at Marvin and Joan's house. They were sitting quietly on their patio, coffee cups on the table.

Once again, he flashed back to when he'd arrived.

* * *

On his first evening as a resident, Barbara had invited him to her house for a welcome to the neighborhood dinner. "Come on over. After moving in you won't want to cook."

"You don't have to do that, Barbara."

I don't have much to move.

"Don't be silly, Mister Cabella."

"Please call me Salvatore."

"Certainly. If you don't mind me asking, do you ever go by Sal?"

"No."

"Well, good to know that. Now I'm inviting a neighboring couple over that you should meet as well. In fact, Marvin and Joan Haigh live right next to you."

Salvatore frowned. "I thought you said the house next to me was empty."

"It is. The house between you and I is empty. Marvin and Joan live on the other side of you."

"Great, then I'd like to meet them."

If I don't try to blend in, this could be a disaster.

The dinner turned out to be a simple and casual affair. The company was delightful and helped Salvatore feel welcome.

The topics of conversation were all vanilla. There were no prying questions about what work he used to do or why he wasn't married.

Why are they avoiding asking me all the personal questions I'd ask them?

Within two days, Salvatore had gotten to know his next-door neighbors Marvin and Joan even better.

4

S alvatore returned to the present moment.

Marvin's waving me over.

Salvatore touched his nose to make sure he was wearing his black-rimmed glasses. He left his coffee cup on his own outdoor table.

Only then did he carefully crunch his way across the gravel that connected both lots. Marvin had already explained that rattlesnakes liked to hunt their prey by hiding near the cacti and shrubs.

He saw Joan go inside.

"Good morning. Have a seat."

Joan was so white and frail that Salvatore was tempted to ask Marvin if she had a serious illness. Instead, he asked Marvin how they liked living on the golf course.

Suddenly, Marvin pointed out to the fairway.

Salvatore was surprised by what he saw. "What in hell are those things?"

"Those Salvatore, are Javelina."

They seemed to come in three sizes: adults, young ones and in-betweens. Salvatore was amazed as he counted the herd of twelve.

Coming up behind the Javelina were two maintenance men in a motorized green fairway maintenance cart. The men were frantically waving their arms and honking the cart's horn. They were obviously trying to chase the creatures off the golf course before any golfers became frightened or were attacked.

The Javelina found an unfenced yard and used it to access the desert.

The men pumped their fists in the air then drove away down the cement cart path.

Marvin said, "Okay, we're safe."

"Those were ugly creatures but they kinda looked like boars."

"They do but boars are part of the pig family while I think Javelina aren't. Someone once told me that they were a giant rodent but I don't think that's true either."

"If they're rodents, then those were some giant rats."

"Here we go." Joan placed a fresh pot of coffee on the table and an empty mug in front of Salvatore. "Oh, I forgot the milk."

Joan walked back inside.

Marvin spoke softly. "I'll let you in on a secret. Whenever Joan walks in a room and comes close to me, my heart does a little zing. You understand what I'm saying. That's not to say she can't be a giant pain in my tuchus, but she does make my life worth living."

God, how I wish I could feel like that some day.

"May I?" Salvatore pointed at the coffee cup.

"Absolutely."

Salvatore poured himself a half-cup then took a big swig of the fresh coffee.

Marvin told him more about the local wildlife. "The coyotes are a bother at night but otherwise they leave people alone. But don't let a cat or small dog out alone. Between the coyotes, bobcats and occasional mountain lion, they won't last a month before they're eaten."

"What about the Javelina?"

"They have nasty razor sharp teeth. If you're out walking at night when you see them, turn and walk away. They'll leave you alone. They will however rip out and eat your agave plants."

"I have agave plants?"

Marvin grinned. "Yes, they're the blue spiky ones in your front yard."

Salvatore asked, "Isn't tequila made out of agave?"

"It is, so make sure they don't eat yours."

So far, they haven't.

Salvatore realized it was time to get back to his own house, so he stood up.

"Thank you for the coffee and the entertainment but I really should get going."

"Any time, Salvatore."

As his feet crunched on the gravel, Salvatore considered the newly arrived people next door.

I wish I could verify that it's four adults.

He made it safely onto his own brick patio.

Salvatore went into his duffel and retrieved his cleaning kit. He placed a terry cloth, a bore snake and 22-caliber brush along with cans of gun cleaning solvent and gun oil that he'd bought at Walmart on the table in front of him. He also grabbed q-tips from his toiletry bag.

First, he made sure the magazine was empty and that nothing was chambered.

Safety first.

He pulled down on the lever and slid off the barrel casing. He wiped off everything although it didn't need it. *I already cleaned it on the fourth day I was here for something to do. Oh well.* Salvatore sprayed the powder blast into the barrel and elsewhere to let it soak in. Then he wiped off the excess.

The feed ramp was gunk free so he wiped the hammer then the front of the barrel.

He dropped some Powder Blast on the bore snake then did a couple of passes. Then he repeatedly fed the 22-caliber brush through the barrel and made sure it was shiny inside *It isn't the most accurate weapon but it's fun to shoot.*

Salvatore wiped down the slide rails. He then sprayed the rails with the Powder Blast.

If it's not clean, it can misfire and I'd be screwed.

Then he used the oil on the slide, trigger assembly and hammer spring before reassembling it.

I'm ready.

5

On the remote chance someone unexpected should visit him during the daytime, Salvatore liked keeping his Ruger in a small hall table that stood beside the front door. It had three decent sized drawers.

As he placed it inside the middle drawer, he decided to shower.

Stopping in front of the master bedroom mirror, he looked at himself. Salvatore made sure his hair was parted on the right side and his relatively new goatee was the correct length.

Satisfied, he picked up his phony black-framed glasses. He'd copied the real Salvatore's look by wrapping a piece of white medical tape around the left arm of the glasses.

The arms were a little loose.

Next time I get a chance I'll stop in and get them tightened up.

He turned on the television news just to have it on in the background.

Salvatore turned up the sound. The local weather girl was speaking. "It's that time of year folks. Today, it'll be beautiful again as it'll be in the mid eighties and it'll stay that way for at least the next two weeks."

If it always stayed like it is now, I might even move here.

"It's also that time of year folks when dust and pollen counts are both high. Over to you Heidi."

He chuckled as the good looking and well-endowed traffic gal was warning commuters about several accidents on the freeways.

I've already done my commute today.

I really should be going outside to enjoy this glorious weather. Back in Chicago, it's still winter. Everyone there's on their third head cold by now.

He poured himself another partial cup of coffee.

I'm addicted, what can I say?

Savoring it, he thought about how he loved that everyone in the Graceful Waters Resort community said they were here to enjoy their last few years in the best way possible.

Who you used to be, what you used to do and how much money you used to make or had, is inconsequential.

Barbara had been advising Salvatore to attend a 10 AM newcomer's Coffee Talk at the clubhouse.

"I don't know, Barbara."

"It's just a simple introduction and orientation to the community. It'll be harmless and it'll help you fit in."

It was Monday and he had nothing else to do so he decided to go so she'd stop bringing it up.

Salvatore wasn't sure what to expect.

The clubhouse was busy with about fifty people gathered in the rotunda.

At first, he stood on the outside of the ring, next to a pillar.

If it's too boring, I'll slip away.

Two grinning people in their thirties were already up front. They were wearing golf shirts with Graceful Waters Resort logos.

The first one to talk was an energetic chap named Tom. He started by highlighting what they would hear at the Coffee Talk. "Here in Graceful Waters Resort we are about much more than offering you the nicest real estate. We also provide you with more than activities and amenities. Our goal is to equip each of you with a feeling of being in Heaven on Earth where social interactions and cultural life are like you've died and gone to Heaven."

Really?

The crowd applauded and someone even whistled.

I can't wait to get out of here.

Tom then told the assembled about several trips that would be taking place over the next several months. "If you're interested in joining us on one of them, please register with the front desk. By the way if you are interested in the bus trip to Los Algodones, Mexico, for drugs or cheap dentistry it's almost sold out, so hurry."

Tom turned to introduce the next speaker.

"Hi, I'm Tiffany."

A perky female waved at the crowd then spoke about special events. "If you want to join in any of the special dinners, dances or performances we'll be bringing to the club over the next few weeks, please buy your tickets at the front desk. Space is limited so please act quickly."

Tiffany paused for a moment. "In case you don't know, we also have a medical doctor who is also a naturopath on staff to help you with health needs. Appointments can be made through the spa desk."

The crowd applauded.

He felt a tap on his arm.

6

A petite young blonde-haired woman who was also wearing one of the club's logoed golf shirts was looking up at him. "Are you new here?"

He nodded.

"Then welcome; why don't you come up front and stand next to me?"

Salvatore knew better than to volunteer for anything.

However, she's cute.

Salvatore followed her to the front of the crowd.

He pushed up his glasses as if to calm his nerves.

She addressed the Coffee Talk group. "Hi, my name is Tina. Let me welcome all of you to the Graceful Waters Resort. I'm a Life Coach here."

A grinning Tina scanned the attendees to see how everyone was responding. "You're probably asking yourself; what does a Life Coach do and how can she help me?"

Salvatore watched most of the crowd nod their heads.

"Well, I help newcomers like each of you to enter into an enhanced awareness of yourself and our community. If I do my job right, your new perception will serve as a gateway leading to the achievement of greater fulfillment in your life."

Say what?

Tina paused and looked over her crowd. "Now I'd like each of you to please try this. Close your eyes. Now inhale deeply. Focus on the sensations within your nostrils. As you shift your energy, you will shift your reality."

What in hell is she talking about?

"Please keep your eyes closed. Your Graceful Waters Resort community believes in helping everyone break down barriers to help you in your pursuit of making new friends. Today, I hope to make it easier for each of you. Now will everyone please take another deep breath?"

He tentatively followed along.

Tina looked at Salvatore. "Now turn your lips into a half-smile."

Salvatore smirked in embarrassment.

"Now softly gaze at the people next to you… On your left… now turn to your right… Notice your thoughts and feelings as you consider them… Now imagine they are your very dearest and best friends."

Salvatore followed her directions and found each person was smiling back at him. His instinct was to recoil at the attention. He looked downward to avoid eye contact. But the beaming smiles began to draw him in.

Who are these people?

Within seconds his natural veneer began to melt away and he found the experience…actually… rewarding.

"As you go on your way today, always wear a smile. Try

being the first one to break the ice and to introduce yourself as you meet new people."

Everyone applauded.

Is the secret to living a happier life really this simple?

"Now I must tell you that if you want to experience more personal growth I am available for individual training. You can sign up in the Spa. Also Graceful Waters Resort boasts over fifty charter clubs run by our members. As you discover that your fellow residents are participating in groups or clubs that you might be interested in, just join in the fun. You have nothing to lose. If it turns out not to be for you, you can always stop going. The important thing is that the more you join in, the more good friends you'll make and the happier you'll be."

Salvatore was surprised with himself.

I'm going to give this lesson a try.

He hesitated, then even joined in the applause.

I'm still not even sure about the gateway part of what she was talking about.

Tina turned to him. "Thank you for joining me upfront today."

Salvatore nodded as he stepped away.

A stranger spoke to him as if he were a long lost friend. "When you realize you've got more road behind you than in front of you, you try to enjoy what's left."

Salvatore smiled and nodded his head as if he were in full agreement.

With a fresh outlook and new way to fit in, Salvatore walked home thinking positive thoughts.

The sunshine in Arizona does seem brighter than any I've ever experienced. It's appropriate. The way people in here deal with each other is refreshing.

It really does make me think of each stranger as a friend. Now that I know the secret, if I practice it, I might be able to change who I am.

Salvatore spotted yet another For Sale sign with Barbara's face and hat on it. He guessed Barbara was selling quite a few homes.

He unlocked his front door and checked on his Ruger.

It's there.

Since he'd arrived, Salvatore had used most of his waking hours to reflect on his past life, what he was about to do and what he wanted to do after the task was completed.

Salvatore stepped onto his rear patio. He glanced next-door hoping to catch some activity at the new neighbors.

That's when he saw something furry out of the corner of his eye.

It's probably a coyote.

He slowly turned his head to see a black cat with white paws.

What is it doing here?

"Meow."

The cat came over to Salvatore and rubbed against his leg. It purred, so Salvatore bent over and scratched the cat's neck.

Damn, it must be hungry. I wonder if it belongs to the new neighbors?

I hate the idea of having a pet. They require constant attention. Caring for one could mean I'd lose my edge. I should send it on its way.

"Shoo kitty, go home."

He shook his head and changed thoughts. Touching the glasses, he went back to being Salvatore Cabella.

They kept slipping every time he looked downwards.

Feeling bad for shooing it away, he went back inside the house.

I'll have to buy a small thing of milk just in case the cat comes back tomorrow... What am I thinking? A coyote will probably have killed it by then.

7

E veryday since moving in, Salvatore explored his immediate neighborhood by going on long brisk walks. When he walked to the clubhouse and back he timed and mentally recorded the results.

At first, I thought it was weird that every time I went out for a walk, everyone I passed looked me in the eyes and said hello.

But after attending that Coffee Talk today, I think I understand.

In the normal world, in regular neighborhoods, everyone goes to work, comes home, watches television and then goes to sleep. No one gets to really know their neighbors or even wants to. It's as if they'd be mentally uncomfortable doing so.

If I said good morning to a neighbor or a stranger in Chicago, they'd call the cops or shoot me. They'd say I was invading their privacy or personal space.

He glanced at his watch.

It read 2:35

He saw Marvin sitting outside so he stepped out onto his

patio and waved at him. Salvatore enjoyed having a genuine friend next door.

Marvin smiled and waved him over. "Come and have a seat."

"I went to a Coffee Talk today."

"How did you find it?"

"I'm not sure. People seem too willing to be nice to each other."

"Relax, Salvatore. People here are very friendly. They've raised their kids and paid their dues. Now they're just looking to have a little fun."

Salvatore nodded as if he understood.

"As you get older you'll discover that having friends you can spend your last years with is far more important than any hobby, interest or sport."

Salvatore then asked, "What about family?"

"Ours live in San Francisco and we live here." Marvin had lost his smile.

"I don't mean to pry but I would think people in their golden years might want to be closer to their families."

Marvin hesitated then spoke. "Our children are grown with kids of their own. If the grandkids want to talk to us, all they have to do is use Facetime or message us... But of course they're too busy playing with their friends. Our kids have their own problems and don't want to hear Grandma and Grandpa complaining about their aches and pains. Out of sight, out of mind."

Salvatore grinned as if he understood. "Ah."

Other than Sonia, I have no one to give a shit about me.

Marvin made a small waving motion with his right hand. "Everyone here is from someplace else. We're all here to make the best of our golden years. So of course, everyone goes out of their way to make friends. And that means no one here is too nosy."

I like the last part.

"I find that very interesting."

"Everyone is welcomed with open arms."

"No matter their pasts?" Salvatore was incredulous.

"All that matters to most of us is associating with people who are pleasant to be with. For me anyway, retirement is a time to get ones affairs in order, make peace with your Maker and settle ones debts."

That suited Salvatore just fine.

Soon I'll settle my debts once and for all.

Marvin winced as he tried to move his leg.

Salvatore couldn't help but notice. "Arthritis?"

"If you spend an evening listening to our fellow residents, you'll hear about bypass surgeries, hip replacements, new knees, arthritis, hearing aides and cataract surgery just to name a few."

Marvin adjusted himself then continued. "Most of us are half bionic. We take dozens of different medications that make us dizzy, winded, and subject to blackouts. Then we wonder why we have bouts with dementia. But, thank goodness, we all still have our driver's licenses."

Salvatore had to chuckle. "Are you saying it isn't safe to be on the streets in here?"

Marvin joined the laughter. "Once you've survived living in here for a couple of years, ask me that again."

Salvatore couldn't help but crack a grin. "I understand. So, why did you move here Marvin?"

"It's a long story."

"I've got the time."

"I was only 73 at the time." Marvin took a deep breath then

confided in Salvatore. "I went out for a walk and collapsed on the sidewalk near my home. Everything changed. I didn't want to go out of the house anymore."

"Where did you live Marvin?"

"At the time we were in San Francisco. But the streets are hilly, crowded and the housing has too many stairs with no elevators. That's why I found it easier just to stay inside. My son told us about this place. We came for a visit and never went back. I'm not afraid to go outside here."

"What about the summers?"

"They aren't too bad. In California when it heats up the humidity can kill you. Here there's no humidity." Marvin grinned. "When it heats up here we make sure we drink lots of water and stay in the shade. Besides the dry heat helps to ease the aches and pains"

"Iced tea anyone?"

Joan placed a tray with three glasses of iced tea on the table and sat down to enter the conversation. "About the same time as Marvin fell back in San Francisco, I lost most of my hearing which is why I wear a hearing aid now. We both felt lonely there even though we had each other and our little family there."

She obviously over heard what we've said.

Marvin patted his wife's frail hand. "Loneliness is common among senior citizens. We're lucky to have each other."

Salvatore grinned then nodded as if he understood.

"The usual social connections we had when we were younger ended up changing as we grew older," Joan said.

"Ya, most of them died off." Marvin said dryly. "Let me share a secret with you Salvatore. The older you get, the more you realize you have no desire for drama or conflict. You just want to be surrounded by people who don't piss you off."

Ain't that the truth.

"Is that even possible?"

Marvin chuckled. "That's a great question. All I can tell you is that I tell everyone not to talk to me, or email me about religion or politics."

"That's a great idea. I'll do the same. I must admit that at my first happy hour, I was approached by a lady with large green eyes who asked me if I wanted to join her bible study group."

"What'd you say?"

"I told her it wasn't my thing and walked away."

"There you go. Although I must admit, I have many friends in here who are devout… Now let me tell you a well-known fact around here. Happy hour is rumor central."

"How's that?"

"If I were to tell someone something juicy, like two guys were having a verbal argument over at the bocce courts, by the end of the evening someone will ask me if I heard about how two guys pushed each other then got in a fistfight. By next week's happy hour it'll have turned out that one of them was murdered with a bocce ball by the other guy."

I love Marvin's sense of humor.

"I'll definitely watch what I say then."

Marvin paused then asked, "Say Salvatore, do you smoke the occasional cigar?"

"Why do you ask?"

"I've smelled and seen you sneaking one out on your back patio."

"Guilty as charged."

"The reason I ask is that we have a great cigar club that meets on Wednesday afternoons to enjoy a smoke and shoot the shit."

"What happens there?"

"We sit around and solve the world's problems. However, I should warn you that the boys are overwhelmingly Republican, so if you're a Democrat, I'd keep your opinions to yourself. If you want, we can go together this Wednesday."

"Sure. I'll go with you. What time do you want to walk over?"

"On Wednesday afternoon. I'll knock on your door at quarter to two. How's that?"

"I'll be ready and waiting."

8

TUESDAY

I t's been over twenty-four hours and there's still no sign of whoever who moved in next door.

With his last sip of morning coffee, Salvatore proceeded to the shuttered side window in the front of his house.

Using the center bar, he fully opened the shutter's blades so he could see out.

The SUV must still be in the garage.

Don't see any movement. I'll keep my shutters open just in case someone goes outside.

With everyone being so friendly here, I'm sure they'll wave at me.

Salvatore chuckled at his private joke.

I need to fit in here just a while longer.

I've lived most of my adult life without many social connections. I've had to be like a turtle that withdraws into its shell to avoid anyone's questions.

Meeting Sonia changed all that.

Pushing a chair so he could look out the window without being seen, Salvatore settled in. He was trying to use his time in the retirement community to his advantage. He reflected.

Sonia's my soul mate. We click.

Sonia fills my needs for intimacy and meaningful conversation.

His mind stayed on the woman he'd left behind on St Kitts, Sonia.

The smooth oval of her face, her warm embrace; the brightly colored dress she had been wearing the last time I saw her. She's the color and warmth of the Caribbean.

At first Sonia had been only a friend with benefits, but he had grown fond of her passion and her love of living each day to the fullest.

Not since he'd lost his long dead wife had he felt such a bond with a woman.

If his thugs have harmed a single hair on her head, I'll kill them all.

In his prior life, he'd thrown himself into his work and had denied himself any extended personal time or steady companionship. He felt married to his job the way a priest was married to the church.

If his employer had sought companionship, he would usually pay for someone else to service him as well.

He'd never made the mistake of having a casual or purchased encounter while on an assignment.

Sonia started out as a one-night stand and slowly became more of a casual relationship.

I wasn't on assignment.

At first, Sonia offered only the necessity of sexual release. After all, he was a healthy male and every shapely body that responded with a willing smile was fair game.

He knew that Sonia, like most women, was emotional. As a man he avoided dealing with emotions whenever possible. *Sonia has many positives going for her. She has no children and other than a brother, doesn't have a close family.* He had explained to her that he worked for the man in the large estate on the cliff overlooking the sea.

"I can't discuss anything about what I do for him."

In addition, he'd told her how his time wasn't his own; he was always on call.

"Look, I'm trying to retire. Until I do, I can't spend as much time with you as I'd like."

She hadn't complained the way he thought she would. In fact, he had never met anyone so easy going. It wasn't Sonia's beauty or smile or cooking that had captured his heart; it was her honesty and joy of living.

I know she exaggerates her reggae slang only because I told her that it turned me on. The only reason I'm doing this is for her.

He heard voices.

Bang!

Salvatore went on full alert.

He rushed from window to window searching next door for what had fallen.

It's just a chair.

Someone had knocked over a metal chair on the rear patio.

Whoever did it is already back inside.

It must be the right people.

No one else would be hiding like this.

He spent the rest of the morning watching silently for anyone to step outside for a smoke, a window shade to be raised or for the garage door to open.

By noon, nothing had happened and Salvatore walked over

to the clubhouse where he bought a ham and cheese Panini with an iced tea to go for lunch.

He thought of the cat. "Can I get one of those pints of milk as well?"

At a normal clip, the round trip itself had only taken twelve minutes to walk and he'd spent ten minutes waiting for his order.

Inside he put the milk in the fridge. Then he went onto his own rear patio and went directly to his favorite chair. He moved it to face the new neighbors empty patio.

After finishing his lunch he found the book he was reading.

He half read and half watched for his neighbors to appear. After several hours, he gave up for the day.

"Meow."

Salvatore saw that the cat was back.

He went inside and found a small soup bowl. He poured half of the pint of milk into it and took it to his patio. As he bent down, the cat immediately started slurping.

Poor guy, must be hungry.

The cat came over to his leg and rubbed against him.

He picked up the cat and scratched its neck and chin.

The cat started to purr.

Glancing at the clock on the kitchen stove Salvatore saw it was close to five o'clock. "Sorry kitty, but I've got to go out now."

He put the cat down and closed the patio door.

It's strange that nothing is happening next door. They must really be hunkered down.

He glanced at the clock.

It's time for me to mingle, smile and meet more people at Happy Hour.

9

The Graceful Waters Resort held Happy Hour events twice a week: on Tuesdays and Thursdays. Depending on the time of year, the club would set up one to three portable bars manned with two to four bartenders in the ballroom. Residents could buy cheap cocktails, beer and wine served in plastic cups.

Salvatore's first impression was that Happy Hour appeared to be a convention of smiling, chatty grandparents.

This is Middle America at its best; neatly coiffed and trimmed, comfortably dressed, friendly folk.

Here, people look at each other with smiles. In Chicago, everyone's looking at the ground or in store windows. No one ever looks directly at another person. If you dare to glance at someone, you'll probably be slapped, slugged or shot.

As with the previous Happy Hours all the residents seemed content to be drinking and mingling with each other.

The clubhouse featured a well-equipped workout gym that was constantly busy.

Next to the gym was a full spa he hadn't been to or felt the urge to use.

Barbara had highly recommended it. "Whatever you may need, they can help."

"How?"

"If you're feeling low on energy, they can put you on an array of supplements to slow down the aging process. They even do Botox shots to erase wrinkles. I myself like getting a weekly B-12 shot to rev up my metabolism. Being a realtor requires you to be on the ball seven days a week."

If I were actually interested in hooking up with someone, it'd be a great spot to hang around.

The spa was next to a large indoor pool with racing lanes and only steps away from the huge outdoor pool.

Walking farther down the hall, Salvatore passed his favorite cafe. It was small and had a limited menu, but it served his purposes.

No need to fill up the refrigerator. Cooking for one is too much work.

It's within walking distance, has relatively fast service and most importantly it allows me to be seen.

Across from the cafe were a membership desk and a community mailroom.

Although no one else seemed to obey the small sign asking everyone to swipe their membership cards as they entered, Salvatore swiped his across the desk reader to ensure there was a record with a time stamp of his checking in.

It's damn nice that renters are allowed to use the facilities.

Salvatore stood off to the side, about thirty feet away. He watched others as they walked in.

No one else has swiped a membership card in the last five minutes.

The rooms designed for more intimate socializing were at the other end: billiard room, ballroom, library, card rooms, sitting areas, a large television watching area and the main bathrooms.

All the rooms were spotless and smelled fresh.

The floor to ceiling walls of glass across from the membership desk and cafe opened up to let the outdoors in.

Salvatore estimated that the glass walls were thirty feet high and about eighty feet wide. This time of year, the sliding doors were wide open allowing a twelve-foot by forty-foot portal.

He loved the way the designers had blurred the flow between the areas of indoors and outdoor living.

Salvatore counted twenty doors through which he could enter and leave.

There are six doors in the front of the clubhouse. I can use any of them for a quick exit and return. I haven't seen a single hidden camera.

No one can possibly keep track of who is where, at what time. Then again, why would they?

Happy hours were supposedly designed for residents to meet and get to know each other. The developer used the bi-weekly event to have prospective buyers wander among the booze bribed residents.

When Barbara Goldberg had shown him the entire community, he'd been impressed. "This is what it must be like to live in a country club."

"It's better than living in a country club because the club itself costs an arm and a leg to join and belong to. If you don't join, you're ostracized and are shunned. Here, everything is included and you automatically belong. The only thing extra is the golf."

Salvatore had been taken. "Sounds perfect to me."

This Tuesday's Happy Hour turned out to be a special evening as the club management had hired a local oldies band to entertain the community.

Surveying the hairscape, Salvatore noted that the men that had a full head of hair were predominantly grey while the women had recent colorings and were well coiffed.

He'd spent a great deal of his life just people watching. Part of his job was to figure out if someone was a potential problem or if they were simply part of the background scenery.

It's the observant ones that I never trust. They may be like me and are hiding their agenda.

Because of the band, the parking lot had overflowed, and the adjoining streets were crowded with vehicles. The inside of the clubhouse was packed, and there were twice as many members who had overflowed out onto the patios and grass.

The buzz of conversations almost drowned out the amplified music.

The band looked like they had come from another retirement community. They specialized in oldies music of the fifties, sixties and seventies. It was transporting Salvatore back to his childhood and teen years when he thought rock and roll would never end.

Now all the kids seem to listen to is that hip hop noise.

As he turned into a hallway to make his way to one of the bars, Salvatore was humming along to a classic a cappella song about a lion.

He remembered to smile at each person he passed.

It's amazing but every single person is actually smiling back at me.

The concept of being friends with everyone is bizarre. It means you are letting people get close to you and you're letting down your guard. I need to be careful. I need to keep my interactions with them at a superficial level.

10

He came to a dead halt.

From out of nowhere, an unfamiliar woman stopped and stood directly in front of him.

She had apparently given him a thorough once over and thought he was interesting. When she had not seen a wedding ring, she'd pounced. "Hi Salvatore. My name's Darlene, are you new here."

At first, he was shocked this woman knew his name. Then he remembered that he was wearing a nametag on his shirt.

Of course.

Salvatore's eyes immediately dropped to her open blouse where a half visible tattoo was screaming 'look at me'.

What is that?

He replied slowly. "Yes. I've only been here a few weeks."

He raised his eyes.

Her breasts are too wrinkled to have a tattoo.

"Then welcome." A smile crept onto Darlene's face. "Is your wife with you this evening?"

Salvatore pushed his glasses higher on his nose. "No, I'm single."

Darlene's smile showed off her too-white teeth. "How nice. Where did you move from?"

Salvatore noticed her too smooth cheeks and realized that beneath her facelift she was probably ten to fifteen years his senior. "Oh, I've lived all over. How about you?" He replied without any vigor. He was glancing around hoping to see someone he knew.

"New Jersey... I'm from the Garden State of New Jersey. I'm a divorcee and I'm here all alone."

Curiosity got the better of him and he glanced once more at the tattoo.

Is it a bird?

Darlene accommodated Salvatore by thrusting out her breasts removing a few wrinkles.

Now that's a misshapen mistake.

Darlene exhaled and the breasts deflated. Salvatore watched the bird's wings flap once or twice as the wrinkles resettled on her chest.

He raised his eyes to her face. "Well it was nice to meet you, but I'm looking for one of my neighbors."

Darlene's face deflated next.

Her enthusiasm waned; she knew she was being brushed off. "Fine. I was just going to tell you that we have a table for our singles club near the patio doors. That is, if you'd like to meet other singles."

"Thank you. Perhaps later." Salvatore walked towards the nearest bar and got in line.

There were two bar maids and one bar lad. All appeared to be in their twenties or thirties.

"At my age, wine is the only thing I'll stand in line for."

Salvatore turned to find a total stranger. "I have to agree with you."

He looked the crowd over.

The husbands were all dressed for comfort in either denim jeans and golf shirts, or golf shorts and Tommy Bahama shirts.

The women were all much better dressed than their husbands. Most were wearing slacks and elaborately designed t-shirts.

Or are they called blouses?

The majority of the women were also looking their best with makeup and jewelry.

The women here are all out to impress each other.

Ten minutes later, it was finally his turn to order. He watched his bar maid closely as she found the open bottle of Cabernet and poured him an almost full short plastic glass. She was wearing a tight black vest that emphasized her breasts, over a white blouse and tight black slacks.

Too bad she has her blouse done up.

With a plastic glass of red wine in hand, Salvatore walked over to the cafe where he ordered a quesadilla. After he paid, he received a notification buzzer.

He shoved it in his pant pocket and stood aside.

As he stood and waited, he made sure to smile at anyone who looked his way. It was a conscious act on his part.

The more that remember me the better.

He also made sure he pushed his glass frame occasionally so that it sat firmly atop his nose.

Suddenly, he felt a vibration against his thigh and jerked.

Salvatore almost spilled his wine.

11

H e pulled out the now buzzing piece of plastic that had a rotating circle of red flashing lights.

My order's ready.

The pickup line had no one in front of him and he was handed his plate straight away.

With his order in hand, he looked for an empty spot to sit but could only find an empty table that was big enough to seat four. He decided to take it anyway.

No sooner had he taken a bite when he heard, "Can we join you?"

Salvatore looked up.

He found a couple that looked to be closer in age to himself. "Please."

The man held out his hand for Salvatore to shake. "I'm Fred and this is my wife June."

"I'm Salvatore."

Salvatore discovered his table partners were from Minnesota.

June asked, "How are you finding living here full time in God's waiting room?"

"God's Waiting Room?"

She giggled. "Yes, it's what everyone calls it, isn't it. It has the same initials as Graceful Waters Resort. I find it oh, so cute, don't you?"

Salvatore smiled at June's creativity. "I get it. That's cute."

Just then, a man at the next table swore at his wife. "Bitch!"

Everyone around the cafe stopped to stare at them.

With the wife's flawless hair and makeup she looked like an ex beauty queen. She appeared to be at least fifteen to twenty years younger than he was.

Must be a trophy wife.

Salvatore watched as the blushing wife stood up, rubbed away a tear from her eye and walked down the hallway towards the main bathrooms.

Salvatore had finished his food and his plastic wine glass was empty. "Excuse me, but I need to get a refill on my wine. It's been nice to meet you."

He stood up and headed towards the nearest bar.

Half way, Salvatore ran into Marvin. "Hey Marvin, nice to see you. Where's Joan tonight?"

"She wasn't feeling up to socializing so she told me to come alone. Said it would do me good to get out for an hour or two. While I've got you I should warn you."

"Warn me about what, Marvin?"

"Apparently some of the women in here have their eyes on you. They think you're a great catch."

Salvatore smirked. "Who told you that?"

"Joan and Barbara were talking about it and wondering how they should tell you. They decided I should be the one."

"But all the women in here are older than I am."

"Ah, but they all still think of themselves as being young and attractive. And since you're the most eligible man in the community, you're bringing out their inner cougar. The only reason I'm telling you this is so you've been forewarned."

"Ha." Salvatore shook his head. "I can handle myself. As for Joan, please tell her that I hope she feels better soon. Now if you'll excuse me I'll be right back. I need to go to the men's room."

As he entered the main hallway, the woman from the table next to him bumped into him.

She left her hands holding onto his arms. "Excuse me, but aren't you a virile looking man."

Salvatore moved his head backwards and tried to step away.

She held onto his arms then leaned in and whispered in his ear. "My husband is almost twenty years older than I am. If you're interested, I would love to enjoy a younger man once in a while." She licked his ear as she placed her right hand into his left pant pocket.

She found her target and stroked him as she whispered. "I'm glad you're not one of the repressed, dysfunctional men around here."

Salvatore wanted to cringe; afraid she'd share details with him.

She kept her hand busy until she got the manly response she was looking for. She winked, released him and then stepped away.

"What about your husband?"

"Oh, I just ignore him. He has chronic hemorrhoids. And whatever drugs he's taking ain't making him any smarter."

"Well thanks, but not tonight. Try me another time." He looked toward the ballroom.

Thank God, no one saw us.

She raised her eyebrows, blew him a kiss and sauntered away.

God, I hope she doesn't break her hip doing that!

What do ya know? I got hit on by two women in one Happy Hour. I like this place!

S alvatore stood still as he composed himself. As he felt his manhood settle, he scanned the hallway to see if the trophy wife was still on the prowl.

Thank God, she's gone.

He thought about how, before moving here, meeting women who were interested in middle aged men who came across as being introverted was a chore he'd enjoyed with mixed results.

He flashed back to the time he was in a store in Basseterre when an attractive woman walked in, talking on her phone. He recalled how he'd overheard her tell her friend, "I have to go, there's a cute man in this store."

Before he could even react, she'd turned to him and said, "Sorry for lying like that, but I really wanted to get off the phone with her."

My ego was shattered.

He re-entered the ballroom to see everyone peering outside. He looked at his watch.

6:36.

Salvatore had thought about buying a phony wedding ring to discourage single women, then dismissed it.

Salvatore Cabella is single.

If he found a woman he found attractive, he had a lifetime habit of looking at her hands to see if she was wearing a wedding ring. It had paid off several times, as females seemed to sense his attentions and if they were interested, they would usually glance his way and smile.

More often, they look away.

Then he recalled how he'd spotted Sonia in the parade back on St Kitts.

If I make it back there and she still wants me, I'll buy her a ring and propose.

Salvatore walked outside to be completely awed by another Arizona sunset. The reds, gold and purples rose in brilliance over a few awe-inspiring moments then slowly faded. He had already seen many in the desert over the few weeks he'd been there but each one still held his attention.

Mother nature sure knows how to put on a show.

He scanned the seating around the fire pits and saw no empty seats. Next, he looked at the tables full of people eating the cafe's evening special and washing it down with wine or cocktails.

He kept on wandering through the crush of people.

Salvatore said hello to several people he'd met before moving on. He didn't remember any of their names so he would just mutter. "Sorry, I've gotta find someone."

His thoughts flashed to Sonia and how much she had changed him. In the past, he'd always avoided small talk.

Ten minutes later, Salvatore saw Barbara. She was talking to three other women. He compared the four.

Barbara is by far the most attractive. Her hair is perfect;

she dresses well, socializes well and listens to client needs. She's a consummate realtor.

Salvatore smiled at her as he raised his empty clear plastic glass.

Barbara excused herself and made a direct line towards him. She was a good three inches shorter as she stood beside him. "I was wondering if you were coming this evening."

He pushed his glasses further up his nose. "I've already been here for an hour and I must say it is much nicer now that I've found you."

She glanced down then back at his face. "You are such a flatterer, Salvatore. How are you getting along in your new home? Settling in okay?"

"Everything is going well, thanks."

"I'm pleased. Let me remind you to make mental notes about the model you're in and what you like and don't like about it. That way in a few months, once you're ready to settle in you'll be able to tell me what it is that I need to find for you."

Salvatore nodded his head as if he agreed. "I really like my neighbors so far."

"Then perhaps I can talk the owner of the home you're in into selling it to you."

"That may be an option. But I'm really not ready to act yet, Barbara."

"No problem. Say, how do you find living on the golf course?"

Salvatore gave a half grin and nodded. "It's nice not having any neighbors behind, looking in on me. On the negative side, there are golfers constantly looking for their balls in the bunker behind me."

"Well just so you know, golf lots always hold their value

better and increase faster than regular lots. You aren't the only one who enjoys privacy."

"I'll file that away. Oh, I was going to ask you, how do the desert wash lots compare to the ones on the golf course?"

"They offer privacy but they're also a runway for wildlife. Javelina, coyotes, burros, bobcats and even rattlesnakes seem to use them, especially at night."

"Good to know."

"Have you had dinner yet? A few friends are going over to the golf course restaurant after the band stops playing. Would you care to join us?"

"Thanks, but I've already eaten. I was planning to leave in a few minutes to get home and finish a great book I'm reading."

"What's the title?"

Salvatore looked blank. "Damn, I can't remember, but it's about a really gruesome murder and a slimy lawyer."

Barbara shook her head while grinning. "Gruesome isn't for me."

Salvatore leaned into her and spoke softly. "I'll say good night then."

Salvatore glanced back at Barbara and saw that she was watching him as he walked away.

As he passed a garbage receptacle, he donated his empty glass.

The crush of people had thinned dramatically and the band was playing a slow dance to end their performance. Salvatore left through the front double glass doors. Stepping into the quiet of the new darkness refreshed him.

He glanced at his watch.

6:59

Happy hour ends at 7PM sharp. By then, most residents are

feeling their liquor and are headed home or out for dinner with friends.

Salvatore glanced at several people outside the clubhouse mailroom. There was a steady line entering and exiting. All left with a daily dose of junk mail in their hands.

He recalled how, when he'd accepted the keys to the house, he was also given a key to a mailbox.

I couldn't tell Barbara I wouldn't be getting any mail.

So once a week, he would gather whatever advertising was stuffed inside and would then dump it into the nearest garbage receptacle.

Gotta fit in.

Salvatore headed home through the parking lot. He dodged several drivers who weren't watching.

One too many drinks.

He was enjoying the warm temperature. For a moment, the warm breeze and palm trees reminded him of St Kitts.

He was singing about another day in paradise to himself.

As he turned the corner onto the street where he lived, he heard someone's voice. "Are you talking to yourself, Salvatore?"

It's Les Bush.

Salvatore recognized him from the clubhouse. "It's because I'm a writer. I'm used to living in my own little world where my characters are always talking to me."

"Then I hope you and your characters have a good evening together." Les laughed as he waved goodnight.

13

A s he walked down his street, Salvatore glanced up to see that the evening's first stars were starting to appear.

The brightest one is Venus and the one closest to it must be Mars.

The houses on his street were all silent and dark. People were either out for a late dinner or more likely sitting in their great rooms watching television.

Nearing his house, Salvatore looked at his watch.

7:06.

He thought he heard someone yelling.

Salvatore stopped in front of his normally vacant neighbor's house and listened carefully.

Either someone has turned up the volume on the television or there is a real argument underway.

Keep walking; don't get too nosy.

Salvatore walked past and went up his own walkway to his front door.

Inside, Salvatore went into the kitchen where he mixed himself a real drink, straight scotch on the rocks.

Fortified, he returned to the chair by the window. He lifted the window open in an attempt to hear any voices.

Salvatore heard a vehicle.

He watched as the black SUV re-entered the garage. Its windows were heavily tinted so he had no idea who was driving or how many passengers it held.

I bet it's been on a food run.

He glanced at his wristwatch.

7:25.

A fortyish year old man carrying two large pizza boxes peeked out from the garage then went back inside.

The garage door hummed as it closed.

It was probably seeing the pizza boxes but suddenly he remembered that tomorrow was Wednesday and that meant it was garbage pickup day.

He checked in the garbage container under the sink to see if it were full; it wasn't.

It didn't matter however, since the garbage needed to go out.

Salvatore pulled the white plastic bag out and tied it closed.

Then he went into his garage, hit the door button and once the door was up, moved the garbage can to the curb.

Marvin and Salvatore had become garbage can buddies. Since the garbage cans were emptied early Wednesday mornings, they had a pact to wheel the other's empty garbage cans up next to his garage if the other one wasn't home or was away.

Neither one had needed to assist the other so far, but Salvatore figured Marvin had asked because he might forget or have troubles some day.

Too bad I'll be long gone.

14

WEDNESDAY

On Wednesday morning, Salvatore was up before sunrise. Once again, he was watching for any signs of life in the house next door.

He tried spying on his new neighbors from every window inside his house that faced them.

No lights on.

Light was about to break in the East.

No one's wandering outside for a smoke, fresh air or to make a private call.

What are they doing in there?

The coffee pot beeped at him.

He poured himself a mug then savored two hot sips.

Next, he retrieved a muffin from his freezer that he'd bought at the local Walmart and placed it in the microwave. Not being a morning person meant Salvatore never made the time to prepare a proper breakfast.

I do miss the cooks we had on St Kitts.

He slipped into his old life.

For the last twenty-five years, I always had to put my benefactor's needs and wants first. My own desires had to come in a distant second.

He'd never felt shame, anxiety or guilt over what he'd done. His boss had always praised and thanked him for forcing someone to pay up, change their ways or eliminating those deemed to be a drag on his business.

Early on, I developed a hard shell that allowed me to ignore the rest of the world and focus on the best ways to do my job.

The shell was of his creation and he never let anyone get close to him.

He slipped back to the here and now.

I wonder where the cat's at?

Salvatore wandered outside and saw Marvin reading the local newspaper.

"Say Marvin have you seen a black cat with white paws hanging around your patio?"

"No. Why do you ask?"

"Oh, I've seen one twice now. Just wondering if you had as well? Anyway, I should get going. I have a telephone call I need to make this morning. See you later."

"Will do."

Salvatore went back into his house.

In the past, he would have found people like Marvin, Joan, Barbara and the others he was meeting in Arizona aggravatingly ordinary and boring. For the first time since he was thirty, he was enjoying spending time with regular people.

Even if they're older than me.

His exposure to them was changing him.

Funny, but since I've turned fifty-five, old has become much older than I am.

Salvatore had no telephone call he had to make. He just

wanted some time alone. Being social and pretending to be a nice guy was rare for him, especially so early in the morning.

He ate his muffin and watched a few minutes of the local morning news.

Other than perfect weather, a hit and run in Scottsdale and a drive by shooting in Phoenix, nothing else interested Salvatore.

He turned off the television and looked out his windows at the house next door.

What are they doing in there?

Frustrated he looked over at Marvin's.

He slid his patio door open and stepped outside. Joan and Marvin were now sitting together. They were next to each other, holding hands.

"Joan, I missed seeing you at Happy Hour last night. Are you feeling better today?"

Marvin waved Salvatore to come over.

Salvatore crunched over the rocks.

Once Salvatore arrived, Marvin looked at his pale wife. "Joan isn't feeling well since her darned doctor changed her medications again. You'd think he'd know what he was doing. Plus, he's going on vacation for two weeks. What if Joan has a reaction to the meds, then what."

"Didn't you complain?"

"I told him that when he returns he could find out how the meds worked from Joan's autopsy."

Joan shushed Marvin and shot him a dirty look.

Salvatore grimaced.

He wasn't sure how to react. Salvatore tried to change the conversation. "How are your kids doing?"

Joan shook her head but didn't speak.

Salvatore tried again. "Marvin told me that you have a new grandson. Are you going to visit to help out for a few days?"

Marvin answered. "We were, but yesterday our daughter-in-law told us that we have to pass a grand parenting class first."

Salvatore winced. "A what?"

Joan sat up straight. "You heard him right; a grand parenting class. Apparently what we did as parents for our kids was all wrong." Her voice was weak.

Salvatore couldn't believe what he'd just heard. "You've got to be shitting me. Sorry, I meant joking. I mean, we all turned out alright."

"Well just as the experts tell us some foods are good for us one day and bad the next, it seems a lot of what we did as parents was wrong and our daughter-in-law is demanding we take a class before we come to visit."

"Did your daughter-in-law give you an example of what you're gonna learn?"

Joan sat up straight. "Apparently when I placed my son face down in his crib to avoid choking if he spit up, it was the wrong thing to do. Apparently new research shows that sleeping face up, on their backs is safer for infants."

Marvin entered the conversation. "I looked it up on the internet. What my daughter-in-law didn't mention was that many children can develop a flat spot on their skulls from doing that."

Salvatore had never even thought about the issue. "Figures… I guess in twenty years we'll have to place babies in hammocks or something."

Joan continued to vent. "We aren't allowed to give a child a spanking when they act out or do something bad." Joan crossed her arms in front of her chest.

"Really? Whatever happened to spare the rod and spoil the child?"

Marvin answered. "Apparently spanking devalues a child, telling him that he's weak and powerless."

He hadn't heard anything about it. "How do you discipline an unruly child then?"

"You talk to them. They now claim that spanking is linked to mood and anxiety disorders later in life."

Salvatore thought of his own childhood. "Is that why we all blame our parents for all of our problems."

"Perhaps it is." Marvin chuckled. "I was curious so I looked up how raising a child has changed over time on the Internet. It turns out each generation does things differently. In the start of the nineteen hundreds, apparently we gave Bayer's Heroin to children if they had a strong cold and opium to help newborns sleep well."

Salvatore chuckled. "No wonder they called them the good old days. Everyone was stoned."

Marvin looked at Salvatore. "Are you still interested in joining me at the cigar club this afternoon?"

"Yes. My only problem is that I don't have a cigar at the moment."

"No problem. I'll give you one of mine."

"Great. I'll pay you back as soon as I get over to the mall."

Marvin gave Salvatore a nod. "Then I'll knock on your door at quarter to two."

15

A t 1:30, Salvatore combed and parted his hair the way the real Salvatore had. He picked up the pair of heavy framed black glasses in which he had replaced the original lenses with blank ones.

The young lady at the eyeglass shop had questioned him.

"You say you don't have a prescription."

"That's correct."

"And you want blank glass in the frame that you've just picked out?"

"I'm an author and I want to look more studious." That was all he could think of to tell the girl.

The look she gave him made him feel like a nutcase. Nonetheless, she rang up the purchase.

She must have been on commission.

He put the blank eyeglasses aside and picked up a pair of the cheap sunglasses he'd also recently bought.

Every day's the same here: bright and warm with pleasant evenings. So bright, I can't drive without the sunglasses.

He looked in the mirror and stroked his goatee.

If anyone who knows who I really am were to walk past me, they wouldn't recognize me.

Salvatore went outside through his front door and stood on his driveway.

As Salvatore waited, he thought about the grand parenting class Marvin and Joan had told him about.

Five minutes later Marvin came out of his house and joined him. "Let's go."

They walked towards the clubhouse.

Salvatore thought Marvin walked at a decent pace for a man as old as he was. "Your comments about your grand parenting class made me think."

Marvin looked at Salvatore. "About what?"

Salvatore said, "I thought about what my parents told me when I was growing up and how a lot of it was pure bull."

"Like what?"

"Every day they lied to make me do things their way. I couldn't drink coffee although they did because it would stunt my growth and make me darker. If I swallowed watermelon seeds, a watermelon vine would grow in my stomach. Shit like that."

"I was told the same. But we only lie to our children and grandchildren to protect them so they'll do what is best for them."

"I guess we all survived anyway."

"True. Maybe that's why I like drinking wine so much. Say, do you have any children Salvatore?"

"Unfortunately, no. My wife died soon after we were married."

"I'm sorry to hear that... Well in my opinion, grandchildren are better than children; you can feed them sugar then send them home."

Salvatore laughed at the old joke. He knew his jealousy of other's children and grandchildren was a wasted emotion. *I'm too old to have any kids now.*

Marvin said, "I've thought of a sure fire way to get my kids and grandkids to come here to visit me and Joan."

Salvatore played along. "How will you do that?"

"Easy," declared a smiling Marvin. "When I send them checks at Christmas, I'm gonna forget to sign them."

"Haha." Salvatore lightly brushed his fist against Marvin's shoulder. "I like it."

It turned out that the cigar club met in the rear of the clubhouse.

Salvatore saw a group of about twenty-five men sitting in metal chairs in an attempted circle on brick pavers. Over their heads were the branches of a single tree.

Salvatore noted that they were as far away from the main patio area as they could be without sitting out in the golf course.

"Salvatore, we need to take a couple of empty chairs from the tables over there so we can squeeze them in with the guys."

Salvatore grabbed two of them. "I got these."

Several of the men stood up and moved their chairs backwards to enlarge the circle as they approached.

"Hey Marvin, did you bring us a new member?"

"I sure did."

Salvatore did a lazy wave to all the guys. "Hi, I'm Salvatore Cabella."

A slender man wearing an Arizona Diamondbacks baseball cap took his cigar out of his mouth. "Where you from?"

"Chicago. I've only been living here a few weeks."

The man touched his Arizona baseball cap. "I heard the

Cubs were taking a batting practice today and the pitching machine threw a no-hitter."

Several of the men laughed.

Salvatore deadpanned his response. "That joke died in 2016."

The slender man held up both hands in front of him as if to say he was sorry.

Several members in the group muttered their welcomes to Salvatore.

Salvatore sat between Marvin and a man with thin salt and pepper hair who introduced himself as Big Al.

Big Al asked, "Have you gone to our website and registered yet."

"Not yet. Why, does the cigar club have an annual membership fee?"

"Yes, it's a big zero." Everyone chuckled.

Must be a newbie joke.

These guys are nuts, but they're okay.

Salvatore turned to Marvin. "Is this where the club meets year round?"

"We do this time of year. When it gets into the hundreds in the summer months, we either drive to a nearby cigar store which has an indoor smoking room or to a smoking lounge at one of the Casinos."

Big Al chimed in. "I don't like smoking cigars outside during the summer because of the oven we turn into and I also don't like golfing if the temperature is lower than my age."

Salvatore played along. "Do you golf a lot?"

"No, not much. However some of the guys in this group golf four or five times a week, all year round."

"Why golf, if it gets that hot?"

"Cause if you don't take it seriously, it's no fun. Besides they're still trying to find their games."

"I think I understand."

"Good, then would you mind explaining it to their wives?"

More group laughter.

Big Al pointed at Salvatore. "You must be a golfer, right?" Salvatore paused for a few seconds trying to think if the real Salvatore had ever mentioned that he'd golfed. "No, I don't golf. Why do you ask?"

"Because you're wearing a golf shirt."

"Oh, but I've noticed that most men wear golf shirts in here."

"Most men are golfers." Big Al took a puff of his cigar as if he'd earned it.

"Oh well, you've caught me just trying to fit in."

Big Al spoke. "My wife told me that she was going to make our dinner great again. I asked her how. She said that she was ordering out from now on."

There was a collective groan followed by multiple puffs of cigar smoke.

16

Salvatore looked up from the circle and was surprised there wasn't a circle of smoke hanging over the group.

"Hey Salvatore, I'm Barry. Have you noticed the pink flamingos yet?"

"Arizona has flamingos?"

Barry laughed. "No. But our little community has plastic pink flamingos."

"You mean if someone has a birthday, his friends will prank him with the plastic birds on his lawn."

Barry said, "Good guess, but no cigar. We have several sexual swingers in here who like to party. They place pink flamingos in their front yard if the event is being held at their house that night."

Salvatore felt he was being pranked. He cocked his head. "Is this another newbie joke?"

Barry chuckled. "No, I'm dead serious. I figured that being a single guy, you'd have already been invited to a swap by one of our single ladies."

"Is that why they call this an active adult community?"

Everyone laughed.

Someone said, "You belong in this club, Salvatore."

Salvatore squinted. "If I get invited, will I see you there, Barry?"

"Perhaps." Barry smiled at him and puffed away.

A rather serious looking and frail chap asked Salvatore if he played chess.

"Not much."

I've been a pawn for the last twenty-five years of my life.

"Do you understand the basics at least?"

With a straight face Salvatore said, "I think the little guys always are sacrificed to protect the big guys."

"That's one way to look at it."

"Oh, and the lady has the best moves."

"Alright, I think you understand enough to come join us one afternoon. We meet every day during the week in one of the card rooms in the back of the clubhouse around two o'clock."

"Thanks, I just might join you one day."

A solid looking man wearing a bright red baseball cap with America written on it spoke up. "Howdy Salvatore, I think Marvin told us you were an author?"

"If he did, then yes I am."

"How many books have y'all written?"

Sounds like he's from a southern state.

He held up his index finger. "Just one so far. You can find it on Amazon if you're interested."

Salvatore was happy that Salvatore Cabella had not filled out his Author Page on Amazon or included a picture of himself in the book.

"Marvin said ya'll write crime mysteries."

Probably Texas.

"That's right." Salvatore pushed up his glasses to appear more nerdy.

"What's your book about?"

"Well, in the first chapter a male librarian in a large library is checking on a book for someone when he discovers a dead body set inside a pentagram."

"Is it fantasy novel?"

"No, it's a crime novel where the librarian uses the Dewey Decimal system to decipher clues and eventually beats the police in solving the crime."

"That sounds pretty close to that Da Vinci Code book to me."

"It's similar."

"Interesting, what happens to the librarian?"

"He solves the crime."

"How does his character change as a result of solving the crime? Does he become a private eye or a cop?"

"No, he becomes a famous author but he stays a librarian."

"Does he get his love interest as a result?"

"No. He doesn't have one."

"Oh, I see. Well, if ya'll have a draft of your next one and need a beta reader, I'd be happy to read it for ya."

"I don't have a draft."

"How about just emailing me a few chapters then?"

"Sorry, can't do that either. So far I only have hand written notes in a notebook."

The fellow in the red baseball cap looked perplexed.

Salvatore tried to explain. "Call me old fashioned but I don't own a computer right now."

The red baseball cap said, "I see. Then how do you make changes?"

"Scissors and tape."

Everyone pondered what had been said until someone chuckled, then they all joined in laughing at the joke.

Another fellow jumped in. "Don't mind old Harlan. As they say in Texas, he's all hat and no cattle."

The men all chuckled again.

Except for the redneck, these guys are great!

Too bad I won't be able to make any more of their meetings.

Salvatore needed to turn the topic elsewhere. "Say Al, what do you like best about living here?"

"It's simple. We're all adults. There are no ankle biters and no obnoxious teenagers. And besides there are so many damned activities there's no way anyone can do them all."

Most men nodded in agreement. Others just puffed away.

A man wearing a black baseball cap spoke up. "Do you guys remember how as kids we went outside, played in the streets, talked into tin cans tethered with string and played kick the can. We were active and had fun. Kids today just sit on their butts and play games on their phones or tablets."

The guy sitting next to him answered. "Have you played any computer games?"

"I wouldn't waste my time."

"Maybe you should try them. I find them fascinating. They keep me busy and are a lot of fun."

Marvin chimed in. "My wife's told me that a lot of the women in here go to the clubhouse to play mindless games like Bunco, Mahjong and Mexican train just to get away from their husbands."

"Isn't that one of the reasons why we formed a cigar club?"

"That's another good reason; besides telling jokes, solving the world's problems and enjoying a good cigar."

These guys are just trying to entertain themselves as they wait for the grim reaper to come.

Another fellow asked Salvatore if he'd found a good doctor yet.

"Haven't had the need for one yet."

"Then you're lucky. If you do need one, I've found a great one not too far from here."

Salvatore played the straight man once again. "Why do you think he's so great?"

"Cause he's got a large candy bowl full of free Viagra in his waiting room."

Some chuckles.

Salvatore shook his head and grinned as if he understood.

The mention of the sex-enhancing drug caused him to think of Sonia.

Sonia's all I need as a stimulus in bed.

Her sense of humor can probably get her through anything life throws her way but I wonder if she'll still want me after what has happened to her?

17

S alvatore had a restless sleep and Thursday got off to a shitty start. He was woken by an awful high-pitched noise.

Damn coyotes.

Shit! It's not coyotes... It's too loud.

Damn it must be a friggin' smoke detector.

It took him thirty minutes of cursing to discover which smoke detector it was and replace the battery.

Once it was quiet he looked at the time on the oven.

5:38.

Salvatore flipped on the coffee pot.

I've got a lot to think about before I go to tonight's Happy Hour.

Waiting for the coffee to brew he sat down at the table and rubbed his face.

It's unexpected events like the damned smoke alarm that can ruin the best-laid plan.

His mind went back to Sonia.

She told me that when she's having a bad day she makes pottery.

He recalled a conversation they'd shared one lazy afternoon when he'd arrived seemingly upset.

"I find making pottery relaxes me. Spinning clay, you'll find your mind and body be in natural synergy. You should try it. It'll open up your mind and relieve your stress."

"I doubt that." He'd scoffed at first.

She'd told him to go over to her wheel. It was next to an open door that led outside. "Go ahead and put your hands on the clay."

Cautiously he did as he'd been told.

"Now close your eyes. Do you hear it?"

"Hear what?"

She whispered into his ear. "Listen. Do you hear the sounds of the waves crashing on the beach?"

He focused. "Yes, I can." They were distant but he could hear them.

"Now, how about the leaves?"

He focused. "You're right. I can hear the leaves of the palm trees in your neighbor's yard."

"Good. Now let the feel of the clay guide your hands."

"What am I supposed to make?"

"It doesn't matter. It's not about the end result. Let your hands guide you. When you're finished, you be feeling pure joy. It makes even a crappy day better."

This is going to be a busy day. I need to be sharp.

I wish I had some clay.

18

B y noon on Thursday, he felt as though he was mentally prepared for the Happy Hour event.

I have five hours to kill.

He decided to walk to the clubhouse and grab a sandwich.

The more time I spend at the clubhouse today, the better.

He passed by the small park with the swing set.

How did that song go?

He started humming an old rock song he thought he remembered. "The time has come today." Then realized he'd forgotten all the lyrics.

I'm having a senior moment like the rest of them in here.

Salvatore tried to focus by alternating his thoughts between getting ready and why he was doing it.

I've never wanted to know who my target is as a person. If they have children, are God fearing people, donate their time to charity; it doesn't matter.

Nope, all I care to know is what their habits are and can I use those habits to kill them without being caught. That way I can free Sonia.

As he neared the parking lot, he saw a woman wearing a floppy hat pass him in her car.

It must be Barbara.

He watched as Barbara waved at him.

Salvatore waved back.

Ninety seconds later, he started to pass by Barbara's parked car. He saw her come around to open her trunk.

She started rearranging some large things.

Except when she's in a parade, Sonia isn't a flashy dresser like Barbara.

He walked over. "Need some help?"

Barbara seemed startled. "Oh Salvatore. I didn't see you standing behind me."

Salvatore saw several large items in her trunk. "I didn't mean to scare you. I just thought you could use a hand."

"Why how nice of you. I just picked these up and as I was driving I heard something fall over so I thought I better stop and have a look."

"Let me look for you."

Barbara stood aside.

Salvatore was surprised by what he saw.

Medical stuff.

"I think this thing was the culprit." He reached in and up righted a wheeled contraption. "What is it?"

"It's a walker. And those are crutches that I'm taking to someone living over in the newer section. They just had a knee operation and will need them for a few weeks."

"Really. Do you have medical supplies in your garage or something?"

Barbara touched the brim of her hat and smiled at him.

"Heaven's no. If you go on our community website you'll find that we have a section where people can list items others can borrow at no cost. Many are medical things like wheelchairs, crutches and slings."

Barbara paused then went on. "People also make available extra beds, cribs, high chairs and even strollers in case grandchildren come to visit. I borrowed a dog crate once for a client that had a dog staying with them for a few days. Why go out and buy something when you can just borrow it from a neighbor for a while."

"Gee, that's great." Salvatore felt like he was learning new reasons to like the community even more every day.

"Say, I'm going in to grab some lunch, care to join me?"

"Thanks for asking but I've got to deliver these, then I have to show another client some homes. Will you be at Happy Hour tonight?"

Oh, yes.

"Yes, I'll see you there."

Damn, I'm going to miss this place. Helping others and not expecting something in return is special. Something I haven't experienced before.

Salvatore walked into the cafe.

He saw ten people already in line.

I'll try again in a few minutes.

Salvatore decided to check out the club's outdoor swimming pool. It was a sprawling area of water surrounded with umbrellas and chaise lounges.

Where can I sit?

Salvatore walked the contour of the pool and found no free chairs and over a dozen noisy children.

Must be grandkids here for spring break. I'm outta here.

19

B eing March, it was the busiest month of the year in the Phoenix area. Every snowbird that could get into the seventy-five to eighty-five degree warmth had done so.

There were also the devout baseball fans wanting to see their favorite teams and players in Spring Training.

In total over four hundred thousand temporary residents clogged the vacation homes, hotels, restaurants and roads.

Salvatore grabbed a sandwich at the café and decided to spend the rest of the day inside his house.

It's tonight's Happy Hour or else.

His mind wandered to thinking about how as a child and as a younger adult he'd been a bit introverted. That had made his lack of social interaction under his benefactor easier to deal with. Being in the retirement community he felt as he was finally becoming more social.

I think I'm evolving.

At ten minutes to five, Salvatore looked himself over in the mirror. He felt himself retreating even deeper into his own brain.

This is it.

Hair - check.

Goatee - check

Glasses - check.

I look like Salvatore.

Next, he picked up his Salvatore Cabella nametag and pinned it to his shirt.

I can do this.

He walked to the clubhouse while waving at everyone he saw.

Gotta fit in just a bit longer.

He noticed that the palm trees outside the main clubhouse still had white lights around their trunks from the holiday season.

They're festive. I think they should keep them up year round.

A man he didn't know held the door open for him.

"Thank you. By the way, my name's Salvatore."

The man nodded his head. "Yes, I can see it on your nametag. I'm Joe." Then he pointed at his own tag.

Salvatore was determined that this evening he would make every effort to be as outgoing as possible.

I'll give my name to as many people as I possibly can.

There was no outside entertainment to draw even more residents in on this particular Thursday. It didn't matter to Salvatore that the Clubhouse itself wasn't quite as full as it had been on Tuesday.

It might be easier for people to remember seeing me.

He smiled to the two women behind the member desk as he scanned his community card.

Now I need to find some people who know me.

"Salvatore." Barbara had found him.

He made sure he gave her a warm hug, as she hugged back.

"Why Salvatore," Barbara winked at him. "You must be enjoying yourself here."

"I am. You were right about this community. It's starting to grow on me. I'll bet the people you delivered the crutches and walking thing to appreciated them."

"They did."

He felt a pat on his shoulder. "Will you be back to the cigar group next week?"

Salvatore turned to face Big Al. "Yes, I had a good time. It's a great bunch of guys."

Barbara stood next to Salvatore waiting for the man to leave.

She knew Big Al was known as an inconsiderate neighbor who sat on his patio smoking stinky cigars several times a day.

Two more men Salvatore had seen at the cigar club joined them. The conversation soon turned to the increased activity of the jets from the local air base.

"Those darn jets are sure getting loud. I think they've doubled their training runs."

"That's because they're the new F-35 models."

Barbara said, "You would think they would route them over the desert instead of over us homeowners."

Big Al replied, "They do most of their flying over the desert, but they still need to land at Luke Air Force Base. Besides, when I hear them, I think it's the sound of freedom."

20

B ig Al noticed Barbara's sneer and excused himself. The other two men followed him.

"Hey Barbara." A couple walked over to Barbara.

Barbara was gracious as always. "Salvatore, this is Elaina and her husband, Bob, from Seattle."

Salvatore held out his hand.

Bob responded with a smile and firm shake.

Salvatore was curious. "I'm still new here. Do you mind if I ask if you get bored living in here?"

"There's no way I'm bored. In fact, I can't do all the things I want to do each day."

"I don't want to intrude, but can I ask what is keeping you so busy?"

"Elaina and I are living the good life. We're biking, hiking, reading, gardening and having meals with friends. And we're doing it together which makes each thing even better. The nice thing is that we've downsized and can live on a fraction of what it used to cost us."

"Do you agree with all that, Elaina?"

"When Bob first retired, he started supervising me and how I ran the house. And I've never been happy at being supervised." A frown crossed her face. "Since we moved here we're now both busy doing things together. And when I need some girl time, I play mah jongg and bunco with the ladies in one of the game rooms."

"Thanks. Good to know." Salvatore didn't really care but he did want the couple to remember him.

Salvatore pointed at four card tables that had been set up. At each table there were several people standing and conversing. "What are the tables for Barbara?"

Barbara grinned. "Each booth is manned by volunteer residents. One is selling tickets to a musical being performed by our talented residents. We have some very talented singers and dancers in here. If you can do either, you should audition."

Salvatore raised his right arm to his chest. "Me? Sing and dance, I'm afraid not. When God was giving out entertaining talent, he overlooked me."

Barbara showed a sad face, turning down the corners of her mouth.

Salvatore pointed at the next table, which had a small sign on it. "What is the newcomers club?"

"It's for people like you that are new to the community. I thought I'd told you about it."

"You may have but I forgot, sorry."

"Don't be silly. Anyway, the club organizes all kinds of social events so that newbies can meet and make friends. They have cocktail parties and go out as a group to restaurants. Would you like me to introduce you to them?"

"Maybe another night. What about the other two?"

"Those are local charities that we support. One is raising

money to help abused mothers and children while the other is raising funds to feed needy children."

Salvatore stood close beside Barbara and whispered. "If I give you some money, would you please donate it to them for me?"

Barbara looked surprised. "But if I donate it on your behalf, you won't get a tax deduction acknowledgment."

"I just want to help out, not reduce my taxes." Salvatore pulled out his wallet and selected four one hundred dollar bills. "Here, give each of them two hundred. Just say it's from one of your clients."

Accepting the cash from Salvatore, Barbara smiled at him. "You're a very generous, big-hearted man."

She walked over and gave a volunteer at each their share of the money.

Salvatore watched as the women hugged her and then spoke to her.

Barbara shook her head then looked at Salvatore. Then she waved at Salvatore to join her.

"I know I said I would donate the money for you, but these ladies really wanted to thank you personally."

Salvatore blushed. "Hello, my name is Salvatore Cabella and I think you ladies are wonderful to be helping mothers and children like you're doing."

The ladies beamed and offered their hands, which he shook.

Barbara saw a chance to give Salvatore a chance to get away from the women if he wanted. "Salvatore, I have a new couple that are clients I'd love for you to meet next."

"Good idea, I'd love to meet them."

Together they went through the open doors to the patio.

Barbara stood next to Salvatore as they enjoyed the

panorama. From where they were standing, the palm trees were front and center. They framed the view.

Barbara said, "I hope you didn't mind my little white lie to get you away from the tables."

"No, I appreciated the gesture."

After a long minute, Salvatore looked at Barbara's nearly empty plastic glass. "Drink it up and I'll get you a refill."

Barbara smiled and handed him her glass.

Salvatore wandered towards the bar.

Barbara watched him.

After returning, Salvatore handed Barbara her glass.

Then he tried to be even friendlier than normal for thirty long minutes.

Salvatore looked at his watch.

Then he excused himself. "I need to visit the boy's room. I'll be right back."

21

Thirty minutes later Salvatore reappeared and asked Barbara if she needed another drink.

"There you are, Salvatore. I thought I'd lost you so I got one already."

"I'm sorry but I ran into a guy from the cigar club and he just kept on talking and I didn't want to appear rude."

"I fully understand. That's what's great about this community. Time flies."

Salvatore grinned. He knew he'd just passed the one thing that could ruin his evening.

"Have you had dinner yet tonight, Barbara?"

"No, I was just going to warm up something when I got home."

"It's seven and Happy Hour is over. I haven't eaten either. Can I buy you dinner over at the golf course restaurant?"

"Oh, that would be lovely."

It took them fifteen minutes to say their goodbyes and walk to the restaurant.

They were lucky and found a booth immediately.

The special was cheeseburgers with fries.

"Do you eat cheeseburgers, Barbara?"

"Oh, I can splurge for one night."

Salvatore kept asking Barbara about herself. He seemed fascinated in her background, how she liked being a realtor and the Graceful Waters Resort community.

As he'd hoped for Barbara did most of the talking.

Forty-five minutes later, Salvatore paid the bill. "I love having the café and this restaurant within walking distance of the home I'm renting."

"So do I, Salvatore."

"May I walk you home now?"

She seemed thrilled.

Halfway home, Barbara brushed Salvatore's hand with hers. "Don't you think the street lights are like candles making the mood romantic?"

Salvatore squeezed her hand then let go of it. "I think you should write poetry or romance novels."

"Really?"

"Sure. You see things in a unique way."

Barbara was about to ask Salvatore what he meant by that when they turned onto their street.

They both saw flashing red and blue lights.

Barbara spoke first. "It's unusual to see the police in here."

Salvatore said, "Now that I think about it, I've never even seen a patrol car or a speed trap in here. How can that be?"

"It's because we have private streets so the police have to be called or invited in."

"You mean like a 9-1-1 call?"

"Exactly." Barbara grabbed Salvatore's arm. "Oh my, I hope Marvin didn't need to call an ambulance for Joan."

As the curvy street straightened out they saw the flashing lights of several police cars, a fire truck, ambulances and several large black SUVs.

They stopped in their tracks and took in the scene. After a long moment, they looked at each.

"What time is it Barbara?"

"Twenty minutes to nine. Why do you ask?"

"I'm just curious, that's all."

The street ahead was full and they could see an officer behind a traffic barrier directing traffic away from the mayhem. Their street was closed to traffic.

Another officer appeared to be stringing additional yellow tape around a house and property.

Salvatore knew immediately that it was a crime scene and went on full alert.

Barbara said. "I think it's the vacant house next to you and not Marvin and Joan's."

"I hope you're right. My first thought was it might be Joan. Did you know she hasn't been feeling well?"

"I did." Barbara looked at him. "You're one of the most thoughtful men I've ever met, Salvatore."

Salvatore grinned. "Did you also know that someone moved into the empty house between you and me on Monday?"

"Really? I haven't seen anyone or a moving van."

"They came in a single black SUV in the early morning hours and woke me."

"How very odd."

They both stood and watched as if they were trying to understand what was happening in front of them.

After thirty seconds, Salvatore squinted at Barbara. "Do you think we can get into our homes?"

Barbara took a deep breath and spoke with authority. "We

both live down there so I don't see how they can deny us access to our homes."

Salvatore thought she sounded as if she were making a presentation to a group of interested homebuyers.

Two police officers picked up the traffic barricade and moved it twenty feet closer to them.

They decided to try to get past it.

At the barricade's new location, a young uniformed police officer held up his hand to stop them. "I'm sorry but you can't go down this street."

Salvatore said, "I live on the other side of the crime scene tape where everyone is coming and going. Barbara lives two doors this side of it. We're tired and need to get into our homes."

The officer touched a button on his communicator and spoke to someone. Then he held up his palm to them. "Stay here."

As they waited, Salvatore sorted out the scene in his mind. The area was crawling with all sorts of people one didn't see every day except on television. He saw several officers acting as perimeter security, four with kit bags who appeared to be Crime Scene Investigators and two SUVs marked 'Glenwood Pathologist'.

The Crime Scene Investigators intrigued him. They were all wearing full Tyvek body suits with hoods, masks, booties and gloves. They looked just like he had seen on television.

One of the CSIs was carrying a box marked evidence while another was hauling a garbage bag out of the house and into a van.

He also spotted three or four men in suits walking in and out.

Salvatore assumed they were detectives or supervisors.

Probably local police and the suits might be federal agents.

Within a minute, a more senior officer joined them. "Where do you both live?"

This time Barbara spoke for both of them and pointed. "That is my house. Mister Cabella lives on the other side. Can you please tell us what the problem is?"

"We have an active crime scene here Ma'am. As you can see, we are securing and preserving evidence. Is there any place the both of you can go to spend the night?"

"Heaven's no. We have every right to sleep in our own beds. Besides, it would take us half the night to gather our medications and pack. No, we're staying in our own beds tonight, thank you officer."

"Have it your way Ma'am. Nonetheless, I will have to have another officer escort you to your homes as long as you promise to stay inside your houses until we leave."

They looked at each other.

Salvatore said, "Sure."

Just then, a local news station van drove up.

The senior officer called to another junior officer. "Get that news crew the hell out of here immediately."

They watched as the junior officer waved both hands and stood in front of the van's driver. "You can't be in here. This is private property and you weren't invited. Now leave."

Salvatore saw the driver throw up both hands as if he were saying, who me?

The senior officer motioned for Barbara and Salvatore to come around the barrier.

He held up his hand. "Before I let you go I'll need you to give me your names; a detective will need to talk to you."

The officer pulled out his notepad and looked at Barbara. "May I have your name Ma'am?"

"Barbara Goldberg."

"Sir, your name please."

"Why do you ask?"

The officer didn't appreciate the question. "Look I'm trying to do you a favor. Our detectives will need to interview all of the neighbors. Your full name please."

"Salvatore Cabella."

The officer wrote in his notepad. "Are you just getting home, sir?"

"Yes, we've been at the Happy hour over at the clubhouse then we had dinner."

"What time did you leave and how long were you there?"

"Happy Hour started at five, lasted two hours then we went out to eat. What happened next door?"

The officer took his eyes off his notepad. "I'm not at liberty to say, sir. Perhaps one of the detectives can tell you. I'm sure they'll want to talk with you tonight or tomorrow morning."

"Fine, can we go into our houses now?"

"Certainly." The officer stepped aside.

Barbara's house was first.

Salvatore said, "When the cops ask you questions, and they surely will, you should only tell them what you know or saw for sure, otherwise you may take them down a false trail."

"How do you know? Oh, I forgot, you're a crime writer so you know these things. Thank you, Salvatore."

Salvatore watched Barbara enter her home, then turned to wave at him.

Without hesitating, Salvatore stepped onto the road to get around the crowded sidewalk and walked straight past the crime scene and into his house.

As he closed the door, he stood still and tried to analyze what he had just seen.

Multiple police cars. Whatever happened it wasn't a minor domestic incident.

Multiple ambulances. That means several people are injured or dead.

Salvatore went to his window and peeked out. He saw two medics wheeling a gurney outside with a fully zipped black bag. The gurney was guided inside the rear of an ambulance.

That means whoever is in it, is dead.

22

T he next morning Salvatore woke up and instinctively checked to make sure his gun was under his pillow.

Apparently, people have to protect themselves in this neighborhood.

He went about his normal routine. First, he flipped the switch on the coffee pot. For only the second time since he had moved in did Salvatore turn on the television because he wanted to actually sit down and watch.

He found the local news immediately. The female anchor was talking. "We are watching footage from our helicopter taken over the Graceful Waters Resort in Glenwood. It is normally a quiet retirement community. That was, until yesterday evening."

Salvatore could make out the overhead view of the outside of his neighbor's house. The flashing lights and yellow crime scene tape dominated the screen. "Yesterday evening, the police were called to a disturbance in this local retirement community.

Inside one of the residences, they made a grisly discovery. There were three murder victims."

The reporter paused for effect. "We now go to our on the scene reporter. Gail, do we know more at this time?"

Salvatore took a step closer to the screen.

The screen showed a younger field reporter. "No, the police department has made no other information available at this time. I did however get to talk to one of the neighbors last night."

The screen cut to a neighbor Salvatore had seen farther up the street but had never talked to. He recognized him as the man who walked his small dog and sometimes feigned not seeing where the dog did his business.

I've had to pick up twice from his mutt pooping on my gravel. God's Waiting Room has poop bag dispensers near most of the grass areas. Why is that guy such an asshole?

"All I can tell you is that I thought the house was empty. Until the police arrived, I didn't know anyone lived there. For all I know it was being used as a meth lab or some other drug related activity."

I hope the police follow up on the drug angle.

Salvatore turned off the television and got a muffin out of his fridge. As he ate, he mulled over what he should expect next.

The U.S. Marshal's or the police should be questioning the neighbors today to see if we saw anyone or anything suspicious.

I need to find out what the other neighbors are saying.

After he had eaten the last of his muffin, he had a quick shower and got dressed.

Later, I'll get a few things at the store.

Before he left the bedroom, he made sure he was wearing his glasses and his hair was parted on the correct side.

He even combed his goatee.

Ready to go, he stepped out onto his driveway and noticed several neighbors congregating on Marvin's. He waved and then decided to join them.

As he walked over, he saw Barbara, Marvin and Joan. He then recognized John Peterson and his wife Mary who lived across the street from him.

Barbara had introduced John by saying, "Don't pay attention to John. He's retired, thinks he knows everything and has plenty of time to tell it."

There were also several neighbors that he didn't know, other than to wave to.

The man with the small defecating dog wasn't there.

Salvatore noticed that the crime scene tape was still surrounding the property.

They haven't released the crime scene yet.

The group all seemed to be agitated by the events in the normally empty house.

Salvatore decided to stand beside Barbara.

Barbara smiled at him. "Did you get any sleep last night?"

Salvatore squinted at her. "Not much. I really wish they would tell us what the hell happened in there last night. The local news just said three people were killed."

Barbara cocked her head. "Do you think we're safe here... given what just happened?"

Marvin chipped in. "Probably as safe as any place else and safer than most."

Barbara ignored him. "Being a single woman, I'm concerned I could be vulnerable."

Salvatore looked at her.

A woman with a slight English accent spoke. "It's shocking that something so horrifying could happen in our community. Everybody's on edge waiting to see what happens next."

Another woman Salvatore had never met chimed in. She was chewing gum like it was chocolate fudge. "I think it's terrifying... I mean are we all potential victims... Where is our security?"

A chunky man said, "It's making me reconsider buying a gun. Arizona is an open carry state after all."

The English woman replied in a snippy tone. "And you think carrying a gun would have prevented the murders?"

The man's cheeks became flushed. "Absolutely. At the very least I would have had a chance to shoot and kill whoever did it."

"Or shoot yourself."

The chunky man stood up straight and raised his finger at her. "Suit yourself. All I'm telling you is that if you have a weapon and someone attacks you, at the very least you have a chance to survive. If you don't have a gun, you're going to be dead meat." Then he turned and walked away.

Marvin turned and spoke to Salvatore. "What do you think Salvatore? I saw them remove three body bags last night."

"As I just said, that's what the local news station is reporting."

"Right."

23

J oan spoke weakly as she held onto Marvin's arm. "Does anyone know who they were yet?"

Salvatore looked around as everyone shook his or her head.

A man with a bushy grey mustache who seemed jittery chimed in. "Do you think it's possible they were killed by someone who lives in here?

"I wouldn't think so." Salvatore shook his head.

Then he thought of the man with the dog. "Not unless they had a dog and he crapped in someone's yard and then didn't pick it up. Then that person might get killed one day soon."

Barbara winked at him.

The woman with the English accent ignored Salvatore's bad joke. "When was the last time this community had a murder?"

Everyone shook their head that they didn't know.

Barbara touched Salvatore's arm with her hand. "How would the killer or killers get in here? We have a gated community." She looked at Salvatore with puppy dog eyes.

John jumped in before Salvatore could answer. "I thought the guard was at the gate to prevent us from sneaking out."

Salvatore noticed that John was probably suffering from some type of degenerative disorder where his hand shook ever so slightly.

Barbara sniped at John. "This is not the time for humor, John."

Salvatore took a deep breath before he answered. "From what I've seen, they don't turn anyone away at the main gate. The only reason there is even someone at that gate is to direct potential home buyers to the model homes and the sales office."

Barbara agreed.

Marvin followed up. "Besides, if someone has the gate codes they can easily get in. Just think of all the gardeners, house cleaners and service people who get in here every single day. They could easily know if a house is empty and if it has stuff that they want."

Barbara squeezed Salvatore's arm. "It's scary."

John spoke in an exaggerated deep voice. "They were probably drug dealers."

Salvatore asked, "Had any of you seen the people in that house before?"

Everyone either said no or shook their head.

John finally got serious. "Hard to say, as no one here actually saw who any of them were. Having said that, a few months ago I did see a couple who arrived by SUV, but they had two children with them and only stayed a day or two."

As Salvatore listened, he was tempted to explain how easy it was to commit a crime and get away with it. He'd been controlling his ego for twenty-five years.

Keep your mouth shut or play dumb!

"Is that house a short term rental or something?"

"It must have been. However, I've never seen it advertised. Usually, the owners use real estate agents who put up signs that it's available."

Salvatore asked, "Has anyone met whoever owns the property?"

Everyone, including Barbara shook their head.

Marvin said, "We've probably lived in here the longest. During the housing collapse way back in around 2008, many homes were foreclosed on and went up for sale. That home had a sign up one day and it was gone the next. Never did see anyone who claimed to be the owner though."

Marvin turned to Barbara. "You're a realtor Barbara, do you know who owns it?"

"I looked it up last night. It's some corporation. There were a number of corporations who scooped up bargains back then."

Joan whispered something to her husband.

Marvin said, "I'd better take Joan inside, she isn't feeling well."

Everyone watched as Marvin and Joan walked into their home.

Then they all started drifting away.

Salvatore turned to Barbara. "I've got a few things to do this morning, maybe I'll see you later."

"I would like that Salvatore. I don't feel safe alone right now. Why don't you come over for lunch at my house at noon."

Salvatore bobbed his head. "Okay, I'd like that." He turned towards his house.

As soon as he entered his house, Salvatore grabbed the keys to the Toyota and drove to the grocery store.

So far, so good.

After finding a bottle of wine, a few produce items and a six-pack of muffins, Salvatore headed for home.

On the drive back, he got behind another car as they passed inside the gates. The community speed limit was twenty-five miles per hour. The car in front of Salvatore never made it past fifteen.

He flashed his lights at he car in front of him to no avail. He had to stay behind the tourist as he gazed at the golf course and water features.

Hurry up, I've got a lot of living I need to cram into the few years I've got left.

24

GLENWOOD POLICE DEPARTMENT HEADQUARTERS

The meeting was being held at the Glenwood Police Department Headquarters.

Chief of Police Stan Everett stood in front of a white board.

To his right was Assistant United States Attorney, Ingrid Johanson. To his left was Chief Everett's Media Relations person, Haley Souza.

Seated in front of them were four Glenwood Homicide Detectives and one U.S. Marshal Services Assistant Deputy, Kevin Brown.

The Chief called the meeting to order and started reading a prepared statement he intended to read to the reporters waiting for him outside. "Yesterday evening, we had a triple homicide in the Graceful Waters Resort retirement community. We lost two witnesses in the WITSEC program as well as a U.S. Marshal. Since the murders occurred during the community's Happy Hour, the press is already calling it the Happy Hour Murders."

The Chief looked up from his statement. "Until we have the Pathologist's report and the crime scene analysis from the lab, the five of you will be working together as a team to apprehend the perp or perpetrators involved."

He stopped to emphasize his point then glanced at Haley Souza.

She nodded back at him.

He went back to reading. "Heading up this investigation will be Detective Bill Garcia. Joining Bill will be our newest Detective, Charlie Fontaine along with veteran Detectives, Harry Elm and Tom Averell. Also joining the investigation will be Assistant Deputy U.S. Marshal, Kevin Brown. Kevin is based here in Phoenix and works for the Major Case Division of the U.S. Marshal Services. As you know, the U.S. Marshal Services normally works on court security, transporting prisoners, and fugitive apprehension."

He looked up at Kevin Brown, then continued. "Since it was very rare for the U.S. Marshals Services to lose someone under the WITSEC program to a murder and since they do not normally investigate crimes like homicide, Deputy Brown has been assigned to the case and will provide assistance to the four local Glenwood Detectives I just named."

Police Chief Everett turned to AUSA Ingrid Johanson. "Is there anything you would like to add at this time?"

Johanson nodded her head and took a step forward. "It is my duty to make sure that the right person or persons are prosecuted and to bring those offenders to justice. I will be working with you to ensure you are able to provide sufficient evidence so that I have a realistic prospect of conviction. My door is always open if you should need my assistance."

Police Chief Everett continued. "Unless there are any questions, I need to address the press next."

Detective Garcia spoke up. "Will you be telling the press who the victims were?"

"The families have not yet been notified, so no, we will not give the press their names. We will however let them know that two of the victims were in the WITSEC program."

Detective Garcia nodded.

Haley Souza held her right arm out to guide the Chief to leave through the door.

Before he left, the Chief looked at his Detectives again. "Alright Detective Garcia, have your team go catch our killers."

AUSA Johanson and Haley Souza followed Chief Everett as he left the room.

Assistant Deputy U.S. Marshal Brown didn't like the idea of having to collaborate with local detectives. He was used to being able to call on the resources of the federal government whenever he needed help.

Likewise, Detective Bill Garcia didn't like having to collaborate with a Fed. He knew the U.S. Marshals Service would take most of the credit should they catch the shooter.

If I get a mention, I'll be lucky. If we fail, the Feds will blame Glenwood PD.

Bill Garcia had been on duty yesterday evening and had rushed to the crime scene.

This morning he needed to extract as much information out of Detective Brown as he could.

Who were the WITSEC people and who were they in town to testify against?

Once we know who they were here to testify against, we'll know who hired the perps and very likely have a list of perps to interview.

In addition, how in the world did someone find out that the

WITSEC people were being held in the Graceful Waters Resort until the trial?

Garcia held out his hand for Kevin Brown to shake. "Let's find a meeting room. Follow me."

They withdrew to a small windowless meeting room.

Garcia took control. "Before we begin can you please tell me what happened to the second U.S. Marshal that was on duty with the witnesses?"

"As of last night he was assigned to desk duty until this investigation is completed."

"Can I talk to him?"

"I already have." Brown's eyes went hard. "He was the junior Marshal so he was the one who went to the pizza place to get dinner for the four of them. He claims to have left the house around 6:15. He stopped at a drug store to get a few personal items and then picked up two pizzas. He returned around 7:15 to find the deceased. He immediately alerted the U.S. Marshall Service as well as 9-1-1. As for information; he knows nothing."

Garcia started to object.

Brown interrupted him. "Before you get all bent out of shape, let me tell you that I've been told we're doing an internal investigation into his bank records, and so on. If anything turns up, you'll be the first to know."

Garcia didn't like what he'd been told but accepted the politics of the situation. "Is this your first murder investigation Marshal Brown?"

"It is. The U.S. Marshal Service rarely loses witnesses so we don't have our own dedicated investigative unit. While you do the local angle, I'll be utilizing federal resources. As leads turn up I'll keep you in the loop."

Here we go.

Garcia ignored the political statement. "If people aren't normally murdered in the WITSEC program what do you normally do in the Major Cases division?"

"I hunt down the most dangerous offenders who leave the WITSEC program as well as anyone who escapes from federal custody."

Garcia nodded that he understood. "Then I understand why you need our help. I spend my days trying to figure out who has committed a major crime and gathering the evidence to make a case stick."

Brown didn't like being pissed on by one of the local boys. "Good, then by pooling our resources we should figure this out quickly. When will we have your coroner's report?"

"First off, Glenwood has a Forensics Pathologist that dissects the organs and determines cause of death."

"I'm sorry; did the Pathologist give you a timeframe?"

"Due to the high profile of the case, he promised to have it to me by tomorrow morning."

Brown felt in control. "Good. How about the crime scene forensics?"

"The forensic team collected everything they could and delivered it to our Lab techs for analysis. It has been moved to the head of the line. But it will take at least three days for the initial findings."

"Does the retirement community have any security cameras?"

"Not that we know of. It's a low crime area."

"Do any of the neighbors have security cameras?"

"Not that we know of." Garcia knew he was being managed. "Now please tell me who the witnesses under the U.S. Marshals

Services protection were and what in hell were they doing in one of our retirement communities?"

"The man was a witness against the head of a Chicago crime syndicate that we have been trying to take down for many years. The other victim was his wife."

"No children?"

"No."

"If your syndicate boss is in Chicago, then why was the witness here?"

"Over the past thirty, thirty-five years, Vincent Rizzo along with his cousin, Anthony Rizzo, made billions of dollars investing in and taking control of companies. Several were here in the Phoenix, Scottsdale area. Our witness was with one of those companies."

"That seems like a hard charge to make stick considering all the time that's passed."

"The witness was prepared to lay out all the details including how he saw Vincent Rizzo ordering one of his henchmen to murder an uncooperative owner. The statute of limitations never expires on a murder."

"When was he scheduled to testify?"

"In another three days time."

"Three days; why didn't you bring him in the night before to cut down the window for something like this to happen?"

Brown felt the sting of the question. "I've been told that the witness claimed to have an allergy problem so he asked to come a couple of days early so his nostrils could adjust."

Garcia frowned. "Do you have a list of hit men Vincent Rizzo has used in the past?"

"We're working on it." Brown raised both his hands as he spoke. "Once we have the Pathologist's Report and the Crime

Lab Report we might have a better idea if this was a local hit or if a shooter was brought in. If you can put together a list of potential local shooters, as I said, I'll have my operations team produce a list of potential shooters Vincent Rizzo may have imported."

25

S alvatore waited until it was exactly noon before he knocked on the door.

Barbara greeted him wearing a silky yellow and pale blue spring dress that Salvatore hadn't seen before. "You're right on time. Come on in."

As Salvatore entered, he pulled out his hand from behind his back.

"My goodness Salvatore, what have you brought me?"

Salvatore produced a bottle of white Chardonnay. "I hope you don't mind but I thought we could have a little sip to take the edge off of all we've been through since last night."

Barbara stood on her tiptoes and gave him a kiss on the cheek. "Aren't you the thoughtful one? Please come in and open the wine while I get our lunch."

Barbara found a corkscrew and cutter in a drawer and handed it to Salvatore.

He cut the foil and pulled out the cork.

Then he caught an unusual scent. He sniffed the air. He

could smell magnolias. Looking to his left, he saw a bowl of potpourri. It was sitting on what looked like an open treasure chest.

That's what smells.

If you don't mind me asking, "What's in your chest? Is it a pirate treasure?"

Barbara glanced over before she spoke. "Believe it or not, I moved here from Michigan kicking and screaming. My husband passed away right after we had visited this place. The idea of downsizing and moving here without his help seemed impossible."

Barbara paused for a moment. "Selling off my furniture was heartbreaking enough without putting my fading photos and crumbling newspaper articles into a shoe box. I was devastated from losing my husband and the idea of putting my memories of him in a box was like cutting out my heart. Then a good friend suggested I make a memory box with my most precious things. I couldn't get everything I wanted in a shoe box so it became the treasure chest."

"What a great idea."

"Memories are what most people have to focus on when you get to be my age. It's the mementos of the special moments in your life. The day you marry the love of your life, the births of your children, the days they marry, your grandchildren."

My memories are of the people I had to terminate.

I was like a soldier, just following orders.

Barbara was setting two plates on a round dining room table. "Please ignore the dust. I haven't had time to clean for the last week. As I tell any overnight guests: you can write your name in the dust, just don't date it."

Salvatore chuckled. "Works for me. Do you have any wine glasses?"

"To your left, in the upper cupboard."

Salvatore poured then brought the glasses to the table.

He held up his glass. "To helping us relax."

They both took a sip.

"I hope you don't mind but I just made us sandwiches."

"That's perfect. However, I must tell you that I was beginning to think nobody in here cooked. Everyone seems to eat out at the early bird specials."

"That's because many ladies in here are sick of cooking dinners every night." Barbara paused for a long moment. "Then there's also the fact that we all need to eat less as we get older so snacks and hors d'oeuvres are all we need."

Salvatore sat kitty corner from her since that was how the plates were set up. "Ah, that makes sense."

He looked at Barbara for a long moment. "I just realized that you're not wearing one of your trademark hats. You look lovely without one."

Barbara blushed as she touched her head. "Well, thank you Salvatore. I hope you like my hair."

Responding to her smile and flirty voice he said, "You look great both ways."

"Thank you. Now I must ask; since you're a crime fiction writer, what do you think happened last night?"

Salvatore prided himself on his knowledge of police procedures that he had gleaned from the many books, both fiction and non-fiction that he'd read.

He sipped the chardonnay before he replied. "On the eleven o'clock news they announced that two of the victims were in a federal witness protection program."

"Yes, I saw that as well."

"So what you're asking me is if I were going to use this in a murder mystery, how would I write the plot?"

"Yes."

"Hmm, now who would kill a couple as well as a cop?" Salvatore rubbed his chin. "Since they were in witness protection I guess they were here to testify against someone."

Barbara looked into his eyes with admiration. "What do you think?"

"From what I saw, no one so much as stuck their head outside to enjoy the weather or look at the golf course. That leads me to believe they were in the Phoenix area to testify in a major trial."

Salvatore was enjoying himself so he rewarded himself with a larger sip of chardonnay. "Now ask yourself Barbara, when you watch crime dramas on television who always has a black SUV?"

"I've seen enough television to know that would be a government agency."

Salvatore grinned and pointed a finger at her. "Bingo. That would mean that they had at least two protectors from the U.S. Marshals Service. One of whom must have been the third victim."

Clasping her hands, Barbara grinned. "Go on, you are making this fun."

Salvatore put his right hand to his goatee and mused, "Now who would be in the program? Hmm, most are criminals ratting out on other criminals or people who do business with big time crooks and gangs. Odds are they were here to testify against drug traffickers, crooks, or terrorists."

"This is exciting Salvatore, but please eat some of your sandwich."

Salvatore chewed his food slowly.

In a fashion, I'm in a protection program called protecting my own ass. Like them, I've got a new social security card and driver's license... Big difference is those wimpy folk got psychological counseling. All I have are my wits and alcohol.

Salvatore smiled at Barbara. "From what I've read, returning to testify is the riskiest part of the witness protection program because a hit man doesn't have to waste time and resources finding them in the expanse that is our beloved America."

"I see."

After another bite, "Either way, this is an ideal place."

"Why's that?"

"A retirement community like this, where everyone is more interested in making friends than in prying too deeply into someone's background would be ideal as long as the witness is not some young punk. Then he'd stick out."

"I see... I think you may be right Salvatore."

"Once they were inside our gates, they would have basically fallen off the face of the earth. If they didn't talk or socialize with any of us, we'd probably just think they were another old grump."

"That's probably true and we have enough of those already."

"And here I thought the Graceful Waters Resort gates were to keep us inside so we didn't annoy the young people."

Barbara chuckled. "That's very funny Salvatore."

Salvatore drained the rest of his glass. "May I pour you some more wine?"

"Of course." Barbara took a strand of her hair and started to play with it.

Sonia does that.

"Speaking of young men, I was showing a house across the way in another subdivision and had a man in his thirties come on to me." Barbara raised her right eyebrow and stared at him.

Salvatore looked away. "I'm sorry to hear that."

"Of course, I shut him down."

Salvatore looked up again to watch Barbara lick her lips ever so slightly.

Oh, oh.

He was suddenly sorry he'd brought the wine.

I need to change the subject.

"Since this place is so nice, why do people move away?"

"What do you mean?"

"Well, I see your face on a great many for sale signs."

"It's usually because their health is in decline, they can't manage on their own anymore and they require more from caregivers, or they move to help out another family member like one of their children who is perhaps going through a divorce, and they are asked to move in and help out. In that case they may rent their home out instead of having me sell it."

"That makes sense. Did I tell you that I talked to a couple who told me they were moving a couple of weeks ago?"

"I don't think so. Who were they?"

"I never caught their names. However, they did tell me they were moving back to California, to look after the wife's father who is ninety-three. They also said it would only be for a year or two. Then they were planning on moving back."

"Did they say how they knew that the father would be dead by then?"

"The husband told me that if her father hadn't passed by then, that he'd kill him himself."

Barbara stared at Salvatore for several seconds. "You have such a dry sense of humor. I almost believed you."

"Going back to the witness protection program idea, I've read that before the person would have testified, the Federal Prosecutor would have needed to go over their testimony so there were no surprises in open court. That house would be an ideal location to conduct that interview before their testimony in court. Thus, as an author, all I would need to weave into the plot was that there was a big time trial coming up."

Barbara sat up straight and beamed at him. "How you can keep all that information in your mind is fabulous Salvatore. You should tell the police your ideas. I would think they'd appreciate the help."

Salvatore swallowed then faked a grin. "I don't think so. I would guess that they would feel insulted and might lock me up for interfering. Then you'd have to come down and bail me out."

Barbara sat on the edge of her chair and looked into Salvatore's eyes. "I'm not sure I should say this Salvatore, but with the grisly murders here in Graceful Waters Resort, real estate prices will be taking a hit and going down temporarily. If you want a great deal on a home in here, this would be the time to act."

Salvatore dropped his smile. "Let me think about it."

26

S   alvatore was safely in his rental after enjoying his lunch with Barbara. He sat in his easy chair with his eyes closed.

Just a little after lunch chardonnay-induced catnap.

The doorbell surprised him.

He jerked.

Door to door soliciting was banned in the community and no neighbor had ever intruded on him before.

I didn't even know the damned doorbell worked.

Out of curiosity, Salvatore decided to answer.

First, he put on his glasses then checked his hair and goatee in a hallway mirror.

"I'm coming."

Before he opened the door Salvatore glanced at the drawer holding his Ruger.

As he slowly opened the door, he found a grim, fortyish year old man wearing an opened neck shirt and a sports coat standing before him.

I smell a cop.

"Mister Salvatore Cabella?"

Salvatore looked the man over before his simple response. "Yes."

A badge was flashed. "I'm Detective Bill Garcia with the Glenwood PD. May I come in?"

Salvatore touched his glasses. "What for?"

Clearly put off, Bill stared at Salvatore Cabella. "I'm interviewing all the neighbors about what happened next door to you. One of our crime scene officers said that he had talked to you and told you that I'd be coming by to conduct an interview."

"Oh, that's right, come on in." Salvatore stood aside and looked down at the floor.

Garcia tried to look closely at Salvatore's face as he passed him.

With his head still tilted towards the tile floor Salvatore pointed to one of the two comfy looking lounge chairs. "Please sit down."

Garcia sat down while surveying the interior of the home.

Salvatore sat with upright posture in the other chair. "What exactly happened next door?"

Garcia could tell Salvatore was trying to convey power and take control.

"That's what I'm here to find out." Garcia had a specific protocol to follow. Knowing that his department as well as the Feds would scrutinize all of his actions and paperwork, he pulled out a standard Witness Crime Scene form.

Salvatore spoke first. "Before you begin, is this an interrogation or an interview?"

Garcia had been trained to use a soft, normal tone and a friendly demeanor. "How do you know the difference?"

"Oh, it's my hobby. I read and write crime fiction."

Garcia raised his right eyebrow. "Oh, so you're one of them." A grin flashed across Garcia's face.

Salvatore's mouth felt dry. "What do you mean?"

"I understand that most writers spend their days in their own little worlds talking to voices in their heads."

Salvatore felt his ruse was working. "Sure, but it's okay, they know me well." Salvatore pointed at his own head.

Bill Garcia stared at Salvatore.

He's a wacko.

Garcia moistened his lips. "Well, I'm here to interview you as a potential witness."

"Then I have the right to cooperate or not."

Yup, he's an asshole.

"Technically, you're correct. Nonetheless, I must tell you that I can obtain a subpoena to compel you to co-operate. You must realize that refusing to co-operate also draws attention to you."

Cabella nodded. "The only reason I'm asking is that if I cooperate I would like to make it a two way street and ask you a few questions as well. This is the first time I've ever been able to interview a real detective."

Garcia had never met a potential witness like Salvatore Cabella before. Most simply answered his questions as quickly as possible and hoped they didn't say anything incriminating. "If you know anything about the law then I'm sure you realize I cannot comment on or discuss an ongoing investigation."

"Let me set your mind at rest Detective Garcia. I'm excited, as I think I might be able to use this interview in my next novel. Rest assured that my questions are more about procedure and not about this case."

Garcia squinted and gave Salvatore a half grin. "Okay, go ahead."

"The first question I have is why the local police are involved versus the U.S. Marshal Service."

Garcia bobbed his head. "That I can answer. Because the crime happened in my jurisdiction. Now can we proceed?"

Salvatore flashed a grin of satisfaction.

Garcia said, "Good, now can I see your driver's license?"

Salvatore scrunched forward in his chair and pulled out his wallet.

A moment later, he handed over the driver's license.

Garcia examined it for several seconds then looked up at Salvatore. "I see your name is Salvatore Cabella. Are you known by any other names?"

"No." Cabella cocked his head.

"Do you live here by yourself?"

"Why do you ask?"

"In case you have a wife. If you do, I was wondering if she'd heard anything."

"No, I'm single."

As Garcia wrote down Salvatore's license number he compressed his lips. When he finished, he handed the license back to Salvatore. "When did you first meet the people next door?"

"Oh, I've never met them. The only reason I knew someone was there was because they woke me up a few nights ago."

Garcia finally broke a smile. "When they woke you, did you get up to see them?"

"I couldn't really see anyone."

"What was your vantage point?"

"A side window."

"How is your eyesight?"

Salvatore touched his glass frame. "I wear glasses and I'd put them on."

"How is your hearing?"

"Fine."

"Did you hear anything they said?"

"No."

Garcia felt he finally had Salvatore cooperating. "I have to ask my next question only because you reside in a retirement community. How is your memory?"

y memory is fine." Salvatore decided to once again throw Garcia off his stride. "May I ask you an unrelated question?

"Try me."

"I'm sure this kind of crime is somewhat rare. What are the more typical crimes in a retirement community like this?"

"It is rare. Believe it or not Mister Cabella this is my first time in one of our retirement communities. Most times when the Glenwood police are called into communities like yours, it's for domestic disturbances. Most are caused by frustrations with one of the partners becoming senile."

"Interesting."

"Okay Salvatore, now how long have you lived here?" He had been trained that liars tend to touch their face and scratch their nose when they lie. Garcia watched Salvatore's hands.

Salvatore didn't move them.

Instead, he casually crossed his legs. Garcia knew this was a sign of disinterest on Salvatore's part.

"Good question, and I only moved in about a month ago."

"Do you own the home?"

"No, I'm just renting."

"Where are you from?"

"That's the first thing that we all ask each other when we first meet here."

Another non-answer.

"I imagine you have a geographically diverse group here. Now if you don't mind, where are you from?"

"Chicago. Born and raised."

"I would like to confirm what you told the officer yesterday." Garcia looked at his notes. "You went to Happy Hour at the community club house and you returned just after seven in the evening."

"No. My neighbor Barbara Goldberg and I went for hamburgers at the golf course restaurant and then walked home. We came upon the police around eight thirty."

"What time did you leave your house?"

"Just before five. That's when Happy Hour starts and if you don't get there on time, the line to the bar becomes very long."

"Did you notice anything suspicious at the house next door when you left at five?"

"Suspicious how?"

"Like any one hanging around watching the place."

Cabella paused for effect. "No, I don't recall seeing anyone."

"How about earlier in the day?"

"No."

"Had you met your neighbors?"

"No, I never saw a soul. It's dead quite around here, especially on the golf course until the grounds keepers start mowing around sunrise. Anyway, I digress. As I told you earlier, the SUV woke me in the middle of the night."

"Do you know approximately what time they woke you?"

"Let me think. Oh ya, when they woke me I had to pee and when I went back to bed my little clock showed it was something like three o'clock... I think... And oddly I never saw anyone leave the house or the SUV again."

Garcia made more notes. "Why did you think it was odd?"

Salvatore hesitated for a few seconds before he spoke. "Because when most people come here, they immediately go outside and look at the golf course, mountains and take in the vegetation. It's not everywhere you get to see a cactus on a golf course like you do in here."

"I see... Are you retired?"

"Why do you ask?"

"This is a retirement community and I must say you don't appear to be over sixty five."

"They told me that this community was for active adults. Although I must admit, I've since found that most people, or at least the ones I've met, all do seem to be retired. The realtor explained to me that active adult means fifty-five, which I am."

"That makes sense. Now if you aren't retired, what's your occupation?"

28

S alvatore gave a little smile. "As I said when you walked in, I'm an author."

"Really. What do you write?"

"Crime Thrillers."

"You mean like murder mysteries?"

"Yes."

"Would I have read any of your books?"

Salvatore looked away. "Not yet."

"Why's that?" Garcia was trying to suppress a grin.

Salvatore forced himself to swallow. "I've only published one book so far and I published that by myself on Amazon."

"I didn't know you could do that."

"What I did is called self-publishing. It's very common these days. Anyway, I've been working on my next book for a while now but I can't seem to find the time to sit down and write the damn thing. That's the primary reason I moved here, to find some peace and quiet."

Figuring he'd shown enough humility, Salvatore raised his

eyes. "Plus, I don't want the hassle of finding an agent and then a publisher. It takes way too long and besides, I don't handle rejection very well."

"So is there a lot of money in self publishing?"

Salvatore looked down and put his hands together as if he were to make a big confession. "Not yet. So far I've sold less than a million copies."

"A million copies, wow, you must be rich."

"I said less than a million."

"Can you please be a little more exact?"

Salvatore deliberately swallowed hard. "Probably around ten to twelve books."

Salvatore watched as the corner of Garcia's mouth suppressed a grin.

"Then why do you write?"

"To find out who I am."

Nutcase.

"That begs the question of how you make a living then Mister Cabella."

"Let's just say I've worked and saved and now that I've moved here where it's more peaceful and economical to live, I hope to finish my next book and then I'll probably try to find an agent this time."

Garcia made a note in his pad. "What did you do for a living before you became a writer?"

Salvatore paused then sat up straight. "I was a librarian in Chicago. One day, I realized that I was bored with my life. I decided that what I really wanted to do was to write the books that other librarians could recommend to readers."

"Is there anyone that can verify that for me?"

Shit!

Salvatore's mind started to race.

"Sure, but I don't have anyone's phone number handy. I just moved here and I haven't unpacked everything yet."

"Don't you have a list of contacts in your phone?"

He regularly bought cheap disposable cell phones since he never expected to get any incoming phone calls. The only time he bought the disposable phones was when he had to call someone. After each call, he'd remove and destroy the SIM card then trash the phone.

"No. Call me old fashioned but I don't have a smartphone with those app things."

"Why is that?"

"Too expensive and I guess you could say I'm an analog person living in a digital world. I like making personal contact too much I guess. I mean, have you gone into a restaurant lately and seen everyone at the tables all looking at their phones instead of talking to the person they're sitting with. They all look like they are getting directions on what to say from the alien mother ship. I think it's very rude if you must know."

"Do you use a computer for your writing?"

"I did, but I dropped mine when I unpacked it so I tossed it into the garbage. I haven't replaced it yet."

"If you haven't been writing since you got here I can see why you haven't finished your next book." Garcia couldn't suppress his grin.

Salvatore looked away from Garcia as if he had been slapped. "The news reporters said that at least three people died. Is that accurate?"

"At this time all I can say is that deaths were involved." Garcia stood up. "Alright, Mister Cabella, I have what I came for."

Salvatore forced a smile and stood as well.

Garcia returned the grin. "Well here is my card. Please call me once you find your contact list of people who can confirm you are who you say you are."

"Surely I'm not a suspect."

Garcia smiled. "No, I just need to dot the "i's" and cross the "t's". The paperwork we need to complete is like writing a book, so I'm sure you understand."

Garcia turned to leave then turned back to face Cabella. "Is there any additional information you would like to provide?"

"No."

"Is there anyone else that you know of that I should talk with?"

"I don't know all of my neighbors yet, but you could talk to Marvin Haigh who lives next door to me." Salvatore pointed. "Oh, and Barbara who lives two doors down the other way."

"Do you have her last name?"

"Goldberg."

Garcia checked his notes. "Yes, I have her name." He wrote in his notepad. "If you think of anything else that would be helpful to the investigation please contact me."

Salvatore took one of Garcia's cards.

How do you get anyone to cooperate with you when the people you had in witness protection have just been killed?

29

S alvatore walked to a window to watch where Garcia went next.

Next door. Good, Marvin will confirm my story.

Salvatore went to the kitchen and poured himself two fingers of scotch. After a big taste, he sat in his comfy chair and closed his eyes. With the chardonnay still in his system, Salvatore knew the scotch would do its job.

Something made him open his eyes.

He rose from the chair and went to the window. Salvatore couldn't see Garcia's car anywhere. Glancing at a clock on the oven, he saw that Garcia had left him about an hour ago.

It's still early.

He decided he needed to work a few things out in his mind.

I'm sober enough to drive.

Getting in his Camry, he pulled out of his garage and headed south to the local shopping mall. Being in high season, he knew it would be jammed with shoppers. It was the perfect environment to blend in so he could contemplate his options.

It took a few minutes to find a parking spot but once he did, he wasted no time strolling past the multitude of shops.

No one in here sees me. They all suffer from shopping mall face blur.

He was lost in thought and ignored the window displays. He was playing devil's advocate with himself.

I should leave.

But if I leave now, Garcia might get suspicious and try to track me down.

A display window caught his eye.

A bookstore!

His mind always relaxed whenever he entered a bookseller.

He appreciated how his eyes immediately searched for the Mystery and Thriller section.

He searched in vain for something to grab his attention or to spot an older title he wanted to re-read. He settled for a new release.

Standing in line to pay, a magazine article caught his attention. It was titled, 'Science and Crime Solving.'

He picked up the magazine and flipped to the article. From a quick scan he surmised it was an indictment that called into question the scientific validity of the analysis of fingerprints, bite marks, blood spatters, clothing fiber, handwriting, bullet markings, and many other mainstays of forensic investigation.

He skipped to the conclusion.

Salvatore smiled as he read where the author believed that no forensic method could be truly relied on with a high degree of certainty to "demonstrate a connection between evidence and a specific individual or source."

Besides, a good lawyer will always find a way to discredit evidence.

"Next in line."

Salvatore returned the magazine to the rack and stepped forward placing the novel on the counter.

Salvatore Cabella's cash was accepted and he smiled as he was handed the book in a plastic bag.

I almost forgot. I owe Marvin a cigar!

Salvatore found a directory of the mall and found the location of a cigar store.

He went up one level and found it.

When he walked in the smell tickled his nostrils and he inhaled deeply. He had always enjoyed the smell of fine tobacco when it wasn't burning.

From his benefactor he'd learned the art of enjoying the taste as it slowly burned down. Like others in the cigar club, he understood the joy cigars brought to the individual smoking it versus the people being subjected to the odor.

It's like the people in the wine club; they drink to enjoy the different tastes as well as how it looks and smells. They aren't alcoholics.

He bought six Churchill sized Romeo y Julieta cigars for just over seventy-five dollars and asked the clerk to put them into a double sealed plastic bag.

After completing his walk over both levels of the mall he decided to stay in Phoenix a while longer.

Wine! I need two bottles of wine.

Salvatore swung his car into a grocery store where he asked a young man in a vest with the store's name on it for help selecting two bottles.

"What are you looking for?"

Barbara said the wine should cost between ten and twenty dollars a bottle – I can't appear cheap.

"I need two bottles of red wine worth about twenty dollars a bottle."

The young man pointed at an end cap display of wine. "I tried this one last night. It has an explosion of fruit flavors with hints of vanilla and notes of cherry."

Salvatore took two bottles.

At the cashier, there was a display of maps on sale for only a dollar.

"How come the maps are on sale so cheap?"

The cashier looked to be a female teenager who sneered at him. "Are you kiddin', nobody buys maps anymore. Everyone uses the maps app on their phones or in their cars."

"Then I'll buy one for old time's sake."

He selected a fold out map of the United States of America.

The cashier rolled her eyes but rang him up anyway.

30

W alking to his car it hit him.
The cat.
He saw a corner mini mart and walked over.

As he drove back up to the Graceful Waters Resort's main gates, he used his clicker to enter.

He enjoyed seeing the scenic golf course; he glanced over at the water next to the fairway. It was a small creek that was home to everything from Canadian geese to ducks to egrets, running beside the road.

A minute later, his eyes were pulled to a group of people having fun at the bocce courts.

In no rush to get back home, he pulled into the clubhouse parking lot and found a shady space to park under a tree. He placed the wine on the floor so it was away from the sun then went directly to the bocce courts to watch.

He recalled watching the elderly Italian men in his neighborhood play bocce back in the dirt lots in Chicago.

He saw that these courts were probably as rough as those

back in Chicago as these had small pebbles on top of decomposed granite.

No matter how good the bowler is the pebbles mean the ball could end up anywhere. That's why the guy who told me about these courts said it was strictly a social game, for fun.

Salvatore counted about twenty people milling around the court. He decided to watch for a few minutes.

A quick glance showed about the same number at the second court.

I'd like to join a team, but I won't be here long enough.

Both teams were picking players for a new frame. Each team placed two players at each end.

He watched as a man he estimated to be in his late seventies or eighties stepped onto the court. His female partner had to pick up and hand him the pallino.

The man shuffled a few steps before he tried to bend his knees to roll the pallino. A look of pain shot across his face as the pallino left his hand.

The man seemed surprised as the pallino landed in the middle of the court about three quarters of the way towards the other end.

Good throw.

His female partner handed the man a red ball.

He seemed to take a deep breath as if he summoning his testosterone to kick in.

Once again, he tried to bend his knees then stopped, as if pain had shot through his body.

The ball seemed to hit a soft patch and never made it close to the pallino.

Tough luck.

A sneer burst onto the face of one of his opponents from the other end of the court.

Then came the loud heckle. "Does your wife play sweetheart?"

Salvatore's blood boiled.

He looked at the opponent. He was completely bald except for a fringe of white that dropped in a semi circle from his ears down.

He even looks like an asshole.

The woman standing next to him looked no better.

From the couple's mannerisms, Salvatore figured they both had symbiotic inferiority complexes.

That asshole is just trying to upset the other team. He's a Darth Vader without the suit to hold him together.

He needs to go and see Tina, the Life Coach.

His thoughts rushed to how his kin had dealt with assholes like him when they were teenagers in Chicago.

Salvatore thought of going to the next happy hour and finding the jerk.

Then I'll wait outside in the dimly lit parking lot for him.

He could feel the satisfaction of plunging a knife between the hecklers ribs and whispering, "Bocce is for fun, asshole."

He caught himself.

I need to stop.

Instead, Salvatore forced himself to walk away. He decided to grab a quick snack from the clubhouse cafe before he went home.

He decided on a cinnamon roll to go.

The roll never survived the walk to the car.

As Salvatore turned the Camry onto his street, he was happy not to spot Garcia's, or any other police vehicles.

Before he shut the garage door, he scanned up and down the street. No cars were visible that didn't belong there.

Salvatore was prepared to spend a quiet evening reading his new novel.

Maybe I'll smoke one of my cigars while I sit outside reading my book.

Then he remembered he had signed up to attend the Wine Club's Home Social with Barbara.

31

S alvatore checked the time. He had only five minutes to
get ready.

Thank God, I remembered to buy the wine.

Fortunately, the dress code at the home socials was casual,
so there was no need to change.

The Wine Club Socials were held simultaneously at multiple
members' homes. Each host's home accommodated thirty to
forty members. Each attending couple was to bring an appetizer
and two bottles of wine.

He'd initially tried to avoid going. "I'm not a wine
connoisseur."

"Don't worry. No one's comparing the wines. They're all
there just to guzzle as much as they can in two hours while
pretending to be social."

"Guzzle?"

"The police don't have roadblocks within the community.
They know we all need to drink."

Salvatore put on his glasses and grinned at himself in the mirror.

He walked to Barbara's home and found her ready, standing outside her front door holding a tin foil covered casserole dish.

She was wearing a subdued sundress and seemed to be naked without a hat on her head. She beamed as he grew nearer to her. "I was afraid that with all that's happened you'd forgotten about tonight."

Salvatore took the bait. "Heaven's no. How could I forget about spending time with you?"

Barbara blushed. He noticed her blond hair with no roots. "Your hair style's a little different, isn't it?"

"Salvatore, you're such a charming lady's man aren't you." She batted her eyelashes at Salvatore then started walking. "The hosts live just a block over so I thought we'd walk."

It was a beautiful evening with the temperature still close to eighty degrees.

"Is everything alright Barbara?"

"Well since you asked, I'll admit I'm feeling a little down. A client I thought was going to make an offer today just cancelled. He said he didn't want to live in such a high crime area."

"Oh. I'm sorry to hear that."

They arrived at the house. They couldn't miss it. It sported a large multi-colored Wine Party sign hanging from an exterior garage light.

Salvatore grinned as he thought to himself.

At least there aren't any pink flamingos in the yard.

Several cars were just pulling up. Salvatore estimated that there were probably twenty cars and SUVs already parked nearby.

Juggling the two bottles of wine under his right armpit Salvatore opened the front door for Barbara.

He smiled as he also held it open for one other couple.

"Thank you young man."

The home was over flowing with bodies and the din of women chatting.

This was his first wine club event.

Where are the other men?

A horde of women were milling around the kitchen island.

Barbara tapped him on the shoulder. "Don't look so lost. The majority of the men and the wine are probably outside."

"Is this a pot luck and wine event?"

"Remember, it's One appetizer and Two bottles. The food is irrelevant. Now excuse me but I need to find a spot to put this."

Salvatore flashed a fake grin at Barbara then eased his way past several women blocking the sole corridor to the outside.

Stepping outside, he immediately felt better.

It was almost quiet.

It appeared all the men were silently holding court on the extra large patio.

Besides the host's outside table with eight chairs, there were four large comfy looking easy chairs and two lounges where men looked like they were going to be taking a nap until their wives told them it was time to leave.

One long folding table supported a large silver tub of ice and white wines. Another table held even more bottles that were various reds.

As he placed both bottles on the red table, he could already overhear remarks about the murders.

"Until the killings, my biggest fear in living here was scalding my tongue on a too hot latte."

"If I'd seen anything, there's no bloody way I'd tell the police about it."

"Why not?"

"Are you kidding me?"

Salvatore took his time pretending he was looking for a wine opener he liked.

"If the feds can't protect a snitch in witness protection then why should I put my life in danger? I'm not that stupid."

"You've got a point there."

Salvatore looked over at the two men. He'd never seen them before, but given the size of the community that wasn't unusual.

He looked at them again and stared.

They're twins.

He looked at one and asked, "How do you know they were in the witness protection program?"

"I heard it on the news."

"Oh, you're always watching the bloody news." His twin jerked away.

"Oh, I see, thanks."

Salvatore ignored the banter. He knew everyone was different from each other, even twins. He knew that under their skin, personal experiences had twisted everyone to be unique.

With a grin plastered on his face, he proceeded to open one of his bottles of California wine.

It suddenly hit him that he'd forgotten that Barbara had told him to also bring two wine glasses.

Fortunately, he saw that the hostess had provided plastic ones.

Not the same as crystal, but this isn't top-notch wine anyway.

He poured two glasses.

Stepping inside, he saw Barbara and snaked his way through the women to be at her side. "I brought you some wine."

Barbara hesitated then accepted the glass. "I see that you forgot to bring the proper glasses, shame on you."

Salvatore grimaced, asking to be forgiven.

Barbara didn't want to upset him. "Don't worry, these will work well for tonight."

Salvatore said, "Cheers."

Barbara responded in kind.

He couldn't help but hear a woman next to Barbara. He turned to see who she was but she had her back to him. "When you get to be my age everything has either dried up or leaks."

Too much information.

Barbara raised her eyebrows and took Salvatore by the elbow.

It seemed like every conversation they overheard on their way outside was about the murders.

The small talk outside was also only about the murders.

"Whoever killed three people in cold blood has to be an animal. Who could live with themselves after committing such a sin."

He wanted to blurt out, "Perhaps the killer had to do it." Instead, he bit his tongue.

32

*H*anging *with these people is driving me crazy. I like them but they act ignorant of the bigger world. It's kill or be killed out there.*

Salvatore took a bigger swig of the wine in the hope it would help to make the conversations more interesting.

The wine was average.

There was no explosion of flavor. Instead of being able to pick out notes of cherry or hints of vanilla, it was simply dull.

A man dressed in a plaid shirt came up to Barbara. "Say Barbara, don't you live on the street where the murders took place?"

"Yes." She moved her right palm up to bring Salvatore into the conversation. "Salvatore and I both live there, why do you ask."

"Well we were just discussing whether it was an inside job."

Salvatore perked up. "Why do you think that?"

"Well I heard that there were two feds, guarding two people. Suddenly one guard left. Surprise, surprise, suddenly both people in witness protection are dead, as well as the guard who was left behind. Who's to say it wasn't the other guard who killed everyone as he was going out for the food run. It could have just been his cover?"

Barbara looked at Salvatore and said, "That's a possibility I guess. What do you think Salvatore?"

Time for some good old misdirection.

Salvatore put down his wine glass on a side table and steepled his fingers to increase his authority. "I think you may be on to something. However, I've been thinking it could have just as easily have been a murder suicide."

Plaid shirt man asked, "Really, why do you say that?"

"Why not? The first guard may have waited until the second guard left on the food run. Since lust is the oldest motive in the world, first guard probably killed the couple because he was in love with the witnesses' wife. Perhaps the husband had found out. Anyway, then realizing his career in law enforcement was over, he turned his weapon on himself."

Shaking his head, the man in the plaid shirt said, "Barbara said that you made things up for a living. That sounds like something only a professional liar could dream up."

Salvatore turned and raised his wine glass. "I'll take that as a compliment. As a writer and avid reader, I can tell you with certainty that lust, love, loathing and greed are the oldest and most common reasons for someone to commit a murder."

"Since you're an expert, how will the murderer get caught?"

"In almost every mystery, no matter how much planning goes into a murder, the culprit will make at least one mistake leading to his or her undoing."

"I see. Do you think there's any chance the killer was a woman?"

Barbara asked, "Why do you ask that?"

Plaid shirt man grinned. "Cause women like to kill a man slowly, over many years."

Barbara didn't see the humor. She glared at him. "Get serious."

Not to be shutdown, the man turned to Salvatore. "You also said the culprit might make a mistake? Like what?"

"Oh say, like a fingerprint on a shell or perhaps talking too much trying to pull the wool over the detective's eyes. There has to be a clue. Otherwise the bad guy would get away and there would be no happy ending."

Barbara was poking around in her wine glass. "Got the little bugger." She held up a finger with a minute black speck. She shook it, then proceeded to sip her wine.

"I thought you said there weren't any bugs here in Glenwood."

Barbara frowned. "There aren't. How is your next book coming?"

"The characters are all beginning to sound the same and the plot feels flimsy and unbelievable. My confidence is draining away. If I can't turn it around I'll probably have to go back to Chicago and see if I can get my job back as a Librarian."

"Perhaps this murder will inspire you. Does wine help?"

"Wine always helps."

Barbara looked serious. "Now, I'm thinking that we should start a petition to have the developer of this community make us feel more secure. I mean how did the killer or killers get in."

A short bald guy with an east coast accent jumped into the conversation. "I agree. We need twenty-four hour a day armed guards at the gates and a twelve-foot security wall around our entire community, including the entire golf course. That'll keep out the riffraff and killers."

Salvatore responded first. "I would think that the cost of

doing those things for security would probably double or triple your dues." He pushed up his glasses. "Besides, it would also ruin the elegant yet casual feel to this place."

A pleasant looking woman who had been listening chimed in. "I've got a neighbor who reminds me of Norman Bates. He's so scary I wish the killer had shot him instead. I think we should be doing a thorough vetting of anyone wanting to move in here."

"What are you suggesting?"

"I'd like to see the developer use a psychological test to screen out the weird and whacky."

The short guy raised his eyes. "Well if they don't make us more secure then I'm moving. Hell, the police can't even tell us why the murders may have been committed. Was it drugs or mafia hit men? How can they not know?"

Salvatore wanted to respond with something snarky then decided to let it go. "Do you need a refill Barbara?"

"Thank you, Salvatore."

33

When Salvatore went back to the red wine table, he found both of his bottles were empty. He surveyed the labels of the remaining bottles and realized they were the less expensive wine.

Cheap bastards!

The man in the plaid shirt saw Salvatore looking at the bottles. "Some of the people that come to these things are cheap, aren't they. The last time I came to one of these, I saw a guy walk in, set down an open bottle of cheap swill and pick up a better unopened wine. He then walked straight out the door before anyone could say anything to him."

Salvatore couldn't believe what he was hearing. "If they can't afford a relatively inexpensive wine how can they afford to live in here?"

"Now that's a good question. Didn't I hear Barbara say that you are fairly new to living in Graceful Waters Resort?"

"I am."

"It's quite a place isn't it? When we first bought in here, this place was in the middle of nowhere. Nothing but desert all around us. Then the gas station went in, followed by the grocery store and then a restaurant. Now look at us. We don't need to drive very far to get life's necessities. Even the doctors have come to the mountain, as they say."

Barbara walked over and interrupted. "Aren't you going to eat anything, Salvatore? There's a lots of good things inside."

"Sure, but only if you'll join me." Salvatore held up his right arm, waist high.

Barbara took him by the arm and walked into the kitchen. They got into a line behind two women.

The woman in front of them turned to Barbara. "Whoever the killer is must have a screw loose."

Ever the pleasant woman, Barbara replied. "Why do you say that?"

"What kind of person can commit cold blooded murder like that? They must be some kind of psychopath, don't you think?"

"I hadn't thought about it." Barbara looked at Salvatore who seemed to be gazing at a painting hanging on the wall.

I'm not a psychopath!

The woman kept going. "We're not talking about someone who can't control their anger or is frustrated and can't take it anymore. Humans are wired for compassion, to feel guilt, to experience empathy. Whoever did it was a monster. I mean, who can kill another human being just for money? I can't imagine it unless they are unhinged."

Salvatore became upset and wanted to walk away, but it was finally the woman's turn to select her food.

Barbara didn't respond either. She passed Salvatore a paper plate and white plastic fork.

Salvatore took them as he inhaled several deep breaths to calm himself.

That woman's psychobabble is bullshit.

People like me are special.

We are super heroes who make the hard decisions and clean up the scum of the earth

Barbara pointed to a dish. "That is an awesome vegetarian quiche, if you like quiche."

Salvatore snapped out of his momentary depression. "Did you know that vegetarian is an old Indian word meaning bad hunter?"

Barbara looked at him sideways then laughed. "You have such a dry sense of humor, Salvatore."

They spent about five minutes picking items from the table and placing them on their plates.

Barbara handed Salvatore one of the napkins. "Let's sit outside."

They found two empty metal chairs with deep cushions. Each chair had a side table and they managed to eat the finger food while sipping wine.

A woman Salvatore had seen talking non-stop sat down next to them. "I think my next door neighbors were about to be shot next."

Barbara looked at the woman in disbelief. "Why would you say that?"

"When I woke up this morning they'd left."

"What do you mean?"

"I heard a vehicle drive up just after midnight so I got up to look. I saw a man and woman next door get into a black SUV with some bags and drive away."

"Are you sure they didn't call for a taxicab or Uber to take them to the airport for an early morning flight?"

"What plane leaves that time of the morning? No, I'm telling you someone picked them up and they fled in panic.

I'm positive they were also in some witness protection program."

"How do you come to that conclusion?"

"They've lived next door to me for three months and except to return my friendly wave just once, they've never talked to me. They've never gone to Coffee Talk that I know of and they keep to themselves. I've never met the wife. The husband went out for a walk early in the morning and late at night. He wears ear buds as if he's listening to music but I think he wears them to make people think he can't hear them. Even when I wave at him, he doesn't stop. He's either totally rude or in witness protection."

"Why would someone in witness protection live in here?"

"Think about it. This is the perfect community. Probably half the people in here are part timers that come and go, so the likelihood is that one of the homes on either side of you is empty, without prying eyes."

"Okay."

"Then there is the fact that people don't dare ask what you used to do. It's as if we don't care anymore."

Salvatore jumped into the conversation. "You mean people in here don't want to admit that they used to be part of a crime family or drug cartel and are hiding out."

The woman's eyes widened. "Exactly, that's why I'm sure a bunch of our neighbors are probably hiding out in here."

A woman in a blue blouse and white pants, who had been listening quietly, spoke up. "I agree with you that we have other people hiding in here. My next-door neighbors moved in over two months ago. They keep all their window blinds totally covered, night and day and I've never seen them go outside other than in their SUV. And it's got heavily tinted windows so I have no idea who or how many live there. I even went to the

Home Owners Association to find out what the hell was going on."

Barbara asked, "What did they tell you?"

"The lady there looked up the address and then she acted funny. She would only tell me that it was a couple who meet the age requirement."

Barbara offered an explanation. "Perhaps they are sun sensitive so they avoid the sun."

Salvatore wanted to have a little fun. "Or maybe they're vampires who only leave their homes when it's dark outside."

Everyone looked at Salvatore with a smirk.

Ya, I'm just a crazy writer.

Ignoring Salvatore, the woman in the blue blouse snapped. "Then why did they move to Arizona? No, they're in witness protection I tell you. I'm afraid that if someone comes to kill them, a stray bullet might kill one of us. You know how much Harvey and I enjoy sitting outside."

Salvatore was tired of listening. For the first time he paid attention to a fire pit that had foot high flames dancing on lava rock.

The temperature's still got to be over seventy degrees and it's very comfortable, why would they need to light the fire pit.

He suddenly realized why.

They don't need it but they want people to notice it!

Salvatore continued to look around and noticed people thanking the hosts, finding their dishes and leaving for their homes. "What time is it Barbara?"

"You're right. It's time to leave." Barbara stood up. "I need to go inside and get the plate my appetizer was on."

As they walked towards home, Barbara was unusually quiet so Salvatore did most of the talking. "You know on my first visit to the clubhouse by myself, I found the conversations I overheard to be boring. The men all seemed to be talking about golf and various surgeries while the women were all talking about some game with Mexicans and trains. Now it seems all the conversations are about the Happy Hour murders."

"Hopefully it'll be the only major crime we ever have. I mean who commits murders in a retirement community."

"Don't you mean active adult community?"

Barbara laughed. "You got me."

As they came to her house, she stopped and looked at Salvatore. Their eyes met.

Salvatore said, "That was a fun event, even though most of the conversations were about the murders."

"Yes, they were, weren't they?"

"Anyway, I want to finish the book I'm reading, so I'll say thank you for a nice evening."

34

GLENWOOD, AZ

They were working a high priority case. Even though it was Saturday, Garcia's team of Detectives was holding a meeting at the Glenwood Police Department Headquarters.

Charlie Fontaine looked around the room and asked, "Where's Marshal Brown and that AUSA woman?"

Bill Garcia moved his hands as if to say, *who knows.* "They were told we'd be working today. I guess the assistant AUSA went shopping and the Marshal thinks it's a federal holiday or something."

All four men cracked up laughing.

Ten seconds later Garcia pointed at Fontaine. "What were you able to find Charlie?"

"Harry and I talked to the rest of the neighbors on both sides of the street where the crime occurred as well as the neighbors across the golf course fairway from the crime scene."

"Great, what'd you find."

"Most of the neighbors were at the clubhouse during the

Happy Hour event. Only the ones that were invalids didn't attend and they didn't see or hear anything due to their disabilities or they were watching television."

"At their age, you would think Happy Hour would be a nap."

More laughing.

"Do any of them have a home video security system?"

"It's not like they go to work and leave the house alone all day, so that's a big negative, Bill."

"A simple no, will suffice Charlie." Garcia turned away.

"Tom, how about you? Were you able to find any murders with a similar MO?"

"There aren't a whole lot of murders that have been committed with a similar MO. I did however come up with two known offenders. Both are local bad boys who shot up rival gang member's execution style. The problem is both men were convicted and are still serving their time in prison."

"Have we identified and searched likely disposal sites for the weapon?"

"We checked garbage containers at the community clubhouse and all businesses within a mile radius. The biggest target area the gun could have been tossed into is the surrounding desert. A dog team will be searching it tomorrow."

Charlie spoke. "How did your interviews with the closest neighbors go, Bill?"

"One of them is an asshole who thinks that because he's written a fictional book about a murder he knows as much as we do. But he's too stupid to have pulled this off." He took a breath. "The others were nice old people who saw nothing out of the ordinary."

Tom asked, "How's the Pathologist's report coming?"

Garcia replied. "We should get the final report telling us that they were shot to death by tomorrow morning. The interesting stuff should come from the lab on Monday afternoon."

Garcia paused, as he knew he was about to tell a lie in order to motivate his fellow detectives. "Remember guys, we only have to be lucky once to catch this guy. He has to be lucky all of the time. The odds are in our favor."

35

O n Saturday morning, Salvatore woke to the sound of an annoying gas powered leaf blower.

It must be the gardeners.

He had been told they came monthly and were included in the rent.

Ten minutes later, he was sipping his coffee.

What should I do next?

Another sip and he'd made his decision.

I need to continue to show my face and talk to my neighbors a bit longer.

He looked out at his freshly blown back yard. It was now devoid of dead leaves and flowers.

That's why people refer to them as the blow and go guys.

He walked up to the clubhouse and discovered that the club was hosting their Saturday morning Farmer's Market in the parking lot close to the clubhouse.

Salvatore walked through the vendors. Several local farmers were selling vegetables and honey. A pleasant looking woman spoke to him as he passed her table. "Do you have allergies sir?"

Salvatore stopped. "In fact I do."

She pointed at several jars. "Then you need to take a spoonful of this local raw honey every morning. In a few days you'll develop an immunity to our pollens."

"Really?"

"Yes sir. If it hasn't cured you in two weeks just bring it back for a full refund."

"I'll give it a try."

With his brown bag in hand, he passed vendors selling bamboo socks, frozen fish, dog treats, soaps and chips and dips.

He entered the clubhouse through a side door.

When he walked past one of the meeting rooms, he heard a female voice call his name. "Salvatore."

He stopped and took two steps back.

Inside the room, Barbara was waving at him to enter. With her were John Peterson, his wife Mary and two others who were sitting around a card table.

"Come join us Salvatore. John is trying to entertain us with a discussion about moral dilemmas." Barbara rolled her eyes.

Salvatore waved the palm of his left hand and shook his head. "I think I'll pass. That sounds too much like work."

"John here thought it'd be interesting. I really need your help. Please have a seat and join me." Barbara was now pleading with her eyes.

Salvatore sat beside Barbara. "Okay, fill me in."

Barbara said, "John thinks whoever murdered the people next door to us may have been crooks themselves if they were in witness protection.

"That's logical."

John said, "However, I don't think killing is morally permissible under any circumstance. What do you think Salvatore?"

Salvatore looked at John. "When a soldier kills, is he morally wrong?"

John squirmed in his seat. Finally, he answered. "Yes."

"Why do you think that?"

"If a soldier has a duty not to kill then it keeps him from targeting civilians and killing surrendered enemies."

"Of course. But in the heat of battle I would think the soldier's first priority is to stay alive. And if he fears for his life or his buddies' lives then he has to kill and society will call him a hero. Further, when the state kills, we call it justice. If the couple that was killed were crooks as you think they were and were ratting out other crooks, why isn't that killer also considered a hero for doling out justice?"

John didn't look happy. He spoke slowly. "Let's make the decision more personal. I'm going to tell you a story and I want you to agree up front to make a decision. Do you agree Salvatore?"

"Sure." Salvatore crossed his arms.

John proceeded to weave his tale. "Let's assume you are in love with a pregnant woman who is carrying your baby."

"Keep going."

"And you are out walking on a beach somewhere when she sees a cave in the rocks. You follow her as she enters the cave. When you are both inside, a landslide imprisons both of you in the dark. She panics and you try to comfort her but you realize you will die from lack of oxygen before you can dig your way out. Are you with me so far?

"Sure."

"Then as your eyes adjust, you suddenly realize there is some light coming from deeper in the cave. You both crawl towards the light when you see a small opening. Then you feel the dirt becoming damp and realize that the tide must be coming in and that you could now drown."

"Go on." Salvatore glanced at Barbara.

Why did you drag me into this?

"Your girlfriend says, let me see if I can fit through the opening and you let her, only to find that she gets stuck and can't move backwards or forward no matter how hard you pull or push her."

Salvatore shook his head from side to side. "That's a hell of a mess but where's the dilemma?"

"Let's say you have a hunting knife in your pocket. Would you kill her to save yourself or would you let both of you drown?"

"Oh my." Barbara looked perplexed.

John looked at Salvatore. "So what would you do Salvatore?"

"I don't know? That's a very good question." His arms and legs crossed.

"That's the moral dilemma. Now don't forget, you promised to make a choice for us."

Salvatore realized that the problem was close to the situation he was living. Suddenly realizing his crossed arms and legs could be seen as being defensive he dropped his arms. "I would cut her just enough to free her. She would probably bleed a lot but I think I could slice her enough to free both of us while not killing her or the child."

Barbara knotted her eyebrows and grimaced. "Eww."

John shook his head. "Now that's not fair, Salvatore."

Salvatore smirked. "But both of us plus the baby would live. So you see, there is no moral dilemma." He deliberately showed the palms of his hands.

Barbara commented. "You sound more like a butcher than a librarian."

Salvatore didn't comment.

John couldn't win the moral argument so he tried to switch to a dilemma. Jerk.

John broke the silence. "Don't worry Salvatore, there is no right answer. A dilemma never has a right answer. Say, there's a spring training baseball game later today down at the Glenwood stadium between the Mariners and Arizona Diamondbacks. Mary, Barbara and I are going and I know it's not sold out. Would you care to join us?"

He remembered how his father had taken him to a Cubs game when he was ten years old. The seats were in the upper tier but they were the best ones ever to him. "Thanks but I've got a few things I need to do."

"Suit yourself."

Salvatore excused himself and left the room. He headed down the hallway towards the cafe.

People may smile at you, yet underneath it's hard to like those that see the world so differently.

36

SUNDAY

S unday got off to an ominous start.

Salvatore woke to the sound of an emergency medical vehicle increasing its whine while it kept coming closer.

Sweet Mother, can't anyone get a quiet night's sleep around this place?

He glanced at the bedside clock, left his Ruger in its nest, rose and then quickly threw on his golf shirt and shorts.

The emergency vehicle turned off its siren but not until it sounded as if it were stopping directly in front of his rental.

What if it's the cops?

He retrieved his gun.

Holding it down by his side while peering from a window, Salvatore saw the vehicle had stopped in front of Marvin's house.

It's an ambulance.

Breathing a sigh of relief, Salvatore secured the Ruger in the hall table. He then walked across his tile floor and found his shoes where he had slipped them off.

After they were on, he went to his rear slider and opened it.

It was still dark.

Salvatore closed his sliding door behind him and walked across the rock landscape to Marvin's back patio.

Joan must be in trouble.

Through the patio window, Marvin had seen him coming. He went to his sliding rear door to let him in.

"Salvatore, thanks for coming over. I hope the ambulance didn't wake you up."

Salvatore shook his head and waved his palms in front of him. "Don't worry about me, how's Joan?"

"They're wheeling her out right now."

Marvin and Salvatore watched as the EMTs pushed Joan's gurney through the front door and out to the waiting ambulance. She was wearing an oxygen mask and had an IV coming out of her arm.

"They gave her an ECG and said they think she had another heart attack. They're taking her to the hospital over by the mall for more tests."

"Anything I can do for you?"

"No, the tests will take a while so I'm going to go down to see her in an hour or so…. Given all that's happening around here maybe you could just watch the house for me."

"No problem, Marvin. Just let me know if there is anything else I can do."

Marvin grabbed Salvatore and gave him a hug.

Salvatore just stood there. It was the first hug he'd had since he left St Kitts.

Going home, Salvatore had a quick shower in case Marvin needed any help.

About an hour later, Salvatore heard a knock on his front door.

It was Marvin, looking pale. "Joan's just had a stroke and they told me to come right down." Marvin looked shaken. "Would you mind driving me to the hospital?"

"Wait for me on the sidewalk. I'll pull my car out of the garage." Salvatore grabbed his car keys.

Salvatore pulled out his beat up Camry. He was surprised it had gotten him to Arizona without any problems.

Marvin climbed in and took a deep breath. "Thank you for driving me. You're a great neighbor."

Salvatore started driving and waited for Marvin to talk.

The ride to the hospital seemed to drag on for hours but took only twenty-three minutes.

Marvin sat, staring straight ahead out the front window.

It must be worse than he told me.

Salvatore dropped Marvin at the front entrance then went to find a parking spot.

As he exited his car, he looked towards the hospital and felt strange. Shrugging it off he entered the hospital and went directly to the nurse's station. The nurse was on the phone, an orchid sitting in front of her.

It made him think of Sonia and St Kitts.

Orchids grow like weeds there and they're Sonia's favorite flower.

"Can I help you?"

Salvatore snapped out of his moment. "Joan Haight's room please."

He looked at the nurse's vacant face as she gave him Joan's room number and directions.

His gut told him he shouldn't be in a hurry.

Seven minutes later, Salvatore found Joan's private room.

He walked in and felt he was intruding.

Marvin was holding Joan's frail hand.

Salvatore could see that Joan's face was whiter than ever and her eyes were closed.

In his gut, Salvatore knew he was about to watch Joan die and Marvin's life collapse.

He felt nothing.

God, why did you give me such a cold heart?

Marvin looked like he was about to cry.

However, Marvin surprised him. He spoke softly while caressing his wife's hand. His voice never wavered. "Joan my love, we are both old and our bodies are failing us... Our ends are near... Know that I am close behind you and if you'll stretch out your hand, I think you'll be able to touch mine."

Salvatore was shocked when tears came to his eyes. He blinked at them in disbelief as he felt the tears run down his cheeks.

I haven't cried since my wife died twenty-five years ago.

Marvin lifted Joan's hand and kissed it. "Until I join you on our next journey, I will keep you alive in my heart." Marvin lowered his face until his cheek touched her hand. "Goodbye my best friend and forever love. I'll see you soon."

Hearing Marvin's words chilled him. Salvatore was impressed with Marvin's eloquence. He placed his right hand softly onto Marvin's shoulder.

I'm here for you.

Then Salvatore stepped away into a corner.

His mind went to something Sonia had said to him one evening. "Exterior beauty can fade but true intimacy and friendship can stay strong."

Salvatore stood like a statue as two nurses and a doctor seemed to float into the room. They moved with caution.

He then realized they had given Marvin his privacy so he could say his final goodbyes to his wife.

When one of the nurses looked at Marvin, he nodded at her and wiped his eyes.

The doctor pulled out his stethoscope and listened to Joan's heart. He pulled the scope away and looked at the other nurse.

Marvin stepped into the corner beside his neighbor.

The first nurse pulled the sheet up over Joan's face while the other pulled the curtain around the bed.

Marvin turned and gave Salvatore his second hug of the day. This time Salvatore hugged back.

Salvatore felt one last sob leave Marvin's body.

After a few moments, Marvin pulled away. "You should go. I need to stay here for a while and take care of things. Joan was Jewish and must be buried within twenty-four hours. But I'll be holding a Celebration of life for her. Probably on Tuesday and I'd like you to come."

"But how will you get home?"

"I'll grab an Uber. I'll be fine, you go."

"Are you sure?"

"Yes and thank you for everything." Marvin patted his neighbor on the shoulder.

Salvatore walked out of the hospital and headed straight for his car.

Once he was in the Camry, he sat for several minutes trying to understand why he had cried and what it meant.

My emotions have never taken over like that before... am I changing from being around these old farts?

37

As he drove back to the Graceful Waters Resort, Salvatore was in a somber mood.

In the privacy of his car, he stopped playing his role as Salvatore Cabella. Once again, he was Mario Clemenza. The role he had been playing for the past twenty-five years.

Joan is dead.

God's Waiting Room indeed.

Joan's death brought his own wife's death front and center.

When my beautiful wife died so young... back then I was known as Bonaro Lombardi.

He thought of how he had chased her and how she kept putting him off. Finally, she decided she'd toyed with him enough. They were young and poor but deeply in love.

He stopped at a red light and squeezed his eyes shut.

After I located the bastard who'd raped and beaten her to death, I exacted my revenge.

Someone blared their horn at him.

He opened his eyes to see the light was green. He put his foot on the gas.

He recalled being arrested. It wasn't until after his uncle Alfonzo had come to see him in his jail cell that he'd felt any chance of hope.

Alfonzo told him he was going to contact the lawyer Vincent Rizzo to see if he could help. It turned out that Vincent was Anthony Rizzo's cousin.

He recalled how the Rizzos later explained that they had bribed the police captain to erase his birth name and fingerprints from the files.

The only person that even knows that I'm alive is my uncle in Chicago. Since my own parents died in a car crash, Alfonzo's been my only friend and confidante for all these years.

With the new identity of Mario Clemenza, he went to work for Anthony Rizzo. He never worried about being discovered as he knew Anthony was now his benefactor and had paid for the best alias possible.

Mario looked into his rear view mirror and touched his face. He recalled the plastic surgery and Anthony telling him that it gave him a rugged old-fashioned look. Anthony had said, "You now look like an average nobody who would not do any harm to anyone."

He had sworn to serve Anthony Rizzo.

Until I killed my wife's murderer, I'd never killed anyone. Sure, I beat up a few guys who deserved it and I took a few beatings myself. But to kill someone; never. However, I owed Anthony Rizzo my life.

That commitment turned out to be a twenty-five year sentence.

Any personal happiness was like trying to eat soup with a fork.

Mario recalled how he became Anthony's full time body-guard and chauffeur. More importantly, he became Anthony's problem solver.

If someone needed an incentive to pay off their debt, or not testify against Anthony, Mario provided the persuasion. And when necessary, Mario would eliminate the individual.

I never felt guilt or remorse. I was doing what I'd been told to do. After all, it's a kill or be killed world.

I can't help but think that much of Anthony's success was due to my special skills as his permanent shadow and enforcer. Every time Anthony sensed a risk or felt the authorities might investigate his dealings, due to my intervention, potential witnesses changed their minds or disappeared before anyone could testify.

With a new name and identity, he took his job seriously. If Anthony were flying somewhere, Mario would pay the airport fuel supplier to ensure the jet received only the best fuel.

When Anthony dined, Mario would watch in the kitchen, as the food was prepared.

Cash was the lubricant that made everyone accommodate Mario's presence and wishes.

Mario had turned Anthony's estate on St Kitts into a secure fortress. No one had ever gotten close to Anthony.

They'd spent countless hours playing chess to keep amused.

It had all ended badly. Anthony was dying prematurely. Probably from his daily nicotine overdose from chain-smoking his cigars.

I'd just eliminated Anthony's wife in a plane crash along with one of Anthony's long time syndicate members. She'd made the mistake of talking to a lawyer about a divorce.

Mario had received a five million dollar bonus afterwards.

Mario had overheard Vincent tell Anthony, "A few million just saved you billions."

Yup, death is cheaper than a divorce every time.

I've broken legs and arms, poisoned, knifed and shot people... But so what, they probably all had it coming to them. I have no regrets. When I first started, I wasn't paid for my services. Anthony would merely tell me that I'd done a good job.

Later, if the business hits resulted in a large payday for Anthony, he would pay me a small gratuity.

It was only later on when the hits were on Anthony's friends and family that I was paid generously.

Mario felt Anthony's guilt had fueled the increase.

That was when I made the mistake of telling him I wanted to retire.

He recalled Anthony's response. "Well you can't just retire. Not just like that. We need to figure it out. Where will you go? How will I ensure your continued loyalty, if I need you? How will I replace you?"

Mario immediately realized that Anthony would never let him leave.

Chaos hit when Anthony died in his sleep.

The next morning Mario didn't know who he could trust. The night before Anthony's son had told him that Anthony and Vincent were planning a hit on him since he knew too much.

I was stupid to think he could let me go.

Vincent claimed that he was going to let him retire.

I didn't believe him since the rules they played by never let anyone walk away.

He realized his years with Anthony had passed quickly and with those years, so had half of his life.

It makes what time I have left even more precious.

He glanced in the rear view mirror and felt happy he had looked after himself physically, even though his boss hadn't.

I should walk even more and hit the gym on a regular basis.

He recalled a snippet of a conversation between two men he'd overheard at the last happy hour.

"Do you believe in reincarnation or an afterlife?"

"Reincarnation no. I can't imagine enduring old age twice."

Ain't that the truth.

He thought of Joan.

She completed Marvin.

His mind bounced to thinking of Sonia.

For about a year before Anthony's death he'd started feeling isolated and he'd started to think his life was meaningless.

I felt empty.

Even though he was surrounded by Anthony's staff of maids, cooks and security team, he'd always felt alone.

Not one of them was a real friend that I could talk to.

As he neared the gate into the Graceful Waters Resort, he felt as lonely as ever. He knew his answer was getting back to Sonia.

If I don't settle down with Sonia, who'll care when it's my turn to die?

38

M ario arrived at his rental house and pulled into the garage. He sat in his car and remembered the last time he'd seen Sonia.

After driving Vincent and his family to the airport I went to say goodbye to her.

"Where are you going and when will you be back?"

"I need to lay low for a few months. I better not tell you where I'm going just in case someone asks you. That way you won't have to lie. But don't worry, I'll be back soon and then I'll never leave your side. We can start a full life together."

Sonia had sagged and looked heartbroken. She'd even started to cry.

"I love you Sonia and I'll be back before you know it."

I gave her five thousand dollars and left.

Going directly to the docks, he'd hired a boat to take him to the neighboring island of Nevis.

From there, he hired several more boats to make his way to

Florida. He paid each captain extra to forget he'd made the trip. These were all men who valued money over being forthcoming.

Once he landed on the southern tip of Florida he found a backstreet hotel and holed up in the Keys. Each day he passed time by reading the newspapers and browsing in an internet cafe looking for any mention of him or the Rizzos.

Each night he read and enjoyed his solitude as he had for the past twenty-five years.

The reading, both fiction and non-fiction, helped pass the time and expanded my options to performing the more interesting parts of my job.

Living in the Keys, Mario had not shaven and had eaten as lightly as possible. The net result was an even trimmer and shaggier shadow of his former self. He felt like a free soul.

I'm a beach bum.

Forty-five days later, he found no mention in the news of anything he felt he needed to be concerned with.

Mario bought a used late model Toyota Camry sedan and drove up to Chicago.

Upon his arrival in the windy city, the first thing he did was swap plates with a Toyota he found in long term parking at Chicago's O'Hare airport.

Mario found the frigid weather conditions unbearable.

I can't wait to get back to St Kitts!

He then checked into a third rate hotel and telephoned the one person in the world he trusted. "Uncle, it's me."

"Mario, it's good to hear from you."

"I know you keep your ear to the ground. Have you heard anything about Vincent or AJ Rizzo looking for me? Or that they have a contract out on me?"

"I'm glad you called. We need to talk, best you come right over to my house."

"Tonight."

"Yes, tonight."

39

Mario had driven to his uncle Alfonzo's house with no idea of what was about to hit him.

His uncle welcomed him into his home like he was a long lost son. "Come on in out of the cold... What's with the scruff on your face? You aren't turning into a damn hippy are ya?"

"No, I've just been taking it easy. What's so important that I needed to come over right away?"

Alfonzo had made him sit down. "I've got beer in the fridge in the kitchen."

"No thanks, just tell me what's so damned important."

Alfonzo rubbed the day old white growth on his face. "Then I'll come right to the point. I had a phone call from Vincent Rizzo."

Mario swallowed hard.

"He told me that you needed to talk to him as soon as I could find you."

Mario's eyes hardened in anticipation of bad news. "Why would I possibly want to talk to him?"

"He didn't tell me. He just had this envelope delivered to me." Alfonzo shoved his hand down between his chair and its cushion and pulled out an envelope. "It's addressed to you."

Mario took it reluctantly.

It was sealed. His name was written on the front. There was no return address and nothing was visible on the backside. He took a deep breath and ripped the flap open.

MARIO,

I need you to do me and yourself a favor.

You need to take a little holiday down in Glenwood, Arizona. It's nice there this time of year.

As soon as you can, you need to check into the Budget Inn there and find yourself a real estate agent. I need you to rent a specific home on the golf course in the Graceful Waters Resort retirement community. I will have the exact address waiting for you at the hotel.

Within a short time period, two turncoats who are in the federal witness protection program will move in close to you.

I need you to eliminate them and send a message to anyone else who might decide to testify against me.

In return, I will pay you two million. You can either give Alfonzo the account number that you want it deposited into now or after the job is done.

If the money doesn't motivate you, perhaps this will. I have Sonia. If you don't comply fully, you won't be seeing her again.

It was signed VR.

He's kidnapped Sonia!

Mario felt a cold wave of hatred roll through him, squeezing the pit of his stomach.

I'll kill that bastard.

Feeling betrayed and irate, he took several deep breaths trying to control his temper.

He looked around his uncle's house and finally at his uncle who could have been playing poker.

Finally, Mario could talk. "Is this all you have for me, Alfonzo?"

"I'm only the messenger. Don't get angry with me, Mario."

His mouth felt dry.

Finally, he found his voice. "How does Vincent know about Sonia?"

"Who's Sonia?"

Mario shot up from his chair. "Give me your cell phone."

"It's on the coffee table." His uncle pointed.

Mario picked it up and punched in Sonia's number on St Kitts.

He let it ring ten times.

Each ring made the hatred rise inside him.

There was no answer.

He dropped the phone onto the coffee table.

"Tell Vincent that he'd better not harm a hair on Sonia's head." His eyes bore into his uncle's face.

"I'll tell Vincent whatever you want me to, Mario. You look like you need to have that beer with me."

"What I need are a Ruger and a silencer. Do you have them?"

"Sure, down in the basement. My knees hurt too damned much to walk down the stairs anymore. You go. Look inside my old locker. You can take anything you like."

Mario walked down the hallway and found the dark wooden door to the basement.

He opened it and stared into the dark.

Mario found the switch and turned on the light.

The stairs were old wooden ones and creaked in protest as he took each step.

If there's anyone down here, they know I'm coming.

The basement was as cluttered as Mario remembered. The last time he'd been down there was after he'd killed his wife's killer.

He dodged his way around old cardboard boxes and no longer needed furniture as he made his way into the middle.

The locker was still in the same place.

Mario had rested his back against it and hidden from the police before his arrest.

The locker wasn't locked.

From a selection that could start a small street war, he chose a Ruger, a box of ammo and a silencer that he figured had been custom made for it.

Mario closed the locker and went back upstairs.

Maybe I'll use it on Vincent instead.

Then he thought about Sonia and focused on the job at hand. "Alfonzo, is this silencer one of the specials you had made out of automotive brake linings and fiberglass?"

"It is. That one will be good for a hundred rounds."

"I'd be dead if I have to shoot that many bullets."

Mario had always prided himself on never having needlessly injured anyone other than his target.

He knew the silencer would buy him precious time as the gunshot noise wouldn't draw any attention while he was in the act.

The noise will be no more than a pellet gun.

Not needing to hurry means getting the job done right.

Armed with what he needed and knowing it was up to him to free Sonia, Mario said goodbye to his uncle and left.

I have no choice.

Sitting in his car, Mario focused on the job at hand.

First, I need a new identity.

Mario knew the easiest way would be to buy a new identity on the dark web.

Or, I could buy one through Alfonzo.

He discounted both options, as he knew that such identities would come with potential problems he needed to avoid.

What I need is a solid ID that I don't have to worry about.

With his long love of reading about everything related to murders both fiction and non-fiction, Mario had always toyed with the crazy idea about becoming an author.

He went shopping for a smartphone.

Mario had heard about a phone app that allowed people with similar interests to get together. He went on Meetup.com and typed in 'writers'.

He found seven groups located within twenty-five miles that were looking for other writers to join them.

Mario emailed the hosts and then went to all seven group's meetings where he made copious notes.

The groups averaged about twenty-two attendees. The majority of each group was female.

Women love to talk. So why wouldn't they love to write?

The groups met in various libraries, coffee shops and a brewery. The smaller ones were only focused on performing critiques.

He didn't make any notes about the critiques or the art of writing. Nor did he write notes on how to market a book, or how to submit inquiries to agents.

Instead, Mario took careful notes about each of the male writers.

Fortunately, each group had several men his age or older. The one man who was most approximately his age, size and coloring was Salvatore Cabella.

40

M ario had gone to a FedEx Office where he rented a computer to dive into Salvatore Cabella's social media accounts.

He found out that Salvatore used to work at a local library but had supposedly quit to pursue his dream of writing.

From what Mario could tell, Cabella had never been married and was an introvert.

Cabella's writing group met weekly. On his second visit, Mario paid attention to Salvatore's mannerisms and noted how little he interacted with the others.

He never speaks unless someone asks him a question. Instead, Salvatore just seemed to be taking notes.

After the meeting ended, Mario used the ruse of asking Cabella about his writing.

At first, Salvatore didn't respond. But after a few moments he opened up. "I do have one book that I've already published."

"Really, well that's great. Where can I find one to buy so I can read it?"

Salvatore took the bait. "It's available on Amazon."

"Did it take you a long time to write your first book?"

"It took me over four years."

"I don't know if I have the perseverance to actually complete a novel."

"The hardest part was re-writing it to where it made sense."

"Can I buy you a cup of coffee so I can ask you a few more questions?"

"Sure."

Thirty minutes later, they exchanged email addresses. Mario's had only been obtained that day.

Mario was envious of Salvatore and let it show.

He's actually written and published a novel. Never mind that it was self-published. It's out there and available to any unfortunate reader who decides to take a chance on a new author.

When he'd gone onto Amazon to research the novel, he discovered it had garnered a single pitiful review.

Mario figured it was probably from someone in his writer's group who had given it a five star rating but had been mercifully short in its praise. 'It's the best book I've ever read!!!'

Ya, right!

Mario set up a fake account on Amazon and downloaded an e-book version to his new smartphone.

Re-visiting the library, he'd survived the torturous read. It was full of plot holes and grammar mistakes.

Salvatore Cabella likes describing objects more than he enjoys having his two dimensional characters interact with each other.

His librarian hero is so arrogant, he's unlikeable.

What the hell, it's listed on Amazon.

That was something Mario had never done.

One of these days, I'll write my memoirs. The Memoirs of a Bodyguard and Hit Man.

Of course, I'll have to write it under a nom de plume.

Na, too risky. I'll have to take my secrets with me to my grave.

He had widely read the genre and had more knowledge than most would be writers. When it came to how to commit a murder and get away with it, he was a master.

Mario grinned to himself.

That's why I've never been caught.

Waiting for two days, Mario contacted Salvatore saying he'd read his book. "Can you meet with me so we can discuss the plot before I post a review for you?"

"That would be fantastic!"

"Your book is fabulous. I want to buy you a drink."

Mario suggested a lowlife bar.

There, Mario told him what a great writer he was while he bought all the drinks and plied him into a state of intoxication.

Once Salvatore was inebriated, Mario asked a few personal questions. "How do you deal with rejection?"

Salvatore hung his head. "I have to admit that writing is a lonely and painful experience. Everyone likes to take a shot at a writer."

"How so?"

"Critique partners try to show off, agents are downright brutal and uncaring creatures. Editors and reviewers enjoy taking their shot at every little thing you've bled to write. Some say show and don't tell. Others say tell and don't show. At night, the demons of shame haunt me and any desire to being a writer shrivels. Most days I wake up thinking I should go back to being a librarian."

"Well I think your work shows great promise."

After leaving the bar, Mario snapped Salvatore's neck then placed the body in his trunk.

It helps to think of them as meat and not as a former person.

Mario went on a two-hour drive to a rural part of the state where he knew it was mainly pig farms and a few light industrial plants.

Unlike his former boss, Mario didn't constantly smoke, watched what he ate and kept himself in shape. It allowed him to perform tasks like he had to do next.

Mario had read where porcine digestion was fast and thorough.

Perfect for disposing of a dead body.

Mario didn't want anyone to realize Salvatore Cabella was dead. Having the body simply disappear was the first of several steps needed to achieve that.

The swine were being raised inside huge metal sheds.

The odor assaulted him as soon as he opened his car door. Opening the metal door to one of the sheds, almost made him gag.

There were already lights on above the pigs.

Mario guessed hundreds of grunting flesh colored sacks of fat were crammed into each pen. He didn't bother counting the number of pens.

There must be millions of future breakfasts on this farm.

He went through Salvatore's pockets removing his wallet and keys.

As he looked at the credit cards and driver's license, he figured that as soon as he grew a goatee he could pass for being Cabella.

Mario removed the clothes from the body and used a ball peen hammer and pliers to remove the teeth.

The pigs became even noisier than he expected as he lifted then dropped Salvatore's body into a pen.

The evidence should be gone within an hour.

He watched the feeding frenzy. The pigs went through the skin and bones like butter.

Maybe less.

At first, he was afraid the oinking and grunting might wake someone. Making his way back to his car, he scanned the farmhouse to make sure no lights had come on.

All good.

He drove back to Chicago. With Salvatore's drivers license, two major credit cards and social security card he had the prizes he'd been after.

He replaced Salvatore Cabella's photographs and substituted his own. Once the new photos had dried in place, he'd taken a photograph of the new identification to a fellow he knew who had an enlarger.

Once the new documents were ready, they were covered in clear acetate so they looked like the real thing.

He'd bent and twisted the final products to take off the new look.

Now they look more authentic.

He used the set for identification purposes only. He had never used the credit cards. He always used cash or prepaid cards that he'd bought with cash.

Pretending to be Salvatore, Mario telephoned the credit card companies and told them he was relocating and would contact them once he was settled.

He disposed of Salvatore's teeth, one at a time. He tossed them out his driver's door window as he drove towards Arizona.

41

GLENWOOD, ARIZONA

The clock was ticking.

Sixty hours had passed since three people had been executed during the Happy Hour Murders.

U.S. Deputy Marshal Kevin Brown set a meeting with Detective Garcia at the Glenwood PD station on Tulip Avenue. As he walked past the perpetrators of various crimes that were being processed, it was obvious to Kevin Brown that drugs, sex offenders and domestic violence took up the majority of the Glenwood station's time.

At the reception desk Brown said, "I'm here to meet with Detective Garcia in Homicide."

Brown found Garcia at his desk. "Good morning. I need to get an update from you."

Garcia stood up and stretched. "Let's go into a conference room, follow me."

Brown followed Garcia into a small interview room with a metal desk and four chairs. Garcia and Brown sat across from each other.

Garcia went first. "We missed you this weekend."

"I had to work on another case yesterday. Let's go over what we know."

"Ask away."

"Are you thinking it's a lone wolf or did he have help?"

"Too early to tell. So far we have no evidence either way."

"Have you had a chance to run a database search for anyone with the same MO?"

"Two, but both are serving time."

"How did the shooter execute the crime?"

"The witnesses in your protection had two shots each in the head while the Marshal had one to the body then one to the head. Nothing was taken or touched. The shooter brazenly walked through the front door."

"What do we know about how he prevented being detected?"

"The perp executed his plan during the community's regular Happy Hour when many of the residents are away from their homes drinking and socializing."

"Either lucky or great planning. How did he escape?"

"Most likely the same way he entered. Either by vehicle, or on foot. There are in fact four gates where he could have exited by vehicle. If he was on foot, there is nothing to prevent him from entering at multiple locations including anywhere on the wide open golf course."

"How would he know where and when?"

"That's the most disturbing. The fact that the case was coming to trial in Phoenix was public knowledge. How they knew where the witness and his wife were being housed, is the big question."

Brown glanced down at the top of the table. When he spoke,

his voice was weak. "We're doing an internal investigation trying to uncover a possible leak."

Garcia lowered his eyebrows. "That's good to know. I hope that it's standard procedure. Let me know what turns up."

Brown was happy Garcia hadn't drilled down. "One Marshal was gone. How do you think the perp would have known that?"

"Probably by watching the house. I'm thinking he was most likely watching the house parked in a rental car down the street."

"Graceful Waters is a gated community. How would he get through the gates?"

"I talked to the guard at the front gate and they don't record visitor names or write down license plates. The perp could also have entered the monthly code in a keypad, but most likely, they simply followed someone in. The gates are timed to allow those old folks plenty of time to get in and then the gates automatically reopen if they sense someone is still entering."

"Any cameras recording license plates?"

"No. Although it projects security, the gates are not for security at all. They only exist to give visitors directions to the sales office. All the so-called guard does is count the number of visitors they direct. The only place visitor names are gathered is at the sales office."

"What about the bullets?"

"Standard 22's you can buy anywhere. And the perp took the time to pick up his shell casings."

Brown said, "I know, I've read both reports. Everyone was shot with 22 caliber bullets. The Marshal suffered chest and head wounds while the civilians were shot execution style."

"Sounds like a lone shooter."

"I agree with you. First off, whoever did this knew what they were doing. There was no hair, fingerprints, DNA, no trace at all. There are however a few interesting assertions. It would appear the shooter came to the front door where he shot the Marshal in the chest when the door was partially open. The first question then is why did the Marshal open the door?"

"Noted."

"He was then executed by a shot to the head."

"The civilians were both found with shots to the back of their heads. Their bodies indicate they were kneeling when shot the back of their heads."

"What about the weapon?"

"It probably had a silencer."

"22's are common, while the silencer isn't. That would indicate a professional."

"Each victim had two bullets in them. The shot pattern also indicates the shooter was a skilled professional."

"Any finger prints or footprints?"

"The shooter must have worn gloves and the floor was all tile, so no."

"Also, pointing to a professional."

"I concur."

"Since you have no locals with that skill set, we need to explore if the killer was imported. To that end, I've had my resources narrow the list to prospects living near Chicago who Vincent Rizzo may have hired. The list is twenty-seven. We are working with Chicago PD to screen and interview all of them."

Garcia knew they were actually fishing without any real leads or suspects. "I've interviewed the neighbors as prospective witnesses. None seem to have seen or heard anything."

"Nothing?"

"At the time of the murders, all except for one couple were at the community center for Happy Hour which in fact lasts two hours."

"That tells me that whoever planned it knew the local situation. That would take either a local contact who knew the location and what to expect or that the shooter was in place for at least a few days scoping out the territory."

"Good assumption. It looks like a professional hit job. Now, I've read where the Federal Marshals Services claim to have never had a witness killed under their protection. Is that true?"

Brown squirmed in his chair. "If someone follows our rules they will be safe. If someone is stubborn or stupid and doesn't follow our rules to the letter, well you can image what could happen to them."

"Are you saying that they didn't follow the rules then?"

"It's easier for a criminal to have a change of heart than it is for them to change their stripes and suddenly become model citizens. We can't change the person; only lay out the rules and wish them luck."

"What are the odds they succeed?"

"Think about it. What are the odds someone stops smoking on their first try?"

"So you're saying the odds of success are less than fifty-fifty?"

"That kind of data is above my pay grade."

The statement was a surprise to Garcia.

Brown took Garcia's silence to change the subject. "That leads me to ask if any of the neighbors seemed sketchy or were brand new to the community."

"Everyone passed my initial interview. The turnover seems to be about fifteen percent annually so there are quite a few new residents. Of the closest neighbors, there is only one that's relatively new. Been there for about a month. However, that doesn't fit the normal modus operandi for an imported shooter does it?"

"Especially if he's still there as well. No it sure doesn't. Out of curiosity, what's his name?"

"Salvatore Cabella."

"Did you ask to see his identification?"

Of course I did, you jerk.

"I did. He's trying to be an author. I actually downloaded his ebook from Amazon and tried to read it."

"What's it about?"

Garcia replied, "A librarian who discovers a dead body in the library then goes on to solve the murder for the police."

"I see. So he thinks he's smarter than law enforcement does he?"

"Pretty much."

"Well I don't think it's him."

"Why?"

Kevin Brown said, "I doubt the killer was from Phoenix. Most professionals prefer to work elsewhere."

"If you've developed a profile, then let me have it." Garcia mockingly opened his notebook.

"He's most likely a loner. Hit men don't want anyone to remember seeing them. They won't over or under tip and they won't be drawn into any memorable conversations."

Everyone in Graceful Waters loves to talk.

Brown sat back in his chair. "Let's consider how the shooter got here? Driving is too tiring so I assume he flew. We have a large airport here in Phoenix. Where is the next largest airport? Tucson? He could have flown into Tucson and then driven here. Or did he use a reliever airport like the one we have in Scottsdale."

"I'll have Charlie check out the airport angle."

"What about trains and buses? You need to check on those also."

Garcia wrote something in his notebook.

"If he flew, he probably obtained the weapon here; it's too much hassle to try and get one past airport security. Or did he send it via a delivery service to where he was staying? Then where did he stay? Motel or hotel?"

Garcia glanced at Brown with frustration.

Brown continued to orate. "Everything a professional hit man pays for is in cash. Transportation, lodging and food are necessities and are paid for in cash. They will use only bills in small denominations, not crisp new one hundred dollar bills. The last thing they want to do is draw any attention to themselves. That's why your detectives need to look into the car rental agencies. They require a valid driver's license and one major credit card as identification even when you pay cash."

Garcia closed his notebook. "Oh and by the way we did have a resident of God's Waiting Room call in a tip on another neighbor. They said their neighbor was scary and reminded them of the Norman Bates character from that old movie."

"Really, did you check him out?"

"Charlie did, and found out that he's a registered sex offender but has never done anything violent. His preference is to expose himself."

"I guess that an active adult community is as good a place as any to warehouse sexual predators like that."

Garcia nodded his agreement. "There are only four of us. How about helping us by putting some foot leather to work with us?"

"That's not my job. I'm here to assist and see if I can pull strings for you. But talking about legwork, what's up with Charlie? Isn't he a little young to be on this case?"

"He's our newest Detective but he's working with me and two of our most senior Detectives... And before you ask, yes, his father is the Chief for the Phoenix PD."

42

Mario was still performing his role as Salvatore as he poured his first cup of coffee. He started to think of Sonia.

I met Sonia at the Carnival parade on St Kitts. The small parade consisted of costumed dancers and musicians playing loud music.

Instead of open convertible cars, there were a few golf carts; instead of floats, there were groups of brightly dressed children of all ages.

These were followed by several groups of scantily dressed but heavily feathered women of all shapes and sizes.

A Moko-Jumbie stilt walker had just passed him when a woman wearing a brightly patterned long sleeved shirt and trousers with a mask decorated with peacock feathers locked her eyes onto his. She'd grabbed him by the hand and dragged him into the street to dance with her.

Her costume was embellished with mirrors, bells and ribbons and she made full use of each.

I'm not the dancing type but I decided what the hell.

He recalled leaning into her. "What's your name?"

"Sonia."

"Can we go somewhere and talk?"

She looked him over. "Only if you keep dancing da salsa with me 'til the parade ends."

It might have been her costume but Mario thought that her smile was enticingly full of pornographic promise. "I'll try."

He soon followed her lead as they took a step forward then instead of stepping backwards they pivoted and the backward step moved them forward once again.

Mario stayed in the parade and kept trying to dance for another ten minutes before he tired. "I can't keep up."

"Your loss." She kept moving with the other dancers.

Mario decided to walk along with her until the parade ended.

A hundred feet later, she smiled at his attention and waved for him to join her back in the middle of the street.

He held his hand over his heart and shook his head, no.

Mario wasn't sure why he felt so attracted to this woman but he couldn't keep his eyes off her ample curves and erotic moves.

I didn't realize that the salsa was so damn sexy!

It wasn't long before the parade ended.

He walked into the chaotic glut of parade participants and found her. "Remember me?"

She cocked her head. "You da man who can't keep up."

"Can I buy you a drink?"

She put her arm in his. "Lead the way."

Given how she was dressed Mario decided to take her down to a bar on the beach at Frigates Bay.

He hailed a taxi.

Stash the cab driver dropped them off at the Shiggity Shack where Sonia introduced Mario to various rum based concoctions.

That evening they had life-changing sex. He didn't know if he'd just been struck with some midlife thing or what.

Whatever had happened, he had forged a deep connection with Sonia. He could see the trajectory of his life unfolding.

In the morning she served him banana pancakes and coffee.

He knew he'd found someone he liked and tried his best to be more personable than he normally was.

"Are you a full time dancer?"

"I wish. No, I work part time as a cashier down at the big hotel near where the cruise ships dock in Basseterre. How about you?"

"I run security for Anthony Rizzo. Have you heard of him?"

"Mista Rizzo. Sure, everyone knows who he is. He has the biggest estate on St Kitts. You have a big job. What ya doing dancing in my parade?"

"I couldn't resist your charms."

The affair grew slowly over many months. They were from different races and different cultures.

It turned out that there was also a fifteen-year age difference.

I don't know why but man, am I attracted to that woman.

At Sonia's request to see where he lived, Mario had snuck her onto the Rizzo estate. He guided her into an empty villa. It was one of the six stand-alone villas where some of the full time staff resided.

The next morning one of the maids asked him if was visiting the villas and winked at him.

Mario had explained and Sonia said she understood. They agreed that he would visit her whenever he could at her modest bungalow.

43

M ario caught a movement from the corner of his eye. He turned to look out his dining room window.

Relax. There's nothing there.

He raised his gaze to spot Marvin sitting outside on his patio. Mario was afraid Marvin might be despondent.

Poor guy.

He took a deep breath and opened his sliding patio door to wave at Marvin.

If he doesn't want company, I can understand.

Marvin waved him over.

"Let me get myself some fresh coffee."

After topping up his mug, Mario carried it over to Marvin's. He tread across the gravel carefully keeping his eyes scanning back and forth looking for a rattler. Marvin watched him approach then waved him to sit where Joan normally sat.

Okay, I'm Salvatore once again.

He spoke first. "How are you doing, Marvin?"

"Good morning, Salvatore. I would be lying if I didn't tell you I was sad. It's hard to lose someone that you love and have spent most of your life with."

The words tore at Mario.

I know.

Salvatore took a long sip of coffee as he tried to compose himself. "Did I hear you tell me that you're not going to have a funeral?"

Marvin sighed. "A rabbi will be putting Joan to rest today. Tomorrow I'm going to hold a celebration of life for Joan's friends in here at the clubhouse. I hope you can come tomorrow. Joan would want you there."

"Of course, I'll come. If you don't mind, Marvin, can I ask, what a celebration of life is. I've never heard of one."

Marvin was gracious as always. "I'm happy to explain. Instead of funerals in a dreary funeral home or in a church, many people in here nowadays like having something with a more positive feel to it. For Joan, it'll be a potluck with everyone bringing a dish to share. I have a friend in here that's putting together some pictures and making them into a video that I'll show. I will say a few words and if anyone is moved to, they can speak as well."

"That sounds very nice Marvin. I'm sure Joan will appreciate it."

Tears formed in Marvin's eyes. "Thank you."

They sat in silence for several minutes and sipped their coffee with an occasional glance at the golf course.

Even though he had been raised a Catholic until he was around twelve, Mario had grown up not believing in an afterlife.

No one can judge me and if they dare, then I have questions for them.

Being the deliverer of death to people whom Anthony Rizzo

thought deserved it had hardened Mario into believing that death was often a good thing.

Another asshole is born every minute.

Mario also knew from the loss of his own wife that dealing with grief was different for everyone. He had lashed out, found, then dealt with his wife's killer.

In today's world that is frowned upon. Why should that be? What about the victim's right to revenge? What ever happened to an eye for an eye?

Each time he'd carried out justice for Anthony, he found it had been further healing for him.

One can never forget someone you've loved.

Sonia's now my way to re-enter the world. She's my Joan.

Marvin spoke, interrupting Mario's funk. "Have you heard any more about the poor people next to you?"

"No, nothing. I expect we won't hear much until they catch the killer… not to change the subject but if there's anything I can help you with or do for you, please just let me know."

"Thank you, Salvatore, I will."

Mario picked up his mug as he stood.

"Just knock on my door if you even just want to talk."

"Thanks."

Mario carefully walked through the gravel watching for any rattlesnakes hiding in ambush.

44

M ario was watching the local Monday afternoon news broadcast when he heard it. "We now have official confirmation and the names of the two victims of the Happy Hour murders."

The screen changed to a different news anchor. "Jerry and Sheila Webb were a married couple in the Federal Government's Witness Protection Program."

Mario recognized the faces on the screen.

"The other victim was their protector with the U.S. Marshals Service. More information is available on our web site."

Mario heard a car door close.

He shut off the television and went to the window. Detective Garcia was walking up to his front door.

Mario could feel his heart rate starting to race.

Instead of heading to the front door, Mario headed for his bathroom.

He heard a loud knock.

"Wait."

Checking his hair and putting on his glasses, Mario looked into the mirror and saw Salvatore.

I'm wearing a nerdy super hero t-shirt, I'm ready.

Knock, knock.

He yelled out. "Hold onto your horses, I said I was coming."

As he went to the door, he took a deep breath.

Detectives normally handle crimes of passion. Let's see what Garcia is made of.

"Why it's Detective Garcia. What are you doing back here?"

"I have a few follow up questions if you don't mind."

"Come on in."

Letting Garcia go first, Mario trailed. "Have a seat."

"Are you into batman comics Mister Cabella?"

Salvatore placed his right palm on his t-shirt. "Comics inspire me."

Garcia sat and Salvatore joined him.

"I'm curious, since you dabble in writing about crime, what do you think happened next door?"

Mario rubbed his goatee as if he were deep in thought.

If I were to get caught, what would they offer me to turn on Vincent? Witness protection? Ha!

Mario suppressed a chuckle. "I always try to make the motive a key part of any plot so I want to ask you, who were they testifying against."

"I'm sorry but I can't comment on an open investigation. Do any of your neighbors have a theory?"

Mario tried not to smile. "The guesses have ranged from drug dealers to suicides. Can you tell me how they died?"

"Sorry, no. I shouldn't say this but whoever did this was a real professional."

He's appealing to my ego.

Mario sat silently.

Garcia clasped his hands together. "Do you have the list you promised me?"

Salvatore was surprised. "Which list was that?"

"Your list of references from Chicago."

He smacked his forehead. "I'm sorry, but Marvin's wife had a stroke at home yesterday morning. And I had to drive Marvin to the hospital where Joan died. I've been in shock ever since and to tell you the truth it slipped my mind."

Garcia thought about Salvatore's excuse. "I'm sorry to hear about Joan but if you don't want to give me your references I will have no choice but to lock you up in a cell."

Mario furrowed his eyebrows. "Why would you put me in jail?"

"For impeding my investigation."

Mario shook his head. "Fine. I'll do it now. Let me get a pen and paper."

Mario stood up and walked towards the den. As he passed the desk near the front door he glanced at the drawer where he'd placed his Ruger.

That would be a stupid thing to do.

He found a notepad Barbara had given him with her realtor contact information. Next, he looked in another drawer for a pen.

"Found them. Give me a minute."

Mario pulled out the real Salvatore's library card and wrote down the address in Chicago.

Then he wrote down the name of the Meetup group from memory.

Next, he added a cousin's name he'd pulled from Salvatore's Facebook page. For the phone number he wrote a question mark.

Finally, he ripped the page from the notebook.

He walked into the great room and handed the page to Garcia.

Garcia looked at it. "What's this?"

"My list. You now have where I worked, the Meetup group I attended and where my writer friends are, plus one of my relative's names. Surely that's plenty."

Garcia folded then placed the page into his own notebook. "It's a start."

"Good, are we done then? I have things to do."

"If you don't mind, I have a few more questions for you."

Salvatore said nothing and stared wide eyed at Garcia.

"The night of the crime, you told the officer that you were just returning from being at the clubhouse for Happy Hour and then having dinner at the golf course restaurant."

Mario nodded. "That's right, I'm guessing that there were several thousand of us there that night."

"Can you now give me a list of people who can verify that you were there for the entire two hours of the Happy Hour event?"

"You've got to be joking, right."

"No, I'm not."

Mario thought about how he should answer. "Well, it's a Happy Hour social where you spend anywhere from a few seconds to maybe fifteen minutes to half an hour with someone before you move on the next person. As usual the booze was flowing. That's why we all go."

Garcia cocked his head ever so slightly. "I'm sorry but I don't understand."

"People like other people more when they've been drinking. You know; the community that drinks together, likes everyone more. The other motto I've heard is that what happens during Happy Hour stays at Happy Hour."

Garcia's eyebrows jumped and a grin shot onto his face.

This guy is a raving idiot.

"Ah, I see… so give me a list of the names of people you recall talking to when you first arrived."

"When I first arrived I met someone I hadn't met before. He held the door for me. I think he said his name was Joe."

It's not up to me to prove that I was there -- it's up to them to prove that I wasn't.

"Does Joe have a last name?"

"Most surely he does, but he didn't give it to me."

"Who did you talk to that you can recall both of their names."

"Hmm, I think that would have been Barbara Goldberg, my neighbor and realtor. Barbara and I also went for dinner as I've already told you."

Garcia wrote something down.

"Then there was Big Al from the cigar club. I don't think he's ever told me his last name but the cigar club apparently has a website with its members names listed… Then a couple more guys from the cigar club came over… By then, I was on my second glass of wine and things become a blur. It was crowded, I'm relatively new and I met a lot of different people."

Garcia stared at him.

Mario openly glared at Garcia. "What's the matter; did I forget to pull up my zipper or what?"

Garcia didn't smile. "Did you leave the clubhouse at any time during the club's Happy Hour?"

Mario could feel his heart speed up. "No."

"So if I told you that one of your neighbors claims that they saw you walking home before 7PM, what would you say?"

Garcia's just trying to bait and entrap me.

He noticed that Garcia broke eye contact.

He's lying to me. Or did he just do that on purpose; maybe he's telling the truth.

Salvatore pursed his lips. "That they were confused or are in need of having their eyes checked... When I walked home, it was with Barbara and that was after eight, maybe eight thirty, as I've already told you several times. That was when we came across the crime scene."

"I must tell you that lying to me makes you a prime suspect and opens you to charges."

Mario smiled, then laughed. "Haha. You've got to be kidding. The only person I've ever killed was in my bloody novel." He pointed at his own head. "My brain is a very small caliber weapon."

I'm not getting anywhere with this idiot.

Garcia closed his notebook.

"Thank you for your time Mister Cabella. If you recall anything out of the ordinary or hear anything please call me."

"Certainly."

After Garcia left, Mario stood at his front window.

The law is on my side, not a victim's.

He was happy he was still part of the eighty percent.

Cops are happy if they can clear twenty percent of the reported crimes in a given year.

Mario had been shaken by Garcia's sly attempt to trick him.

I wonder if a neighbor did see me walking home before 7PM? Na, if one did, Garcia would've dragged me into the police station... I haven't felt this close to having my life fall apart since Anthony's death.

45

W hen Detective Garcia knocked on Barbara Goldberg's door, he found a pleasant and polite woman.

After interviewing Salvatore Cabella, Garcia was happy to have someone who just answered the questions she was asked, without asking their own.

"Detective Garcia. Please come in and have a seat."

Garcia entered and looked around.

Just as I remember it.

Out of date hutch with frilly figurines.

Lots of pictures of children and grandchildren.

Typical home of a female senior citizen.

Once he was seated, Garcia started the interview. "What can you tell me about your neighbor Marvin?"

"Marvin's wife Joan just passed away. They've lived here for over eight years. If I may suggest, please don't bother Marvin right now if you can avoid it, he's grieving for his wife."

Garcia wrote in his notebook. Without looking up, he asked about another neighbor. "What can you tell me about Salvatore Cabella?"

"He's a very nice man."

"How long has he lived here?"

"I'm his realtor. Oh, let me think... about a month so far. However, he prepaid for an entire year, so he's very committed. He's just trying out the neighborhood before he decides which home to buy. He's doing it the smart way."

"Have you noticed anything odd about him?"

"No, not really. Except..."

"Yes."

"One thing is, I think he spends too much time in his own head."

"Excuse me, but what do you mean by that?"

"He's like most men I've met who are always thinking about something else while you try to talk to them."

Garcia made a note. *Typical female*

"Also, he's not as outgoing as some of the folks who move here. Then again it takes some folks time to adjust and fit in. For a former librarian I think he's coming out of his shell nicely."

"Why do you say that?"

"In my experience most librarians would rather have their noses in books than talking to people, don't you think?"

Garcia didn't answer but pretended to write another note. "Is he on a month to month rental?"

"No, as I just told you, he signed a one year lease. He's very committed to living here and paid for the full year in advance. You know, I think he's saved his pennies. Most of the single women around here view him as a catch."

"Why's that?"

"You know. He's still got his own hair and teeth, the money to live here and he's single." Barbara grinned.

Garcia chuckled to himself. "Let me ask you: were you at the Happy Hours with Salvatore Cabella last Tuesday and Thursday?"

"I wasn't with him in the sense of a date, but yes I saw him both times. You need to understand that Happy Hour is designed to be a mobile social situation where everyone mills around making friends."

"Were you with him the entire time?"

"Of course not. Even wives don't stick beside their husbands the entire time. However…"

"Yes."

"Well, I did see him interacting with men from the cigar club and oh, he also donated four hundred dollars to charity that night so the ladies were paying him special attention as well."

"I see. And you walked home with him on Thursday evening after the Happy Hour stopped?"

"No, Salvatore then took me to the golf course restaurant and bought me dinner. Then we walked home together."

"Did he seem on edge or nervous when he saw the police activity?"

Barbara's eyes widened. "I don't know if he became upset, but I sure did. Now if you have finished asking me questions, I have one for you. What reassurances can you give us that another murder won't happen in here today or tomorrow?"

46

The Celebration of Life was to take place at ten in the morning; Marvin had left his house an hour earlier.

It was now a quarter to ten.

Salvatore knocked on Barbara Goldberg's front door.

She answered and left the door ajar. "Give me another minute and I'll be ready."

He waited in the doorway.

A minute later, Barbara reappeared wearing one of her smaller hats. "Okay, I'm ready."

"You look very nice."

"Thank you, Salvatore." Barbara locked her front door. "I guess we can't be too safe around here anymore."

"I understand."

As they walked towards the clubhouse, they made small talk.

Barbara had a big reveal. "Detective Garcia came to interrogate me yesterday afternoon."

"He must be making the rounds because he visited me as

well." Mario let out an abbreviated laugh. "He even had the gall to ask me about you and Marvin."

Barbara stopped. "Really? I shouldn't admit it but I'm really beginning to dislike that man."

Starting to walk again she admitted more. "I must say, I was surprised when he asked me about you and Marvin. The questions he asked me made you both sound like suspects."

"I think it's standard police procedure to pit people against each other to see if one of them will get scared and make up incriminating statements against the others."

Barbara stopped again. "You know, come to think of it, I think I've seen that in a movie or on television more than once. I guess that means we'd all better stick together. But why is he wasting his time with us anyway?"

"I suppose it means that they've got no real suspects so they're making busy by taking shots at everyone remotely involved to see if something shakes out. But I'm only guessing of course."

"I think you may be right. Is that in your book? Never mind, here we are."

Mario held open the door to the clubhouse. "Have you been to a Celebration Of Life before?"

"Yes, they've become quite popular in here. I think it's because everybody's of different beliefs and we don't want to impose our beliefs and customs on each other."

"I've never been to one."

"Don't worry Salvatore, if you have any questions just ask me. As my grandson keeps telling me, I've got your back."

"Thanks Barbara."

As always, the people inside the clubhouse were nicely dressed. For this event, probably half of the men were wearing suits or sport coats, some with ties as if they were coming to a church service.

"I should have worn a sports coat but I don't own one."

Barbara looked at him. "Relax, half the men in here are dressed exactly like you are. You look very nice. Don't worry about it."

As they walked into the main ballroom there was a small sign saying 'Celebration of Life - Joan Haight'.

It featured a photograph of a younger and smiling Joan.

Mario deliberately walked a half step behind Barbara who said hello to everyone.

Must be the realtor in her.

Or it's the Life Coach training.

Mario said hello as if he'd met all the guests before and just nodded to several he didn't recognize.

They nodded back.

The good news is that Marvin certainly has a lot of friends and neighbors that will support him.

Glancing around, he saw Marvin standing near a podium that had been set up in front of the large glass doors. They were open to the golf course.

A gentle breeze kept the attendees comfortable, while the bright sunshine made the mood seem upbeat.

It was unlike the funerals he'd attended with Anthony, where the parlors always had dim lights.

It was as if the mourners were about to send their departed into the darkness of the unknown. It was if they were preparing the departed to be disappointed.

This setting had a happy feeling to it.

This could very well be an afternoon Happy Hour.

Mario wondered why Marvin was having such a simple but refined event and asked Barbara.

She considered Salvatore's question for a moment. "In here there's no need to one up the Jones. We've all been there and done that. At our ages, all we want is to be practical. Do we leave something for our heirs or do we have one last fling? I can tell you most of the seniors I've met are hoping that their kids will put them in a nice care facility and the way to do that is to dangle dollars in front of them. Look after me and I'll look after you."

"Ah, I see."

Who is going to look after me?

Mario looked around at the sea of faces that were trying to keep up a brave front.

"Everyone, please sit."

Out of habit, Mario suggested to Barbara that they sit in a corner seat in the last row. "That way we can see everything."

"Don't be silly, Salvatore. We should sit up front to give Marvin moral support."

Mario didn't argue.

They sat in the first row.

Mario watched as Marvin took a deep breath, stood as tall as he could, then slowly let out his breath.

He's nervous.

Marvin welcomed and thanked everyone for coming. "Joan would be so happy that each of you were able to come here today to remember her... Joan and I were together for the best years of my life and frankly, I've long forgotten about the rest. Sometimes having senior moments are a good thing."

The crowd let out several chuckles.

Until I moved here I thought this kindness thing was just drivel spewed at sermons in churches on Sundays.

"Joan made me whole. She was my world. She loved life and it loved her back. We were both grateful to have found this community and to have become friends with each of you. Knowing you changed both of us for the better and for that we are blessed."

Marvin paused and winked at Salvatore. "I would like to share a little story with all of you. When my good friend and neighbor Salvatore Cabella moved in, he asked me what Joan thought of my smoking the occasional cigar. I told him that she went shopping with one of her girlfriends every time I went to the cigar club. Salvatore asked me, every afternoon when you go to smoke? I replied yes. In fact, Joan loved to shop so much, that I've had to send Macy's and Nordstrom's sympathy cards."

The laughter was genuine and everyone seemed to relax even further.

A moment later Marvin continued. "Now I would like to share a little video with you that is a series of snapshots from Joan's life."

The photos started out with faded black and white snaps of Joan as a little girl, then as a teenager and then in color as a young woman. Their smiling wedding photographs reminded Mario of Joan's smile as she sat with Marvin on their patio.

Watching the snapshots Mario started seeing Sonia's face instead of Joan's.

Sonia had better not be dead.

After the photographs, several of Joan's friends rose from the audience and gave a few short but loving stories about her.

Finally, Marvin came back to the podium. "Thank you to all for coming and celebrating Joan's life with me. The club has set up a bar in the main lobby and I would appreciate it if you'd all come and share a toast to Joan with me."

Barbara leaned into Salvatore. "I have a house to show at twelve o'clock so I need to run home, but you should stay."

"I'll just say goodbye to Marvin and then I'll walk you home."

They stood up and both walked up to Marvin who was still near the podium.

Marvin hugged Barbara and then Salvatore, thanking them both for coming.

As they walked back to their homes, Barbara said, "You know that house where the triple homicide occurred will be an extremely hard sell now. People don't like a house where murders have taken place. I'll bet I could get you a really great deal, if you're interested."

"I admit that I really like this neighborhood but I'm still not ready to commit just yet. I'm not comfortable the way people are looking at you, me, Marvin and the other neighbors. Why don't we wait and see."

Barbara wanted to sell to Salvatore. "Next time one of those detectives comes to my home I'm not going to talk to him. There's no way I can talk about my best friends in the world as if they were hardened criminals."

47

Playing the gentleman, Salvatore stood and watched Barbara as she entered her home.

She waved at him and he waved back.

Knowing she was safely inside, he headed home.

The fact that Detective Garcia had paid him a second visit was still bothering him.

Why talk to me again? I was planning to stay for a couple more weeks then telling Barbara that I didn't think I fit in here. That I was feeling too young and single.

Mario guessed that ninety-five percent of the residents were married couples.

She'll understand.

He sat down in his easy chair and mentally reviewed the events of the last Happy Hour on Thursday.

* * *

At 5:45 he'd gone into his Mario mode and used the large

crowd of residents that were milling around the clubhouse as the veil to exit through the farthest front door.

He'd cut through the parking lot in an effort to save time.

As he'd headed home, he reviewed reasons he might have to abort the mission.

My timing could be off or the U.S. Marshal decides to do delivery instead of going out for pick up tonight.

Then I'll have to deal with two Marshals instead of one. That could be fatal.

A random neighbor could be out for a walk or getting fresh air and see me. Then I could be recognized and it'll be game over. The police will know it's me and my goose will be cooked.

My gun could jam and I'll be the one who gets shot.

They could have been moved or gone out for dinner. Then I'll be screwed.

Once he was clear of the parking lot, he increased his pace. It wasn't enough to draw attention but he figured he'd shave another full minute off the round trip.

As he walked down his street, he scanned the neighbor's homes. No one was outside or looking out a window, at least that he could see.

A longer glance at the WITSEC house didn't tell him anything.

He entered his rental and removed the fake glasses.

He'd left the Ruger in the console drawer by the front door. Retrieving it, he placed the gun in his rear belt then pulled out his shirt so it covered it.

Next, he went into his master bedroom closet grabbed a pair of blue booties, latex gloves and a clear plastic party mask.

He took a deep breath and left his rental.

Looking up and down the street, he saw no one.

All's clear.

He walked up the neighbor's driveway.

The garage door had small square windows across its width. He jumped up to see if the SUV was in the garage.

The SUV was gone.

Knowing the Marshal was most likely on the food run, he knew he had a window of opportunity but that he had to be quick.

If he comes back before I'm finished, it could be a disaster.

Mario had long ago learned to rely on his gut instincts. Especially when it said things weren't right. Whenever he'd felt something was wrong, he'd follow his intuition and back off.

He scanned both ways along the sidewalk.

I don't see anyone.

Pulling out the pair of the blue booties Barbara had made him wear when she had shown him a new home, he whipped them over his own loafers. Then he pulled out the pair of latex gloves and slipped them on.

Mario slipped the clear plastic mask over his face for insurance.

His last preparation was to check his weapon and attach the silencer.

He gave the door two quick knocks and waited.

Within three seconds, he could hear the muffled sound of a voice. He assumed it was the U.S. Marshal giving orders to the targets.

He also figured that the Marshal had most likely drawn his weapon.

As soon as the door cracked open, Mario shot at the door with his suppressed Ruger then kicked it open.

He swayed to his left and peered inside.

The inanimate Marshal had fallen backwards and lay before him. There was a growing red spot on his chest.

With a clear shot, he aimed for the forehead and pressed the trigger.

He watched as the crimson appeared on the Marshal's head.

Protection down.

Mario crouched and peered inside.

Now for the targets.

He saw no one.

Mario stood up, stepped over the Marshal's body and moved inside.

He used a back kick to shut the front door. Even though Mario was confident the Marshals wouldn't have armed the witnesses in their protection, he held the Ruger in front of himself.

He heard the sound of heavy breathing and a whimpering female voice.

Stepping behind the kitchen island, he found the male and female targets were on their knees, crouching and cowering.

The woman had tears running down her cheeks and her husband was begging for their lives.

They both looked up into his eyes.

Finding no compassion from the gunman, they both closed their eyes and started to beg.

Mario was already stepping back to minimize the blood spatter.

He was five feet away before he squeezed the trigger four times.

Two in each head.

Normally he would check after the second shot to ensure the heart had stopped pumping and the blood had stopped flowing.

Tonight he was in a hurry.

He did however make sure he picked up the shells.

As he did, Mario could smell the sour tang of the blood hitting his nostrils.

He turned and headed towards the front door as he shoved the weapon into the small of his back.

He stepped over the Marshall and pulled the front door open. He also glanced at the small hole he'd made.

Glancing left, then right, Mario took a deep breath and casually closed the door and turned to return next door.

Once he was inside his rental, he placed the Ruger back in the drawer.

Next, he removed his latex gloves, mask, black golf shirt and black shorts and placed them in a garbage bag along with his blue booties.

He carried the bag and placed it in the garbage can in the garage.

Then he washed his hands with soap and water with a small brush to remove any traces of the gunshot residue.

Finally, he put on an identical shirt and shorts to what he'd just been wearing.

He had bought two pairs of identical black shorts and seven golf shirts when he moved into the house.

Four were black and three were dark blue. That way he could go a week without doing a wash.

Before he'd left Chicago, he'd also gone to a thrift shop and purchased three t-shirts emblazoned with Super Heroes.

Why would Salvatore have liked those crappy t-shirts?

Hair was good.

Glasses were on.

As Salvatore once again, Mario left his rental and returned to the clubhouse using a side entrance.

When he glanced at his watch, it was 6:10.

The entire mission had taken only twenty-five minutes.

The place was still crowded and was even noisier than when he'd left.

The wine and cocktails are loosening everyone's tongues.

He spotted Barbara, smiled at her, then walked over.

Thankfully my breathing and posture relaxed me enough to hide the fact that I was still full of adrenalin.

Salvatore made a point of waving at people he had met and had even asked Barbara to introduce him to some he hadn't met yet.

Once Thursday's Happy Hour ended, he'd taken Barbara to the restaurant at the golf course and afterwards they'd walked home together.

* * *

The second U.S. Marshall must have arrived home just after seven, discovered the victims and alerted the police.

48

I t was day five of the Happy Hour Murders investigation. Detective Garcia and U.S. Marshal Kevin Brown once again met in the Glenwood Police Headquarters to discuss progress.

Brown turned to Garcia. "Did you listen to the public appeal for witnesses to come forward that your Police Chief made this morning?"

"With no leads and very little to go on, it was time to do it."

"How are the interviews of the neighbors going?"

"They're finished. No one seems to have seen anything out of the ordinary. If they did, they're too scared to say anything."

"Anyone seem out of place?"

"Both next door neighbors are singles, living alone. The female is a realtor and long time homeowner. On the other side is a male, one Salvatore Cabella, who is renting on a one-year lease.

"Did you check Cabella out?"

"His former employer, Meetup group members and cousin all verify that he is a harmless, weird duck."

"What in hell's a Meetup group?"

"Meetup is a web application that you use to find others who are nearby and have the same interests. In Cabella's case, it was other writers. If you ask me, all writers are by definition whackos. Who else would spend their lives sitting in a dark room talking to themselves?"

"Ya, I imagine you have to be weird to sit and write all day and night."

"Yes, weird pretty much sums them up."

"How long has he lived in Arizona?"

"A few weeks."

"If he was the killer, what are the odds that his targets would move in next to him?"

"I think we can say they're impossible."

"I agree... Did his timeline check out?"

"Their happy hour is a huge social event held in the ball-room, hallways, cafe and outside on the patios. But yes, many people socialized with him over the two hours in question."

"I see. Then he had no motive or opportunity."

"No."

"Then let me ask you; why are you looking into residents?"

"We aren't anymore. Now tell me, how could anyone know when the targets would be in that particular house?"

Brown rubbed his face. "You didn't hear this from me, but I've found out that the U.S. Marshals website was hacked and we have reason to believe the WITSEC database was also hacked."

"Is that why you think the shooter may have known where that witness was going to be kept?"

"It looks that way. That database held the address of the safe house on the golf course."

With it looking more and more like it must have been an imported assassin, Garcia looked at Brown. "What are the odds a shooter would stay in place after the hit. Why wouldn't he just vanish into thin air by leaving town?

Brown lowered his head. "You're right. It makes no sense. Like I said on Monday, it was probably an out of towner. How is your review of the airline passenger lists going?"

"We've checked with the airlines flying in and out of Phoenix, Scottsdale, Tucson and Palm Springs. We have their lists of all passengers and crew. We crosschecked arrival and departure dates, with passenger names and no one stood out. But it would be easy enough for anyone to use another person's altered identity."

"How about car rental agencies?"

Garcia closed his eyes before delivering the bad news. "We looked for anyone that paid cash and there weren't any."

Kevin Brown scrunched up his face. "If he's not a local and he's not an import, then who the hell could he be?"

"Isn't there a federal agency you can turn to for help?"

"I've checked with the FBI's Behavioral Science Lab in Quantico. They haven't done any studies on contract killers."

"How about from Interpol?"

"All they could tell me is that our best bet would be someone from the Balkan countries."

"That's of zero help."

Brown's face was blank. "Bill, I'm afraid that you and your team are still our best hope for a break in this case."

Garcia closed his eyes for a moment. "In that case, let's hope that my Captain's appeal to the public brings us something."

"I guess the next step will be to offer a huge reward."

49

It was another perfect late Tuesday afternoon in March. The temperature was in the seventies and there was a slight breeze. Salvatore walked over to the clubhouse to catch the end of the Happy Hour.

As usual in March, the parking lot was full. Residents had also parked on the nearby residential streets.

He arrived at 6:15.

It was the peak time and the community clubhouse was packed. As soon as he entered, the bedlam of conversations assaulted his ears.

Looking outside towards the patio area all he could see were more people.

I heard it's so light in July and August that they only need one bar instead of three.

Salvatore chuckled to himself and headed straight for the first portable bar he saw.

It turned out that he'd met the couple standing in front of him.

They were talking to another man Salvatore hadn't met. He couldn't help but listen to their conversation.

"The afternoon news broadcasters are still calling what happened here last Thursday night as the Happy Hour Murders."

The wife said, "Ouch."

"We haven't had this much attention since the rash of coyote attacks."

"When was that?"

"Oh, about three or four years ago."

"What happened?"

"Well the first woman to be attacked was laying down on a lounge chair on her patio having a nap. A coyote bit her hand."

"Goodness gracious."

"Then a day later, a woman had her breast gnawed. She was napping inside her house with the patio door open."

"Were the coyotes rabid?"

"No. But all the victims had to have rabies shots and they hurt like the dickens. You should have heard the woman who had to have it in her breast. She said it hurt like hell. Then a third person was bitten and that's when the Arizona Game and Fish people were called in. They had to hunt down about six coyotes that were living in the washes and ended up shooting them all. None were rabid though."

"Then why were they attacking everyone?"

"Apparently someone living in here thought they were cute so they put out food and water dishes for them. The culprits were only here for the spring. When they left for the summer the coyotes were trying to get people's attention to feed them."

Another woman who was also eavesdropping spoke up. "What do the coyotes have to do with the Happy Hour murders?"

"They don't."

Salvatore rolled his eyes.

Within another few minutes he was finally able to order a glass of Cabernet. With fortification in hand, he walked away.

Spotting Barbara standing with another couple, he walked over to them.

The husband was talking. "You won't believe what Nancy did this morning."

The wife punched her mate in the arm. "Henry, don't you dare!"

The husband moved a step, pretending to have suffered a massive blow. "My wife knows I'm wrong before I even open my mouth."

Barbara turned away from them and looked at Salvatore. "I say, are you feeling okay, you look a little pale."

"You know you're right. I've been feeling a little off since lunchtime. Must be something I ate."

"It could be allergies. Several people are suffering with them right now. Before you go, can I ask you something? Since you're a professional writer of crime, why do you think the police are taking so long in solving the Happy Hour murders?"

"That's a great question."

Salvatore noticed that Henry and Nancy had stopped arguing to listen to his answer.

"Most killers that the police catch are the garden-variety idiots who are apprehended at the scene or fleeing the crime. Others are caught in possession of material that can be easily connected to the crime. They usually turn out to be someone the victim knows and sometimes loves the victim. That's why spouses and boyfriends are the first ones the police look at closely."

Nancy spoke first. "Like when a husband murders his wife for a younger mistress?"

Mario wondered for a moment how he should answer. "Sure, husbands and wives kill each other every night on television and in the movies. Boyfriend kills girlfriend and vice versa. Gay and lesbian lovers kill each other. From what I've read, if you're in a relationship, and you're murdered, your better half is your likeliest murderer. In addition, the ones who aren't killed by their significant others are killed by their parents, by their kids, by their friends, or by their co-workers. That's why the cops always have a board with pictures of the victim and all the suspects with lines showing how they are all connected."

"What about all those CSI shows they used to have on television? Every week they always caught the bad guy because they left trace evidence behind."

"I don't know much about forensics but I think it's only common sense that if someone isn't acting on internal urges, they'd be better able to bide their time and avoid leaving evidence."

"That makes sense." Barbara smiled at him.

"Then if you combine the lack of any relationship to the victim, and the impersonal way in which a victim might be killed, there may not be much of a trail for a detective to follow."

Barbara nodded at Salvatore. "I knew that if I asked you, you'd have a good answer."

"He ran a hand over his forehead. "Glad to help, but I should really head home now."

Barbara touched his upper arm. "Go get some rest."

Salvatore left the table and exited through the main clubhouse doors.

His mind started racing as he returned home.

It's time to leave and go back to being myself.

As Mario walked back to his rental, he didn't pass anyone out walking by themselves or with their dog. Only one car passed him and they didn't wave.

I'm taking that as a sign that it's time to leave.

50

Wednesday morning Mario got up earlier than normal at 4:30 AM.

He flicked on the coffee maker then immediately had a shower to jolt himself awake.

Hearing the coffee maker beep, he dried off then put on a pair of shorts and golf shirt.

It's going to be a lot colder where I'm heading but I can change later.

Wasting no time, he made himself a quick breakfast then slipped on a pair of latex gloves. He washed his dishes by hand.

Mario dried the dishes ensuring all fingerprints were gone and then put them away.

Next, he emptied everything in his fridge into a garbage bag.

With his second cup of coffee in hand, he decided to pack.

Entering the master bedroom, he grabbed and unzipped his large duffel bag. It held his two pair of jeans, underwear, a sweater and four long sleeved shirts normally too warm to wear in March in Arizona. He threw in the shorts he'd worn yesterday then jammed in his golf shirts, t-shirts along with his toiletries.

He also threw in the lock pick he'd found at a garage sale as well as the book he was reading.

Mario made sure to place the Ruger and its silencer on the bottom of his duffel bag.

It took him only four minutes to check that everything that was his had been packed.

He then took another hour to meticulously wipe down every surface in the house that he might have touched.

Noticing his coffee cup hadn't been washed, he took a moment to scrub then dry it.

Finally, he poured a full large bottle of drain cleaner down his bathroom sink and shower drains.

Don't need any pesky hair or DNA hanging around.

It was overkill and Mario knew it. When he'd died in the car wreck, the Rizzos had seen to it that all of his records had been purged.

When he'd become Mario Clemenza, he hadn't had to give anyone his prints.

When he'd become a citizen of St Kitts, they hadn't asked for anything or had any requirements at all. He'd simply brought them a picture and they'd issued him the passport.

Very civilized of them.

And since then I've never been investigated in the United States or in St Kitts, no agency has my prints or DNA.

He grabbed the bag of waste and carried it into the garage. Mario pushed the door button and watched it open. He walked to the trashcan and placed the bag inside before wheeling it to the curb.

When Marvin sees it's there and that it's been emptied he'll put it beside the garage. That's what garbage buds do.

Mario went back inside and while wearing latex gloves wrote a note to Barbara. He placed the paper along with two hundred dollars and a key into an envelope.

DEAR BARBARA,

I had an emergency call from a dear friend in San Francisco when I got home last night. He's had an accident and asked if I could come and look after him for about a month. I have enclosed two hundred dollars to have one of your house cleaning services give the house a thorough cleaning so it looks great for my return. I have enclosed my spare key as well.

I look forward to returning and spending more time getting to know you better.

P.S. If you see a black cat with white paws hanging around, please give it some milk for me.

In Your Debt,

Salvatore Cabella.

MARIO CHECKED that all window blinds and shutters were closed while taking one last look around.

He picked up his duffel and dropped it into the trunk of his car.

With the garage door still open, Salvatore walked over to Barbara's house and placed the envelope sticking out from her doormat.

He returned to his garage and tossed his jacket onto his passenger seat.

Mario backed out, hit the close button and left.

He didn't see any lights on in any of the neighbors' homes.

As he exited through the gate of the Graceful Waters Resort he felt a touch of sadness.

His right hand was firmly on the steering wheel.

Mario glanced in the rear view mirror and watched as the community grew smaller then disappeared.

Within fifteen minutes, he was on his way out of the greater Phoenix area.

The residents may be old but they are more stimulating than Anthony ever was. Anthony was a successful bully when it came to business, but there is a lot more to life than dollars and cents.

Now I need to settle scores.

Vincent blackmailed me. He kidnapped Sonia and took her someplace. That's why I had to kill those people.

I need to verify that Sonia is back home and unharmed. Then we'll need to disappear for a while. I wonder if she's ever been on a cruise or been to Europe. Or maybe we should go to Sedona?

First however, I need to pay a visit to Vincent. Until I take care of him, I'm sure he'll continue to screw with me.

My uncle has kept my secrets and protected me for the past twenty-five years. I wonder if he's gone rogue on me as well?

Once I've settled my debts I can move out of the shell I've been living in once and for all.

51

SEDONA, AZ

The killings in Glenwood were behind him. He felt no sense of guilt. The job he had been forced to do was done and he was moving forward.

The next thing is to make sure Sonia's safe then to free myself from Vincent and anyone else who might want me dead instead of being free.

Since he'd recently made the reverse trip, Mario knew exactly how far it was from Phoenix to Chicago. It was just over seventeen hundred and fifty miles. Since he was the only driver, he decided to break it into easy segments.

No need to speed.

I don't need the cops to run my plates or driver's license.

For all I know the U.S. Marshals Service and the police may soon be on the lookout for Salvatore Cabella.

Mario had left Phoenix heading towards Flagstaff by taking Highway 17 north.

Arizona's saguaros and other weird desert plants sure make for an alien landscape.

A roadside sign said he was passing Deadman Wash.

Arizona sure celebrates its history of violence. Too bad I didn't get to visit Tombstone.

A few miles later, he passed Horse Thief Basin.

Then Bloody Basin Road.

Both names brought smirks to his face.

When he saw a roadside sign announcing he was at four thousand feet he found he was suddenly on a high plateau.

Gazing left then right, he realized the saguaro cacti had disappeared. The surrounding area was covered in a yellow weed or plant of some sort. It was so thick it looked like it had been planted.

Miles later a sign announced that the turnoff to Montezuma's Castle was just ahead.

I don't need to see old Indian ruins.

When he passed a sign announcing that the next exit was Sedona, his mind went to Sonia and her love of pottery. He pictured the red pieces she made.

Long before I met her, I saw some tenacious red clay while on a hike up one of the slopes on St Kitts. I wonder if the red sandstone of Sedona would mix with Sonia's clay.

Then he recalled what Big Al had told him. "Have you experienced Sedona yet?"

"No why, what's there?"

"It's a fabulous place full of red carved sandstone mountains and of course vortexes."

"What's a vortex?"

Big Al made his eyes go wide and a smirk appeared on his cheeks. "It's a magical place where the earth's energy is exceptionally alive. Sedona has at least four vortexes where the earth's energy swirls and draws everything that surrounds it into its center."

"You make them sound like they're a tornado or black hole from outer space."

"In a fashion, that's what they are. You should see how bent and twisted the trees that grow around them are. The woo-woo people love them."

Mario felt his chain being pulled. "Alright, I'll bite. Who or what are the woo-woo people?"

"They're the ones who are more sensitive and can feel the vortex's energy from miles away. In fact, I met a woman while I was up there that claimed she could feel the vortex energy as soon as she got within a few miles of the place. When she actually gets there she can't help but start to cry because the feelings she gets are so strong."

"I don't need to cry so I think I'll skip it."

"Now that would be a mistake. Trust me." Big Al tilted his head when he spoke. "Don't be surprised if the energy of the place draws you in as if it were a magnet and you're iron or nickel."

Mario saw another sign for the exit to Sedona.

Hell, maybe if I visit a vortex, I'll become more sensitive. Sonia would like that.

He took the exit.

Within a mile, the first vibrant red rocks came into view.

He had to admit the sight was spectacular.

Wow, I've never seen anything like this before.

He approached a gigantic rusty red Hersey's Kiss dropped right next to the road. He pulled over and saw a sign announcing that he was viewing Bell Rock.

He saw people hiking on it.

Mario was tempted but decided against it.

I wish I had an iPhone right now so I could take a picture to show Sonia.

After scanning the view, he remembered why he was there.

Do I feel anything yet?

Nope.

Maybe it's because I'm sitting in a car surrounded by metal and a battery?

He drove further and discovered multiple majestic small red mountain formations. Each seemed more spectacular than the last one.

I can see why people think this place is so special.

The traffic was heavy. Every car seemed to be going under the speed limit as the drivers were succumbed by their surroundings.

The actual town of Sedona was tiny.

From the comfort of his car, the shops and signs spoke of a vibrant arts and food scene.

I can see why tourists come to see its beauty and quirkiness.

He stayed on 89A until he saw a sign saying Airport Turnoff. It had an arrow pointing up.

It turned out to be a steep but short climb.

At the crest of the road, lay a large plateau.

Off to the left was a parking lot where there was a sign marked Trailhead Parking.

Mario pulled in and parked.

The trailhead was busier than he'd imagined it'd be. Most of the people he saw were properly dressed for the adventure. Even though he wasn't wearing hiking boots he decided to find the vortex.

Mario spotted a young couple he guessed to be in their late teens or early twenties returning to their car.

"Did you find the vortex?"

The couple stopped to talk to him.

Cute and petite, the girl beamed at the mention of the vortex. "Yes and it's fantastic! I feel more energized than I've ever felt in my entire life."

She seemed to be shaking from an electric charge.

Mario looked at the young man.

"Ya, it has a gorgeous view for sure." He shrugged his shoulders.

He doesn't want to disagree 'cause he wants to get laid tonight.

Addressing the girl, Mario asked, "Did you see or feel anything?"

Still beaming the girl closed her eyes and answered. "I even saw colored orbs floating in the sky."

"Really? Well I look forward to the experience, thanks."

She's a woo-woo girl.

The young man looked at Mario's casual shoes. "It's about a two hundred foot climb so be careful mate."

"Thanks."

This I've got to experience. Maybe it'll be a shortcut to help me feel things faster.

He followed the worn trail as it slowly ascended.

It wasn't too long before it became steep.

Shit, it's straight up.

He started feeling a bit faint.

Must be the altitude.

He passed a couple of twisted trees.

I must be really close.

He took several deep breaths and persevered even though his heart was pounding.

He finally made it to the top.

Breathe, Mario, breathe.

He sat down on a boulder to catch his breath.

Shit, I didn't know I was this much out of shape.

He looked around at the three hundred and sixty degree vista.

This view is outstanding.

52

"Ohmm."

He turned and saw a grey haired woman in some sort of yoga position.

She looked like she might have come from God's Waiting Room. Her clothes were flowing garments that moved with the slightest breeze. Her eyes were closed and she was chanting.

Mario watched her to see if she could give him any clues on harnessing the energy of the vortex.

She opened her eyes.

"Do you feel it?"

"Oh yes young man, I do." Her eyes were sparkling and she seemed full of energy.

"What does it feel like?" Mario felt his heart rate coming down and he realized he'd stopped sweating.

"It's a resonance and it feels like electricity or some form of magnetism is radiating out of my head. Everyone who is sensitive feels it. Do you?"

Mario closed his eyes and waited for a long moment.

"Nope, afraid I don't. Maybe I'm just a little light headed from the altitude."

She smiled at him. "Don't worry. You're off to a good start. The more you come here to the vortexes to recharge, the more attuned you'll become."

Ya sure.

"Well it's time for me to head back. My husband is waiting for me back in our car. We've still got a long drive ahead of us today."

She's a woo-woo woman and her husband's not.

He watched as she left. Hoping to find some sensation, Mario turned in a circle taking in the vista of red mountains.

Come on inner peace. I don't have all day.

Deciding he was a lost cause, he headed to the edge. Being careful to watch his every step, he left the top of the supposed vortex.

They really should put in a proper staircase. Anyone could kill themselves on this damn terrain.

Fifteen minutes later, his knees were getting sore and he was sweating once again but he'd reached the parking lot.

Mario hurriedly opened his car door and sat down.

It was hot inside. He immediately turned the temperature all the way down while he adjusted the fan up to its maximum setting.

Then he aimed the vents directly at himself.

After sitting in the increasingly cool breeze for ten minutes, he felt better.

He opened his eyes and looked around.

Fifty feet away was a flimsy formerly white tent covering two card tables.

They were covered with what he figured was native Indian

jewelry. A grey-haired couple that looked like authentic Indians stood behind them.

Maybe I can find something Sonia might like.

Mario wandered into the tent. He could see the jewelry was either shiny silver or silver with turquoise.

The male Indian looked at Mario. "Visit the vortex?"

"I did."

"Feel its energy?"

"No more than I felt before I climbed up top of it."

"Let me see the palm of your right hand."

Mario evaluated the old man.

Feathers in his hair and wearing lots of buckskin.

He seems harmless enough.

The Indian looked closely at Mario's palm. "You are not an average man who can bond with his fellow man." The Indian looked into Mario's eyes. "You have the soul of a warrior."

He talks well for someone dressed like he's in a bad western movie.

"What does that mean?"

The Indian stood up straighter, as if he were addressing a superior. "You are not anyone's prisoner; you don't need to win someone else's approval."

Mario pulled his hand away.

"Did being in vortex make you feel good?"

Mario thought about the question. "Strangely enough it did."

"That's because all of Sedona is a sacred energy field. Our vortexes have the power to heal and clear emotional blocks."

"What do you mean by clearing emotional blocks?"

"They help you let go of the past, releasing feelings of anger and injustice. A warrior is always seeking release."

Wow!

The Indian must have seen a spark in Mario's eyes. "Do you know about music?"

"I like music."

"Well, everyone hears a different note and appreciates it in their own way. That is the way it is with Sedona. Now, each piece of jewelry before you was made by my wife, here in Sedona. The spirits of Sedona inhabit each piece. If you are giving one of these to someone, they will bond with you. They will become in harmony with you. The more a woman wears each piece, the greater will be the bond you will share with the earth and with each other."

"Really?" Mario raised his eyebrows.

"Trust me. If they don't, just bring the piece back and we'll give you a full refund."

I bet.

With a silver and turquoise bracelet, necklace and a pair of earrings in a small brown bag sitting on his front seat, Mario decided to get back on the road to Flagstaff.

Either Sedona is a complete scam, or I don't have a sensitive bone in my body.

I'll bet that Sonia would feel it, what with her talk about having her mind and body in synergy. Hopefully she'll like the pieces I picked out for her.

Mario glanced at the time on the dashboard.

Maybe I'll stop for lunch in Flagstaff. I think Graceful Waters Resort is more magical than Sedona. Everyone there has already been changed into a super friendly person.

Mario laughed out loud.

53

FLAGSTAFF, AZ

About an hour outside of Flagstaff, the traffic was light so Mario stopped on the road's shoulder.

Putting on a pair of latex gloves, he crushed the silencer. Then he tossed it into a thirty foot deep wash in the desert.

Getting back onto the road, he soon saw the mountains and ponderosa pine forest surrounding the town of Flagstaff.

The effect of living in God's waiting room was very therapeutic. I liked both Marvin and Barbara.

They would make good friends, if I can ever have real friends. Maybe I can soon. Living in the retirement community has helped to change me. Hopefully, I can practice friendship and kindness from now on. Maybe I can start with my uncle and his family. I owe him for all he's done for me over the years.

Mario recalled a conversation he'd had with Sonia one evening. They were in Sonia's bed when she'd turned to face him. "Do you have a big Italian family back in Chicago?"

"I don't have anyone."

Do I tell her how I was reborn into working for Anthony Rizzo?

"Why, were you adopted?"

Anthony and Vincent Rizzo adopted me, ha!

Mario couldn't hide his grin. "Yes, I was adopted."

Sonia's forehead creased as she tried to understand. "Where are your adoption parents? Are they in Chicago?"

"They're both dead."

At least to me.

"Have you ever tried to find your birth parents?"

"I don't see what the point of doing that would be. I'm doing fine… in my own skin. How about you, what family do you have here on St Kitts?"

"I think everyone on St Kitts is related one way or another. Either by blood or by friendship."

"You think of friends as relations?"

"Sure why not. You can't pick your relatives but you can be selective 'bout friends."

Mario knew his strength had always been being able to slip into being logical and deliberate. It had allowed him to focus on whatever task was at hand and not letting emotions get in his way.

Sonia however is the opposite and lives with her emotions on her sleeve.

If we're going to have a life together, I need to move into the middle and find balance.

He heard his stomach growl so he started looking for a place to eat. He spotted a small restaurant that seemed to have parking spots available and pulled in.

Having heard that chain restaurants were increasingly installing video feeds he was now seeking smaller places that couldn't afford the cameras.

This was another of the logical rules he lived by.

Not talking to the police is another one.

I shouldn't have talked as much to that detective Garcia as I did.

For the Phoenix job, he had broken one rule. He had always told himself to never stay in a place where he was making a hit. Never stay in the same hotel, yet alone right next door.

But that was what Vincent wanted me to do.

The only worthwhile witness protection program is the one you run yourself.

If anyone besides you knows who you've become and where you are, the odds are you'll be killed.

He glanced at his dashboard to check on the outside temperature. It was only fifty-two degrees.

Thank goodness I changed into my jeans before I left Sedona.

He found a parking spot, grabbed his jacket and went inside.

A waitress escorted him to a booth and handed him a menu. He ordered a salad and iced tea for lunch. "Why is it so much colder here in Flagstaff than it is down in Phoenix? It's in the mid-eighties there today."

The woman looked at him with disdain. "Phoenix is at a thousand feet while here in Flag we're at seven thousand."

Mario didn't like the server's attitude but he let it slide.

As was his custom Mario surveyed the other people in the restaurant.

He figured by their bent heads that half were on their iPhones texting or surfing the web.

He recalled when he'd first met Barbara how she'd asked him if he was on Facebook or Instagram.

I told her no. She'd asked me why. I said, "I don't want to see people who have their perfect lives and perfect spouses lying to themselves. That's not to mention all the political crap people post."

He decided to try out what he'd been taught at the newcomers Coffee Talk.

He took several deep breaths then tried to focus on each person who didn't have their face buried in their iPhone.

Each person in here is my dear friend.

As he glanced around, he made sure he had a smile on his face. To his dismay, everyone he looked at turned away from him.

"Whatcha looking at asshole!"

A large man with a full beard who was dressed like a lumberjack was now staring at him. With a quick glance to the bearded man's left and right, he saw everyone was now looking at him.

No one's returning my smile.

Mario dropped the smile and held up his palms as if to say he was sorry.

He looked away and stared out the window.

Great, now they all think I'm a pervert.

After an eternity his meal came.

Even the waitress is giving me a funny look.

He kept his eyes focused on his plate.

Fortunately, the salad was fresh and tasty.

I should teach the bearded guy a lesson.

He left a quarter of the salad untouched.

Mario wanted nothing more than to walk past the jerk then turn sharply to slice his throat with a steak knife.

Stop it! I don't need the cops.

Still looking out the plate glass window, he heard his server. "Would you like a free refill of the ice tea in a large plastic to go cup?"

She'd brought him his bill.

"Sure, that would be nice, thank you."

He left the server a decent tip. His face was purposely expressionless.

Mario walked out without looking directly at the lumberjack or anyone at his table.

54

A s soon as he hit the fresh air, he inhaled deeply.

I'm not in God's waiting room anymore, what was I thinking?

Out here in the real world, most people think that someone looking at them is violating their personal space.

He got into his car and locked his doors. He looked towards the restaurant's front door and was glad not to see the lumberjack walking out.

I'm outta here.

He eased his Camry back onto the road.

Next, I'll take Interstate 40 to Albuquerque, New Mexico on my way to Amarillo, Texas.

Mario pulled into the first rest stop outside of Flagstaff.

I should have used the bathroom back at the restaurant.

The place was empty.

He walked around the small building and burnt the Salvatore Cabella identification cards in a large cigarette disposal urn.

He figured if he needed to show identification to anyone, it would be as the person he'd been for the past twenty-five years.

I'm Mario Clemenza once again.

He kept his Salvatore glasses in case they came in handy in Chicago.

A sign along the road stated that he was on part of the historic Route 66.

It made him feel nostalgic. He turned on the radio and searched for an oldies channel. He didn't find one but did find one with classic rock.

He enjoyed that for about an hour before he turned it off.

Sonia and I have a mature love. Like the God's Waiting Room residents, we aren't interested in prior loves or what someone did to someone else.

It's all about living in the here and now, for a comfortable future together. Being in love isn't just holding hands, it's staying focused and looking in the same direction.

The ribbon of highway never ended.

He made sure to wiggle his toes and occasionally squeeze his butt to keep the blood flowing.

Another sign advised him that he was nearing the Petrified Forest National Park. He ignored it and kept driving until he reached Albuquerque, New Mexico.

He decided to stop for the night and found a cheap motel beside the highway.

He prepaid with cash.

The motel room door had a sloppy lock. Mario figured a slight shove could open it.

Others must have complained as it also had a cheap bolt and chain on the inside trying to appease paying guests.

He wrinkled his nose.

WTF?

The room smelled.

Something floral has been sprayed in here in a feeble attempt to camouflage dog urine and God knows what else.

The queen size bed had seen better nights. When he lay on it to try it out, he fell into a six-inch deep depression.

It's only for one night.

Mario closed his eyes. He recalled Sonia's touch as she had rubbed baby oil over his entire body after he'd showered.

I need to get her back!

With his determination reenergized, he placed his Ruger on the small bedside desk, which held the room telephone.

Thanks, Alfonzo.

Mario liked automatics like the Ruger because they were tightly sealed. When it was fired, almost all the powder residue is forced and trapped in the silencer. This prevents the powder from escaping and covering the person who fired the shot. Only a small amount of residue leaks out from the automatic's ejection port.

He proceeded to break it down. Using a rat-tail file, he altered the ballistic markings in the gun barrel, the shell chamber, the loading ramp, the firing pin and the ejector pin.

He made sure that he scraped each item where it made contact with the shell.

Next, I'll lose the pieces one at a time along the way to Chicago.

He also found what was left of the copper jackets of the spent 22's he'd collected at the crime scene.

The night of the event, he'd taken a hammer to each shell.

Now his plan was to toss them, one at a time along with the gun parts.

Before he went to bed, he shaved off the goatee.

I'm me again.

As he tried to fall asleep, he thought about Sonia.

If I were to meet Sonia for the first time today, would I still find her hot?

Damn right I would.

It's not like I have any friends pestering me to get hitched. I know my needs and what I want out of a relationship.

Plus, I know what she says she's looking for. No children, since she says it's too late. I agree, who needs ankle biters at our ages.

When he heard that Sonia had been taken, his blood had boiled and he'd wanted to act out of passion and rip Vincent apart.

He gritted his teeth as his thoughts lingered on Vincent Rizzo.

Vincent could have chosen anyone for the job. To subject me to the task, by blackmailing me was beyond cruel.

If Sonia's dead, I guess I could always find another soul mate.

They now have those soulless apps that apparently ask you too many questions and then have the audacity to tell you who you should marry.

The problem is they don't know about our secret baggage and the shells we've constructed to hide behind.

He made a snap decision.

Using another one of his disposable cell phones, he telephoned his uncle. "Alfonzo, I need you to do me a favor."

55

F or breakfast, Mario had coffee and pancakes in a small Albuquerque diner.

This morning he made it a point not to smile when he glanced at his fellow patrons.

Now I feel as lonely as I did before I made some friends back in God's Waiting Room.

As soon as he finished his meal, he hit the road.

Figuring he had another twenty hours of driving in front of him, Mario decided to cut it in half, if his butt would allow.

Setting out on Highway 40 once again, Mario immediately turned the heater on.

The outside temperature wasn't supposed to get above the mid fifties and the weather forecaster on a local radio station was calling for it to get down to freezing that night.

The sound of the tires was his main source of entertainment. He focused on the thuds, whips and dull roars his Camry's tires made as they ate up the different road surfaces.

WTF?

At first he wasn't sure what was lying on the road ahead of him.

As he drove over it, he was surprised to see a single tennis shoe lying alone in the middle of the road.

It brought a smile to his face.

I'm not alone.

It's probably the shoe of a killer who was getting rid of his clothes and tools as he was driving away from the scene of a murder.

Mario laughed at his own joke.

Having grown up in a Catholic home, Mario hoped that if there was a God, that he would be just and understand that the killings he'd undertaken were simply tasks he'd been asked to perform.

I shouldn't be judged by doing what others ordered me to do.

His gut snapped into a knot as soon as he realized he was in a Highway Patrol speed trap.

Automatically his foot tapped the brake petal as he glanced at his speedometer.

I'm not speeding.

He watched in the rear view mirror.

The panic drained away and he relaxed, as the Patrol Car didn't pull out after him.

Within two hours, he passed through three more speed traps while trying to stay in his happy place -- thinking about Sonia. He recalled how he had asked Sonia if she wanted to travel and go to fine restaurants.

She'd replied that she was already living in paradise.

Then she'd added that if it made me happy she'd try it.

The scenery through his front windshield was mountain and desert.

At one point, he had to swerve to avoid tumbleweed rolling past his car.

He kept thinking of Sonia.

She's willing to try new things.

I wonder if I should help her open a pottery shop for the tourists down in Basseterre?

Nah, that would take her away from me.

Sonia likes the bond she has with her brother Kwame, even if he's a bit of a scoundrel. Maybe I should help him out?

Mario remembered the afternoon he'd asked her why she liked him.

"Because you seem happy in your own skin and treat me right."

If she only knew the things I've had to do.

There were no big cities to bypass or major attractions to distract him.

Most people say that loneliness is downright painful. I've spent too much time on my own to agree with that.

He saw a large billboard advertising the Cadillac Ranch.

Mario recalled seeing the attraction before as he'd driven the old Route 66 on a job for Anthony. He'd been disappointed. To him, it was just a row of ten junky old Cadillac's that had been planted upright in the earth. Someone had called it a work of modern art, but Mario thought of it as a garbage dump and a waste of time to visit.

He'd overdone the coffee and had to make several stops to relieve himself.

At each stop he made sure to take a few extra steps and stretch before getting back in his car.

It's Thursday, I missed the cigar club yesterday.

For lunch, he parked at a strip mall and walked half a block to a McDonald's. He watched the children yelling and screaming in the playpen.

Now don't they make a good case for birth control?

56

Mario needed to stop at a branch of his U.S. bank in Amarillo, Texas. He parked and looked up and down the street.

Ah, an old-fashioned barbershop.

He made a quick decision to further alter his appearance.

Mario entered the shop to find a slim man who looked to be in his seventies sitting in a chair reading a newspaper. "I'm in a bit of a hurry. How long would it take for a quick cut?"

"Depends on what you're looking for."

"I've been missing my old army buzz cut. Can you do one for me, just not as short?"

"That's the fastest cut of all. Grab a seat and we'll get you out of here in a jiffy."

The barber was playing an oldies station. Johnny Cash was crooning about walking the line.

That could be my theme song.

Mario found that a few minutes of music were therapeutic; by the third song, it was annoying.

Ten minutes later Mario was entering the bank.

For the past twenty-five years, he'd had no expenses, as Anthony had paid for everything. The other benefit was learning from Anthony and Vincent how to utilize tax havens and international banking.

All of the bonuses Anthony paid me went into my Caribbean tax havens.

Long ago, he'd formed several offshore corporations and placed the bonuses Anthony had paid him in various accounts. One of the corporations he'd formed was a U.S. land development corporation. It was from this account that he was now withdrawing the laundered and legal funds.

Withdrawing funds took even less time than the barber did.

One last task.

He spotted a used car lot and parked his Camry two blocks away.

Mario retrieved the map of the USA he'd bought back at the Glenwood mall.

He folded it so the state of California faced out.

He took a pen and circled San Francisco then put the map back into the glove box.

Just in case the police ever find it, they'll think I've gone to San Francisco.

Before she'd died in the car crash, his mother had impressed upon him that doing the little things in life were worth doing well.

When he'd gone to work for Anthony he felt he had the time to do exactly that. For his life as well as Anthony's depended on making sure everything was as it should be. If Mario missed or did something wrong, it could have meant the end for both of them.

Mario had always figured that Vincent would get Anthony off while he would die the first night he went into a jail.

The one thing that still bothered him was that he didn't know exactly who or what had killed Anthony.

Whoever it was, I should thank him.

Or her.

Na, it had to be either Vincent to cover up Sarah's loss of Anthony's money or AJ who was pissed at being overlooked by his father.

Or just maybe, it was Frank, who wanted to get out from under Anthony.

Mario left the Camry with its keys in the ignition and the doors unlocked. He also put Salvatore Cabella's Graceful Waters Resort nametag in the glove box.

It should be stolen within an hour.

As he approached the used car lot with his duffel bag, he had to smile. A salesman was grinning while he stared directly at him.

He's licking his lips.

The salesman was hard to miss. He wore a pair of white pants, a white belt, black shirt and white shoes. Above him waved strings of triangular pieces of plastic in an attempt to make a customer believe he was about to enjoy himself.

He could be a Norman Rockwell painting.

Mario knew he was about to be verbally beaten by a man who represented the last vestige of horse-trading in America.

The salesman smiled and shot out his hand. "How can I help you on this fine day?"

"What's the most reliable vehicle you've got?"

"That would be the late model blue Malibu over there. Let's go look at it, shall we."

They started walking together. "It just came off a banker's

lease. It's the best car I have. I'm afraid its not inexpensive but I'll see what I can do for you."

Mario walked around the Malibu then sat inside. "Looks fairly straight; how about we take it for a test drive?"

"Great, I'll just go the keys."

Ten minutes later Mario was behind the wheel. "I don't know this area, how do I get to try it on the highway?"

"Turn right."

An hour later Mario had purchased the Malibu and registered it in his own name.

The U.S. authorities have no interest in Mario Clemenza.

If anyone looks into me, they'll find a guy who moved to St Kitts years ago.

Feeling like a new person, Mario headed for the highway where he was quickly lost in his thoughts.

Working for Anthony, I led a soft life. It was in the lap of luxury even though I was virtually little more than a twenty-four hour a day servant.

He thought back to when he first realized he could kill someone without any emotional response.

I need to change.

By living in God's Waiting Room, I experienced how life should be lived.

My past is holding me back. I need to cut loose of those holding me back so I can find my happiness.

Another car sped past him.

One thing I can't ever change is to let anyone know what I did for the Rizzos.

That's when Mario felt Vincent's suckered tentacles crawl inside his skull.

Wait until I get to Chicago: I'll make Vincent pay for bringing me out of retirement.

Mario turned on the car radio and tried to find a station he didn't hate. After trying for a full minute, he turned it off.

He recalled how Anthony Rizzo listened to classical music because he said he found it calming.

I can only take it in small doses.

His mind started to consider AJ.

That sniveling AJ's the worst kind of parasite.

Mario couldn't believe that after he'd killed Anthony's wife for him, Anthony had ordered Vincent to make arrangements for his son AJ to become the head of his Wheelchair Foundation.

It delivers wheelchairs to people who really need them around the world.

AJ could have lived in his parent's mansion in Chicago and lived a prosperous life.

Instead, he chose a life of drugs and crime. AJ's crazy enough that he might want to pay me back for killing his mother.

He hired an assassin to try and kill Frank. All because Anthony had chosen Frank over AJ to be the heir to his syndicate.

Mario tried to take his mind off AJ but couldn't.

AJ's a spoiled brat and screwball.

Why was AJ so intent on replacing Frank Moretti as heir to Anthony's syndicate is beyond me. Anthony was trying to set AJ up in a cushy job with the Wheelchair Foundation for heaven sake.

To hire some random assassin from the internet to try to kill Frank was foolish and only tells me that I can't trust AJ to leave me alone to live my life with Sonia.

Mario next recalled how Anthony had given him the bizarre order. "It's time that you kill my son for me."

Anthony's own sudden death that very night had changed the immediate need to kill AJ.

I just don't know if AJ will be a problem going forward.

The terrain changed and became a broad expanse of flat land known as the Great Plain. Mario knew it stretched from Mexico to Canada.

His mind wandered and he tried to think positive thoughts once again.

Where you have been has no effect on where you can go.

Unless you let it.

He thought how with all of his practice playing different roles, he might try out for a local theater group.

Who knows, perhaps I'd make a good villain?

When Mario had telephoned his uncle, he'd asked him what he'd heard about AJ. His response had been to the point. "Rumor has it that he's either relapsed into drugs or overdosed."

Mario believed him.

It's also possible AJ pissed someone off and he's now dead.

As he neared his evening destination, Mario spotted the oil derricks populating the landscape.

The heartland.

Man, how I long to live on a clean beach.

He'd only been on the road for eight hours when his butt became numb and sore.

He decided he'd driven far enough for one day.

The next big city he came to was Oklahoma City. He pulled off and spent the night in another below average motel.

57

GLENWOOD, AZ

I t was day eight in the Happy Hour Murder investigation. Detective Bill Garcia was standing in front of the murder board in the investigation room.

On the white board were pictures of the victims and the known facts:

Victims:

• U.S. Marshal: Tim Gladstone

• Witness: Jerry Webb

• Wife: Sheila Webb

Time of death: Thursday March 9, approximately 6:30 – 7:00 PM

Motive: prevent Jerry Webb (WITSEC) from testifying against Vincent Rizzo (Chicago).

Method:

• Webbs - Pistol with silencer; 2 kill shots each to head of each witness

• Gladstone - Pistol with silencer; 1 shot to head after shot to torso

• 2nd Marshal was on food run

Forensic Info: 0

Pathologist Info: all deaths from 22 hand gun

Security cameras: 0

Witness info: 0

How perp knew where witness was – U.S. Marshal Service hacked.

Killer was local? – no perp with similar MO

Imported Killer? – no airline or rental car hits

Known Rizzo Associates – 27

Interesting Rizzo Associates - 0

Working theory: Professional, imported hit man

Suspects: 0

SITTING in front of Bill Garcia were his fellow detectives: Charlie Fontaine, Harry Elm and Tom Averell.

"This morning I was informed that unless we can show that we are making progress, we will be going back to our normal work load. Starting tomorrow, we'll be handling multiple cases. Any questions?"

Garcia knew this would be his last day with Harry and Tom helping. "Harry, you were going to look at options the perp had to get away from the crime scene? Either in some sort of vehicle or on foot, right."

Harry Elm looked at his notebook then spoke. "The community is out in the middle of the friggin' desert. So no one walked in or out. The rental car companies were of no help, so I went back and talked to the Graceful Waters Resort general manager."

"What did you find out?"

"I asked him about parking violations or any reports of

suspicious vehicles."

"I hadn't thought of that, what'd you find out."

"They have a single patrol vehicle which drives the neighborhood each night looking for vehicles parked illegally on the street. If there are, they issue tickets which are charged to the homeowners accounts."

"Were there any?"

"Yes, there were three within a mile radius of the crime scene."

"Did the patrol vehicle collect the license plates?"

"They did and I ran them. Here's the list." Harry passed the list to Garcia. "As you can see, one was from Colorado, one from Minnesota and one from California. All the drivers were staying with residents who claimed they didn't know about the rule about not being able to park a vehicle on the street overnight. I then checked to see if any of them had rap sheets."

"And?"

"All are Joe Citizens."

"So no possible suspects then."

"Sorry but no luck, Bill."

Garcia looked at Tom Averell. "Tom, you were going to check into how the perp may have known the home's layout."

"I did. First, all the floor plans are on the developers web site as a sales tool. Anyone could access them."

"What else?"

"The second thing you asked me was how the perp may have known the front door opened up into a great room where everyone would probably be waiting for the second Marshal to return? Well, I don't think the perp did. He would have been prepared to take out both Marshals. Since one Marshal was on a food run, there was only one Marshal on duty and he would be the one to open the door. Once he was taken out, it would have been easy to shoot the targets."

Garcia frowned and looked toward Charlie Fontaine.

Since Charlie is the Phoenix Police Chief's son it means if this case isn't solved, the blame will fall squarely on me, not Charlie or anyone else.

"Charlie, do you have any new insights about our case?"

"I was wondering if the perp kept the weapon when it would be the key piece of evidence against him or did he dump it in a trashcan somewhere?"

"I doubt he kept the weapon. Everyone with a television knows to dump a weapon as quickly as they can. It would be too easy to convict him if we caught him with it."

"That's what I figured also, so I checked out the community trash cans as well as the doggy station cans."

Garcia winced. "Unless you found a weapon, I don't need to hear anything."

Charlie smiled. "By looking at the board I gather Chicago PD cleared all twenty seven of known associates that may have been the killer."

"You're correct."

58

OKLAHOMA CITY

Mario left Oklahoma City a little later than he'd planned. In an attempt to get blood flowing to his rear end he'd gone for a brisk two mile walk before hitting the road.

He pulled onto the highway just after seven in the morning. Even though he'd enjoyed a decent breakfast of ham and eggs, Mario was already contemplating a barbecue dinner in Memphis that evening.

My favorite barbecue spot in Memphis is Pappy's Smokehouse.

In a good mood, Mario tried the radio once again.

This time he found gold. It was Dean Martin singing about being nobody 'til somebody loved him. His mind immediately went to Sonia.

When I asked her why she listened to dance music she told me that she could listen to the blues and wallow in self-pity or she could listen to upbeat music and find joy in what she had and who she was.

He started humming along.

When the song ended, he turned the radio off and sat in silence. Staring ahead at the white pavement lines flashing by he considered what he would do with Vincent once he got to Chicago.

Do I know enough to send Vincent to prison?

Yes, I do.

When he was working, Mario was obsessed with reflection and planning. As he drove, he wrestled with what to do next.

I could be upset with Vincent but I understand why he would want to have me silenced.

I was well rewarded for the services I performed. I must admit I knew all along that once you're in with someone like Anthony and Vincent, you don't get out alive. I mean, look at all of Anthony and Vincent's closest business associates in the syndicate that I killed for them.

Before the Phoenix job, I was worried Vincent could have a hit out on me if he found out where I was.

In my gut, I know I should really kill off Vincent and AJ.

Perhaps even Frank Moretti, but that would mean killing his bodyguard Naomi as well.

Ah, Frank. I did try to kill his fiancée Ashley and deep down I think he's still in love with her.

Mario always preferred to have one of his murders appear to be suicide or an accident.

Stop it!

Mario didn't believe in ghosts or the supernatural. Reviewing his past hits was like recalling some movie he'd seen years before.

In Ashley's case, Mario had tried to have it appear to be a boating accident. However, Mario had made a major mistake.

He didn't know anything about boats so he asked around and contacted an expert who knew both boats and bombs.

The problem was, the person he contacted worked for a federal agency.

It was only a week later that Anthony had told him that he'd screwed up. In the end however, it didn't matter, as Ashley never testified against Anthony.

The lingering problem is that if Ashley is still alive, some federal agency may have my name flagged and could come after me.

Then he saw the flashing lights in his rear view mirror.

Shit!

He checked his speed, which was bang on. Glancing beside him and in front, he saw no other vehicle.

He's after me.

A quick glance in his mirror confirmed the flashing lights were still there.

He flicked on his right turn signal and slowed down.

Mario glanced once more into his rear view mirror before pulling over onto the gravel shoulder.

The flashing lights pulled in behind him and sat there for what seemed an eternity.

He's running my plates.

Mario's mind started to panic.

What's in my car that can get me in trouble?

I don't have any weapons in the car.

He looked in his driver side outside mirror and saw the police car door open.

A large uniformed and armed officer left his driver's side door open and started walking towards him.

Mario hit the window button to roll it down. "Officer."

"Registration and insurance cards." The officer had his right hand resting on his weapon.

Mario passed him the printout of his temporary registration. "What's this?"

"I just bought this car yesterday in Amarillo."

"Why did you do that?"

"I had a smaller car and found it was too cramped. I decided I wanted something a touch bigger."

The officer was wearing a sour look. "It says here that you live in Chicago." He pulled out the book he used to issue tickets.

"That's right." Mario had used the address of Anthony Rizzo's estate just outside of Chicago since that was where he had lived whenever Anthony had come back for a short stay.

Since Anthony had asked Mario to kill his wife, he hadn't even thought about changing the address.

If I decide to keep American identity, I need to change my address.

The Officer seemed to be deliberating for an eternity.

Ten seconds later he finally spoke. "Well, you need to find the nearest Chevy dealer and have them replace your right rear taillight."

"Why, is it burned out?"

"That's why I pulled you over."

"I had no idea, thank you officer."

"If you promise to have it fixed today, I won't issue you a ticket."

"I promise that I'll have it done today."

The officer closed his book of citations.

"Thank you very much Officer."

The Officer handed Mario his registration. "Drive safely."

Mario watched the Officer walk back to his patrol car.

He turned on his ignition and flicked the turn signal.

Turning his wheel, he checked to make sure no vehicles were coming his way and pulled out onto the highway.

Several deep breaths later Mario drove while still feeling numb.

That was close. I'll find a dealership to change the light bulb and get an oil change just to be safe. Then I'll find a motel before I hit Pappy's Smokehouse.

He kept the speedometer just below the speed limit.

With his stomach guiding him, Mario drove until he reached St Louis, Missouri.

59

CHICAGO

L ast night Mario had savored the ribs at Pappy's Smokehouse. Today was a new day and he knew he couldn't afford to risk another traffic stop.

He made finding a Chevrolet dealer to change out the light bulb a priority. He'd considered trying to change it himself but without the right tools, he knew it was useless.

"How long will it take?"

"Give us an hour. You can wait in our lounge. We keep the coffee fresh in there."

After giving his Malibu over to the service department he spotted an outdoor clothing store across the street from the dealership.

Jay walking across the road he went shopping.

I need some warmer things. Once I have them I'll grab more coffee.

He was rewarded with a black wool beanie to protect his ears and a pair of black wool gloves.

With a freshly serviced vehicle and warmer items for his

extremities he set out on his fourth day of driving. Mario knew he only had a five-hour drive before he'd arrive in Chicago in the early afternoon.

Chicago's always been my bad luck city.

He thought of the Gene Pitney song about the town without pity.

It isn't very pretty...

My father died here of a heart attack when I was only eight.

My wife was raped and murdered here.

For Mario, thinking about his wife was like scratching an old scab only to find the wound was still fresh and bleeding.

Here I sold my soul to the Rizzos.

Then my mother died without my ever seeing her again after I supposedly died in that car crash.

Mario felt cold and alone just like the snow that was falling.

Other than Vincent and my uncle Alfonzo, who knows who I really am?

He also knew he couldn't kill off everyone he perceived to be a potential problem.

Or could I?

Anthony wasn't my friend; he was the God I had to adore and obey.

Now that he's dead, Vincent has yanked me back into working for him. One way or another, I'm through with him. Vincent deserves to die.

AJ? I can't trust AJ to not come after me for revenge for killing his mother so he should also be eliminated.

The snow stopped falling.

Frank could have his bodyguard and new girlfriend, Naomi Dolphin kill me for supposedly killing Ashley. I wouldn't put it past Naomi. Then again, surely he's in love with Naomi and they've forgotten about me.

They're why I need to stay under the radar after I leave Chicago.

First things first.

Mario pulled off the highway when he saw a diner by the road.

Stretching his legs, he made his way inside.

"Seat yourself hon."

He found a booth with a clear view of the front door.

As he waited to order, he thought of Sonia.

Mario supported Sonia and she was always supportive of his need to spend most of his time with Anthony.

She would always ask me how my day went.

Mario loved how Sonia made the mundane events of her days interesting tidbits she would share with him.

In return, he would treat each time they met like it was a special occasion and a time to celebrate.

I found myself emerging from my self-imposed shell.

It was like I was discovering that I was alive.

One day she asked, "Are you going to stay working for Anthony forever?"

The question had never crossed his mind.

It's been over twenty-five years. Anthony's not doing many deals anymore. I've killed off his enemies, his wife and her lawyer and most of his syndicate. Who's left?

Perhaps I can retire. Hell, if I'd been convicted of murder I'd have only been sentenced to twenty years and been out in less.

"What can I get for ya hon?"

Mario looked up.

The server was in her forties and gave Mario the eye. "Let me guess, salad and iced tea?"

Mario decided to try being nice one more time. "As a friend

recently said to me; forget the health food. I'm at the age where I need all the preservatives I can get. Besides I had some of that green stuff yesterday."

"You don't look all that old to me, but hey, it's your stomach."

He ordered a coffee, cheeseburger and French fries.

"How do you take your coffee?"

"Black, please."

I think spending time in Graceful Waters Resort has helped me grow. The way they combine bringing people together and connecting them with fun things to do gives the residents a better way to live.

Then he spotted the telephone hanging on the wall.

It must be one of the last landlines in America.

He waited until the waitress brought him a mug and poured him a full measure.

Knowing it would take several minutes for the cook to ruin his burger, he rose, went to the phone and picked it up.

It had a dial tone.

He inserted the amount and dialed the operator.

Once I know Sonia is safe at home, I'll visit Vincent and collect the two million dollars he promised me.

A few moments later, he was connected to a number on St Kitts.

Mario held his breath as he waited to hear her voice.

"Hello?"

His heart popped into his throat.

I know what I've got to do.

Mario cradled the phone against his heart.

Instead of speaking, he hung up.

Mario got back to his booth just as the food arrived.

"Here you go hon."

Feeling energized by hearing Sonia's voice Mario attacked the food.

He ignored the coughing and sneezing of his fellow diners as he ate. He made sure not to smile at anyone.

Fifteen minutes later, he was in the Malibu heading into downtown Chicago.

As he drove, he thought about his life with Anthony and how his balanced life had unraveled ever since the fateful day he had told his boss he was considering retirement.

I'm tired of living in someone's shadow.

He wondered how he would have turned out if he had just gone to prison and served his time.

I know that I was really just a cutout for Anthony and Vincent. Someone, who if caught would take the fall and protect them or else be quickly killed.

No place is safe when Vincent has the kind of money he has.

No one except Sonia needs me and no one cares if I'm happy or not.

He had hoped this next phase of his life would turn out to be one of living his life to the fullest.

Originally, he was hoping to find several women who could be his special friends. When he'd met Sonia that had changed.

He wanted to live somewhere he didn't need to be constantly looking over his shoulder. So far, he hadn't found that either.

Maybe an active adult community like Graceful Waters Resort.

Anthony, especially in the later years had become lethargic and spent most of his time sitting listening to his classical music and smoking cigars. Many evenings were spent playing chess together. Some nights Mario would whip up sushi for them. Those were the nights Mario remembered with fondness.

It wasn't all bad. But I did delude myself into believing that Anthony thought of me as more than another one of his servants.

Mario suddenly thought of the crazy woman from the wine club who said that the killer had to have been a psychopath.

Most people are sheep who do exactly as they are told. It's the adventurer, the misfit, the exceptional, the hero who can overcome their fears, who can do what others can't, that can be focused; they are the ones who achieve.

Mario had once read where someone had said that happiness in intelligent people was rare. He'd taken that to mean he was smart.

I may not be happy about what I have to do sometimes but at least I have the intelligence and focus to get the hard jobs done.

Then he thought of Marvin and Joan.

I want to live like they did. To be bonded with Sonia and share every moment with her.

If that means I need to become more empathetic and caring, then I will.

I can do it.

Mario turned on the car radio. The welcome was less than warm. "This is Mark your weather man and I'm forecasting another freezing night with three more inches of snow before we hit a balmy high of thirty nine tomorrow."

60

A fter experiencing the eighties in Arizona, Mario swore he could feel the Chicago cold settling into his bones.

Minor aches Mario had forgotten about were suddenly reappearing.

Mario pulled up to a seedy hotel with street only parking in an older area of Chicago.

The wind was driving a wet snow everywhere and clinging to everything it hit.

He was glad he'd bought the beanie and gloves.

While trying to avoid the grey snow and the wettest slush his feet got wet nonetheless.

The hotel was no prize as it had seen better clientele.

No one pays attention to anyone who stays in a dump like this.

It's the type of place where people tend to ignore each other, lest they see something that would get them in trouble.

As he checked in, he saw a woman standing about ten feet

from him. Her nose was running and she was using the sleeve of a sweater.

Doesn't anyone use handkerchiefs anymore?

I wonder if she's been snorting coke or if she has a cold.

She raised her eyebrows giving him a look of availability.

Mario shook his head and went up to his room.

He plopped onto the bed.

After a minute, he sat up and went over his priorities.

First, I need to visit uncle Al, get the lay of the land and the item I asked him to get for me.

Second, I need to have a sit down with Vincent to determine where I stand with him.

AJ and Frank Moretti can wait.

Mario closed his eyes and pictured Sonia's smile. He felt her body next to him.

Even though the sex was great, it wasn't just about that.

He thought about Sonia and how they wouldn't be having children.

I'm fifty-five and she's forty so we're probably too old for that blessing.

For Mario it was about being with someone that wanted him.

I hope we end up like Marvin and Joan where we share all of the day's little events and then years later look back and remember them; even if some of them aren't such good times.

Even though we've had a couple of tiffs we've quickly made up.

He didn't want to chance his uncle having any Saturday visitors. He knew that was the day Alfonzo had always reserved to be with his sons Dino and Leo. Alfonzo had explained that Dino was short for Aldobrandino, while Leo was short for Leonardo.

Being back in Chicago made Mario nostalgic for his childhood.

It was the last time I was part of a real family.

As he unpacked he found Salvatore's glasses. He put them aside.

No one knows me as Salvatore here.

Stepping outside the hotel he was glad he was wearing his jeans, sweater and jacket. The snow was still falling so he turned up his collar.

He decided to drive the ten blocks to where he'd watched bocce being played with lots of Italian vocals and body language.

The residents back in Arizona would be intimidated off the courts by those old Italian guys.

Mario was sure he was in the right spot even though everything was covered in snow.

There's the park; it hasn't changed.

Where there was once an empty lot, there now stood an Italian restaurant - Casa Bocce Pizzeria.

Mario went inside. It wasn't what one could call a classic Italian place that made one feel at home. While it had the red and white-checkered tablecloths and a flag of Italy, the paper napkins and plastic utensils immediately branded it as a fast food place. It was however jammed with customers of all ages.

The place was toasty warm.

No wonder everyone's in here.

Half the patrons in the place were at tables with people eating pizza and drinking beer.

The other half seemed to be playing a refined form of bocce on carpeted lanes.

That court is very fast. That woman barely threw it.

"If you can find a seat, grab it and I'll bring you a menu in a minute."

Mario turned to find a young girl, barely of legal age carrying a tray full of beers.

He looked at her body then chastised himself.

She could be my daughter.

"Okay, thanks."

Times have sure changed. What used to be free now costs by the hour. Hell, maybe I'll open up a bocce restaurant on the beach back on St Kitts.

Instead of finding a place to sit, Mario left.

61

PHOENIX, ARIZONA

U.S. Marshal Kevin Brown was frustrated. It had been twelve days since the murder of a fellow U.S. Marshal and two witnesses under the U.S. Marshal's protection.

So far, the only good news was that the Marshal who had gone for Pizza had been cleared of wrongdoing and had been reassigned.

The bad news was that the agency had confirmed that its database had been hacked on multiple occasions. They were now working on how the WITSEC couple had been compromised. They were working on the assumptions that Vincent Rizzo had commissioned the computer hacks and the assassinations.

Trying to identify how and by whom the databases had been compromised had been turned over to the FBI since neither the Marshal Service nor the Glenwood Police Department had adequate cyber resources.

Detective Garcia of the Glenwood PD investigation had

advised Brown that he had no active suspects and that the daily briefings had been suspended until there was a new development. He'd also told him that Detectives Elm and Gladstone were no longer dedicated to the case.

It was Wednesday morning and both Brown and Garcia had received a text message to come to the District of Arizona's United States Attorney's office in downtown Phoenix for a noon meeting.

When Brown arrived, he found Deputy Garcia had only arrived a few minutes before him. They were shown into a meeting room and were waiting for the AUSA to appear.

Five minutes later AUSA Johanson entered wearing her poker face.

Both law enforcement men stood up.

She waved her hand. "Please sit."

Johanson spoke as if she were addressing a jury. "It's your job to find the killer and provide me with proof beyond a reasonable doubt. So, I need both of you to go back over the evidence and talk to the witnesses again. Find me the killer. It wasn't a ghost. You are missing something."

She paused and looked at each man before she continued. "Either the details, logic or the human factors have caused your investigation to go off the rails… What we do know is that they killed three people. We know that they knew where the targets were and when they would be there by hacking the U.S. Marshal database. That tells us that there was at least one accomplice. The FBI has their cybercrime analysts looking into it. That may produce the break we need."

She paused again. "For now, we know the goal was to prevent them from testifying against Vincent Rizzo who has a reputation for hiring the best hit men. That would suggest to me that the killer was brought in and well paid. Perhaps it could have even been an international assassin. I suggest you contact Interpol and see if they have any suggestions."

Kevin Brown spoke up. "I've already done that. They couldn't add anything substantial to the case."

Johanson clutched her jaw in frustration.

Seeing the blank looks on the detective's faces only added to her displeasure. "This is a different case. You need to recognize other possible avenues of investigation or other possible offenders."

Ingrid Johanson left the room.

Brown looked at Garcia. "I don't know what else I can help you with at this stage."

With a stern face, Garcia said, "In my spare time, I'll start over and try looking at everything with fresh eyes."

Both men sat in silence until Garcia spoke again. "Nobody notices the good work you do but they sure will bitch when you come up empty."

Kevin Brown shook his head. "Perhaps Johanson was right when she said it might be a ghost."

Both men smirked.

62

CHICAGO

M ario was trying to find something good about being back in Chicago.

At least I have less pressure in my nasal cavities. No pollen; no allergies. However, I'm probably going to end up catching a cold.

He could feel himself transforming into work mode. When he had a job to do, he viewed life in black and white. There were no grey areas and no decisions that could be delayed.

This time however there was no need for Mario to rush in or take significant time doing his homework. There was no need for him to create a mental sheet of details about his target.

Mario knew exactly who his target was, where he lived and most importantly, he knew his habits intimately.

I need to meet with Vincent.

Mario knew that all three of Vincent's daughters had married or had moved out and were on their own. Vincent Rizzo and his wife Gina were empty nesters. They had no dog to bark, to warn Vincent or alert the neighborhood.

Best of all Vincent had asked Mario to personally select the home's alarm system, so he knew how to defeat it.

Mario had been inside of Vincent Rizzo's home on many occasions. He knew the home's layout and the best ways one might get in and out without being seen.

It's definitely a mansion with multiple garages housing his most valuable exotic automobiles.

Vincent and his wife shared a love of antique and very expensive classic Italian racing automobiles.

Vincent and Gina were often pictured in online and print magazines driving or standing beside their automotive babies. Even Vincent's daily driver was exotic. Mario had seen it in a magazine. It was a red Ferrari Pininfarina Sergio, one of only six built.

On the negative side, even though Vincent was supposedly retired, Mario knew he was paranoid and kept one weapon in his desk drawer, one in his den and another in the nightstand beside his bed.

Mario was considering potential methods of delivering the hit.

After discounting the mansion, Mario's first thought was to manufacture a well-planned racing accident.

The cars are all old and they break down on a regular basis.

However, he also knew Vincent's vehicles were all pampered by a special crew of mechanics he'd hired on a full time basis to ensure every vehicle he or his wife might race was as sound as possible. That included a pre-race final inspection.

It would be tough to pull off.

Mario also calculated that there would be a thorough inspection of the wrecked vehicle by the crew under the auspices of the police.

He also figured Vincent Rizzo would still have many police

on his payroll to ensure his continued reputation as a Teflon lawyer and not as an alleged crook.

Mario smiled to himself.

I just don't have the skills to make the failure of the car look accidental.

On more than one occasion, Mario had hired a hooker to deliver injections of drug overdoses to his victims.

Unfortunately, Vincent isn't a skirt chaser like Anthony was.

For this hit, I'm the only person I trust.

I want the cleanest, most efficient and professional service possible... Perhaps I should hire a snowplow.

He laughed to himself.

Since he'd already visited his uncle before he'd gone to Arizona, Mario decided to drive by Vincent's estate.

Parked outside the gated home, Mario sat and watched Vincent's premises for any movement even though it was a Saturday.

It was no surprise that Vincent never left his home.

Vincent is officially retired and whatever work he does is probably done from his den.

Mario had seen how Vincent's preference had always been to hire other unscrupulous lawyers to be his cutouts to get things done.

When Vincent's unlimited financial resources were combined with the best hard-assed lawyers Chicago had to offer, the result was usually intimidation that outlasted everyone unfortunate enough to come to his attention.

If a home invasion and snatch was involved, as had probably been the case with Sonia, Mario figured that a criminal defense lawyer would know who the smartest and most successful were at the job.

Besides repaying Vincent for blackmailing me, I need to find out who he paid to seize Sonia.

Mario wasn't too concerned with being seen. Other than his uncle and Vincent himself, virtually no one had seen him up close in twenty-five years. He was invisible in the big city that was Chicago.

It all comes down to common sense.

Mario was feeling his old efficient self. He had a job to do and he was focused on that alone. He didn't let the weather, a good-looking woman or anything else distract him.

The emotions he had re-discovered in Arizona had once again been scabbed over.

Mario knew Vincent was smarter than he was when it came to details within the law.

But when it comes to actually pulling off a hit, or surviving on the run, no one can beat common sense.

Mario wasn't planning an elaborate ruse to sneak in a long-range sniper shot or bludgeon Vincent over the head until he was dead.

Instead, Mario wanted a personally satisfying payback for Vincent forcing him to pull off the death of a couple in the WITSEC program and for whomever he'd hired to grab Sonia.

Mario decided to meet face to face with Vincent.

I'll tell him that I want to look in his eyes and have him tell me that he'll never bother me again. I need something lethal that'll be a bugger to detect.

He smiled as he recalled reading about two such recipes in a medical journal. One was a neurotoxin made from fermented plant alkaloid and the other was a simple mix of fungi & citrus. The reason he had committed them to memory was that they virtually left no trace.

They certainly wouldn't be detected in any normal tox screens.

ST KITTS

S onia was finally feeling somewhat safe in the comfort of her modest one bedroom home on her native island of St Kitts.

Her bungalow was furnished with used furniture which she told herself was shabby chic.

Since everything had to be imported, new furniture was reserved for the wealthy foreigners buying homes to obtain their citizenship in St Kitts.

After the stress of Mario leaving and telling her that he would return in a few months, Sonia had resigned herself to waiting.

Mario gave me enough money so that I don't need to go back to work at the batik shop for at least six months.

Her routine became one of cooking, cleaning and entertaining herself with friends and the occasional visit from her bother Kwame.

That had all changed when two men had paid her a visit in the middle of the night.

She had been alone in her small one bedroom, tin roofed bungalow.

Her only possible savior would have been Kwame, but he lived a mile away with his wife and child.

The day after her return she had summoned up enough courage to go outside and talk to her neighbors.

"There you are Sonia, where you been girl?"

I may as well just tell the truth.

"I was kidnapped in the middle of the night and they finally brought me back last night."

At first, her neighbor's reactions were disbelief. Then they decided to play along with her.

"Did you hear or see anything the night I disappeared?"

"No, notting. We thought you'd run off with that Mario guy you bin seeing."

Sonia had stopped that conversation by saying she had to go to the store to get groceries.

She left to walk down to the local store where they sold food and liquor.

Her experience at the store had not gone well either, so she decided it would be best to keep her episode to herself.

Back at home, she went over what little she knew.

I must have been injected with a drug... I remember they put a black hood over my head before I totally passed out.

She never knew it but they had whisked her away by jeep to the local dock. There they had loaded her onto a boat and taken her to the smaller island of Nevis.

When I woke up, I was chained to a single bed in a room that had its sole window boarded up with plywood. I remember the daylight breaking through the edges.

Her right arm was sore and she'd found a multi colored bruise where they had jabbed her with the needle.

Fortunately, the room had a makeshift bathroom for me to use.

Her captors always wore masks when they brought her food or let her have a bathroom break.

If they don't want me to see their faces, they may not be planning to kill me

Every day one of them would walk her around what she assumed was a large private backyard. They would hold her by the arm and guide her, as she had to wear the hood each time.

It smelt like St Kitts.

That's how I knew I wasn't that far from home.

There was no television but they did supply her with used books to read which she did to pass the boredom.

Most of the novels were romances where white women were smitten by hard bodied rich men or pool boys. What a bunch of crap!

However, every novel she read made her long for Mario. He was the first man that hadn't asked her about her past.

She recalled the time she had brought it up with him.

He'd responded by saying, "As hard as it might be, sometimes things are best left in the past. Why don't we both agree that we've each done some living and with each day going forward we'll just build a new life together."

"And ignore the past?"

"Yes."

Sonia remembered hugging Mario for that.

The attempts she made at conversation with her captors were fruitless.

"Shush now, before we gag you."

She had also glimpsed their white skin.

They be Americans.

One of them did tell her she would be going home as soon as her boyfriend completed a job.

At first, she wondered which of her poor choices they were talking about until she realized that the only man she'd been seeing for the past year was Mario.

When she asked what job Mario had to do, they hadn't answered.

She counted the days by scratching a short line in a corner of the wooden floor each morning. Sonia thought about how she and Mario had bared their souls to each other.

Sonia had explained that she didn't have a particularly happy childhood, especially after her father left her, her mother and her newborn brother.

Her mother ended up supporting the fatherless family by cleaning homes for the wealthy new foreigners as well as doing odd sewing jobs. Her now dead grandmother had guided and raised them.

Sonia had never married. Not because she wasn't attractive, it was just that she didn't want to end up like her mother. She recalled telling Mario that she had turned away boys and then men. "The men I did date all turned out to be abusive bastards."

My dream is to find a man who will respect me.

A week passed, then two weeks, then three.

What job takes this long? Where are you Mario?

She thought back to what Mario had confessed to her one night. "Hell, Sonia, I have no friends, my family all think I'm long dead. The only person who cares about me is you."

Come back to me Mario.

Being held prisoner wasn't exciting, it was terrifying.

Sonia remembered asking Mario if he'd ever ridden a motorcycle.

"Yes, but I'm a cautious rider."

"Good because I'm afraid of them. My brother Kwame had one. One day he asked me to sit on the back as he went to the store. The faster he went, the more I loved it: the banking to the side as we went around a bend, the feel of the wind on my face, the smell and roar of the engine – I just loved everything about the whole experience. Then we banked around a curve in the road where there were several goats. Kwame swerved to not hit them and the bike slid out from under us. Luckily, there was no other traffic around us other than the goats and I got away with cracked ribs and bruising. It scared the bejesus out of me. Since that day, I refuse to ride with him or anyone else. Some nights I dream of that day and I wake up lathered in sweat."

She loved Mario's answer.

"Don't worry, the only thrill I'm looking for is to hold you tight."

Thirty days passed and nothing changed.

What da hell kind of job takes this long?

On the morning of the forty-seventh day, they told her she was going home.

"When?"

"Today. Now drink this up unless you want another needle." They had given her a glass of odd tasting orange juice.

The next thing she knew she had woken in her little bed in her home.

It was still nighttime.

She pulled the sheet up and cuddled her pillow. All she cared about now was that she was home and safe.

She'd waited until morning to get out of bed, make some coffee and then gone outside.

Feeling upset, but also grateful to be home and unharmed, she tried to go about her life once again, as if nothing had happened.

There was no point going to the island police.

What could they do?

She could imagine the conversation. "Let's get this straight. You were kidnapped and then they brought you back to your home. While you were in captivity, they feed you and didn't do you any bodily harm. Is that right?"

Sonia closed her eyes and shook her head.

They'd call me crazy again.

The one question that she couldn't get out of her mind was what had become of Mario.

Mario's such a sweet man. Why isn't he here? I hope he's not dead?

I wonder if they killed him after he did whatever they made him do for them?

64

CHICAGO

S unday night, the temperature in Chicago plunged to below freezing.

On Monday morning, the weather was its trade-marked unpleasant mixture of snow, hail and rain.

It was just as miserable as Mario remembered the start of spring to be.

It's the coldest place on earth.

When he went out to his Malibu, he found that its window had a thick sheet of ice covering it.

How in hell did I ever survive growing up here?

He turned on the ignition, set the heater to full blast, and aimed the air at the window.

Turning to the back of the car, he discovered a thick sheet of ice on the rear window as well. He pushed the rear defrost button.

Next he took out his wallet and selected a credit card.

As he stood in slush, he used the credit card to scrape ice off the front windshield. He suddenly longed to be back in Phoenix where it was in the mid 80s.

The heater worked well as a small area of the foggy, icy window suddenly cleared.

At least I can now see to drive.

Mario used the time he needed to drive to meet his uncle to reflect on his relationship with Sonia.

I think she loves me.

Even if she doesn't, I love her and she sure as hell makes me happier than anyone else has in the past twenty-five years.

Mario's uncle Alonzo was older than even Anthony. He recalled how his uncle had told him tales about working as an enforcer for Anthony's father, Bruno Rizzo, before Bruno had moved to Florida. His uncle was now in his eighties but claimed he was as strong as a bull.

Mario flashed back to how his uncle had come to his aid when he'd found his wife dead and he'd beaten the guy to death.

I didn't know what was worse, my wife's death or being accused of the crime.

Mario's uncle had told him to man up. "Do you want to go to jail or live a life of luxury working for the Rizzos?"

As a result, Mario had developed a protective shell insulating him from the world. He felt like a turtle living in a shell that he never let anyone enter. He was safe and so were those who didn't get close to him.

The first few years were easy as he was still living his own personal nightmare. His shell meant less joy, calm and support that a normal person needed. A close relationship with anyone other than Anthony was forbidden.

I was like a spoiled attack dog. I was stuck in a cage where I

*could see between the bars but I had no door through which I
could escape.*

And everyone knows what's on the bottom of a cage.

He knew it was either let in feelings or stay numb and keep
them out. That's what he'd done for over twenty-five years.

*I told myself it was the only way to survive. Without my
shell, I would probably have felt shamed by what I had to do.*

Killing without remorse is harder if you care about people.

65

His uncle lived in the same modest middle class neighborhood of post war homes that he had his whole life. Alfonzo's home was painted white and needed a fresh coat. The front door was a faded black.

With all of his money, why has he never moved into a better neighborhood?

While the rest of the yard was covered in snow, his sidewalk was clear.

It's part of the code he's lived by for his entire life.

Across the street, some kids had built a small snowman.

Mario was sure his uncle's neighbors thought his small wholesale plumbing business was legitimate.

They have no idea it's used to launder just enough money to ensure his family is well taken care of.

For the life of me, I can't understand why he didn't retire to the Caribbean or Florida, years ago. If my dad had lived, I'm sure he would have.

Other than his uncle, Mario had avoided contacting any relatives since going to work for Anthony Rizzo.

Family can be helpful and they can be fatal.

As far as he knew Alonzo's sons, Dino and Leo had no idea who he really was, or of his history.

Most of them must think I died when Bonaro's remains were found burned in the car wreck.

He sat in the car and remembered the night back on St Kitts that Sonia had brought up the subject of her brother. "He's a small time crook that's had a few run-ins with the police."

"Is he in jail?"

"No, he's never been convicted."

Mario remembered smiling at her. "You're only a crook if you're caught and convicted. Otherwise, you're just another member of the public. The ones that are convicted are bad because they're lousy criminals. The ones that are good at crime are regarded as successful businessmen. Your brother must be good at what he does."

He recalled her looking at him sideways. "Are you trying to tell me something Mario?"

"Not about me. It's the guy I work for."

She put her hand on his. "What exactly do you do for Mista Rizzo?"

"I've already told you, I manage his security."

I've spent most of my life being the strong silent type of man. The guy who doesn't need anything or anyone.

Sonia brought me out of my shell. She taught me to release my inner beast so I can express my hunger for love and to be myself. Sonia said it would allow her to really trust me.

The turning point was the night Sonia had told Mario that she longed for a man strong enough to respond when challenged, who cares enough to fight and who respects himself enough to take his woman on, when needed.

"I'm not some orchid you must baby and protect. I've had one of dem and I dumped him."

Mario looked at his uncle's house one last time. Opening his car door, he made his way to his uncle's black front door.

Before he could knock, the door opened and his uncle was there, grey hair and all.

"I thought you was gonna sit in your damn car all night. Come in, sit, and warm yourself up."

The wood-burning fireplace was cranking out the heat. Mario sat in one of two large, well worn, comfy chairs. "How you doing uncle?"

"What does it look like? I'm still on this side of the grass. There's beer in the fridge and wine on the counter."

"I'm good and besides I'm driving."

"Suit yourself." His uncle stared at him. "What's up with the army buzz cut, you going to war or something?"

Mario ran his hand through his short hair. "Fresh start."

His uncle looked uncomfortable, grimaced, then farted. "It's scary when you start making the same noises as your coffee maker."

Mario grinned. "I understand. Don't forget I just spent several weeks living in a retirement community in Arizona. You're young compared to a lot of the people I met there."

"Non dispiace invecchiare, è un privilegio negato a molti."

Mario understood Italian and knew what his uncle had said, "Do not regret growing older, it is a privilege denied to many."

"I don't. In fact I'm here to see if I should be writing my last will and testament." Mario stared into his uncle's eyes.

His uncle's eyes looked away. "You're talking about Vincent's state of mind, right?"

Mario kept staring. "I've done his blackmail bidding for the last time. I need to know if I'm now a loose end."

"When it comes to men like Vincent, it's hard to know what they're thinking."

Mario blinked and looked away for a second to gather his courage. "Vincent did use you to contact me and pass along his blackmail proposal. I find it hard to imagine you didn't look him in the eye and read his intentions."

Alfonzo adjusted his butt as if the chair had grown harder. "Look Mario, I'm just trying to live out my days with as little drama as possible."

Mario's eye caught a color photograph on the fireplace mantle. Standing up he went to examine it.

It was a color photo of two grown men standing on either side of his uncle. "Are these my cousins? I haven't seen them in years. How are they?"

"Ya, that was taken a couple of years ago. Dino, Leo and I were out fishing on Lake Michigan... So tell me, how was Phoenix?"

Mario sat back in the easy chair. "The job was straightforward. But it was different than I expected."

Alfonzo furled his eyebrows.

"The people in the community were just regular people, but it was as if they were all on their best behavior or something."

"How so?"

"They weren't normal. Until I moved to Arizona I assumed all old people became grumpy and vindictive."

"Are you including me in that group?"

Mario grinned at his uncle. "From my experience, most people, like you, keep to themselves. Not those folks. They go out of their way to be friendly. I gotta tell ya, it opened my eyes."

"Well I ain't leaving here, I can guarantee you that." Alfonzo set his jaw. "So what are you really doing back here in freezin' Chicago? I would have thought you'd be back on St Kitts by now. Have you changed your mind? It would be a shame for someone with your skills to retire. Have you decided to do some work here with my sons after all?"

"I'm here to meet with Vincent and look him in the eye."

66

Mario saw his uncle's right eyelid twitch.

"I can understand that."

Why did he flinch when I mentioned Vincent?

"Tell me, has Vincent kept Anthony's syndicate in place?"

His uncle dropped his head onto his chest. "As far as I can tell, the syndicate died with Anthony. Vincent is pretty much spending all of his time traveling around the world with his wife racing his antique cars. You know, doing their prissy rallies and all."

"Then what was Arizona all about then?"

"It was old news from when Anthony and Vincent started out. Unfortunately, fresh new Feds think they can make a name for themselves by going after old cases where the statute of limitations never dies."

"What about doing deals with Frank Moretti?"

"No. From what I can tell, the syndicate fell apart with the deaths of Anthony's crony, Angelo Basso, then Anthony himself. The other members have all pulled in their horns without Anthony to guide them. Besides, Vincent's wife, Gina, is making more than enough in legit investments to take any risks. No, those days are over."

"What's the word on Frank then?"

"He seems to be trying to go legit as well. Word is he's starting his own investment firm."

"What do you know about his bodyguard, Naomi?"

"I hear she's more of a girlfriend than bodyguard these days."

I knew that was going to happen.

"What about AJ?"

"He's a full blown drug addict living on the street. If he doesn't overdose one of these nights, I'll be shocked."

Mario seemed to be lost in thought. "If there were any contracts out on me, you'd tell me, am I right uncle?"

"Ya, I'd tell ya and no there ain't." Alfonzo's eyelid twitched again.

"Do you think Vincent will leave me alone now that I've done his dirty work?"

His uncle fidgeted while he scooted his bottom back and forth in his chair. "Unless you ever get caught for something. In which case Vincent could never take a chance that you wouldn't talk. In that case, you'd never last a night in a jail… or if he needs another somebody silenced. Once a predator like Vincent knows your weakness, he'll never leave you alone. You know that."

"That's what I figure as well. Were you able to do the favor for me that I called you for?"

God helps those that help themselves.

"It's in the fridge."

Mario walked into the kitchen and opened the refrigerator where he found a small plain brown cardboard box. Knowing it was stable at room temperatures, he opened it up to find the vial of Batrachotoxin. It had the logo of the maker of the research drug on the box, along with multiple warnings.

It's the real deal.

Mario had researched the drug and discovered that it was available to researchers studying the function of small molecule inhibitors of voltage-gated sodium channels. The next step had been to use the web to discover a Chicago researcher who could order it.

Mario figured that his uncle or one of his sons had convinced a researcher to part with a vial for a substantial bribe.

Mario spoke loudly. "I found it."

"Ya, Dino left it in there for you."

Mario walked back and stood in front of his uncle. "Did I wire you enough money or do I owe Dino some more?"

"No, all is good."

"Say uncle, do you know a reliable fence that specializes in jewelry?"

"Sure, but you do know Valentine's Day was in February, right?"

Mario chuckled. "Can you just cut the shit and write down his name and address for me."

"Lately it's too hard for me to get up. Bring me the pen and paper that's on the counter over there."

Mario did as he was told. Once he had the information securely in his wallet, he sat back down. Then he leaned forward and looked his uncle in the face. "I've been wondering: how did Vincent know you could get hold of me?"

Alfonzo stared at Mario as if he were a child that needed to be disciplined. After too long a pause he said, "Lucky guess I suppose."

Mario hated to ask, but he needed to know. "Would you tell me if there was a contract on me?"

His uncle looked away for just a split second then forced a chuckle. "Yes, of course I would. Who are you going to trust if not me, Bonaro?"

Mario stared at Alfonzo.

That's what I'm trying to decide.

Mario nodded his head and stood up. "If you hear anything, let me know right away."

"Of course. But how will I contact you?"

"If I survive the next week, I'll contact you and let you know."

His uncle stayed seated, raised his right hand and gave a limp wave good bye.

Mario picked up his package and walked to the front door where he placed his right hand on the doorknob and paused.

He looked back at his uncle.

Other than Vincent, his uncle was the only one who knew who he was and that he was alive. His uncle was the one who had persuaded Anthony and his cousin Vincent to save him from prison. He recalled how his uncle had told him there was lots of work for someone with his skills in Chicago if he ever left Anthony and survived.

If I can't trust him, who da hell can I trust?

67

Mario was upset about the way his employment of the past twenty-five years had ended. He felt sad and hurt that all of his dedication and deeds on behalf of his now dead employer had turned out to be for naught.

Deeds that ranged from strong arming people into compliance, to erasing their lives.

All had been done successfully to the point that neither he nor his benefactor had ever been charged with anything.

When he'd broached the subject of retirement he had been rebuffed and thought he might even be whacked himself.

For as long as Mario had known the Rizzos, he'd never known Vincent to ask what was the right thing to do; all he wanted to know was what outcome his cousin Anthony wanted.

Now that he's the de facto boss, Vincent's creating the outcomes he wants without regard to anyone else.

Mario couldn't have cared less about what Vincent was

doing; except he'd once again been dragged back into the cesspool he was so good at.

I can't wish the world to be the way I want it to be. Whatever the cost, I must make the changes myself.

I need to be the warrior that Indian back in Sedona saw in me.

Mario knew there was the distinct possibility Vincent Rizzo had placed a contract out on him now that the couple in witness protection had been eliminated.

Vincent doesn't like loose ends and I'm a loose end. He can easily find and afford to pay someone to waste me.

Mario left a message with Vincent Rizzo's secretary. "Please tell Mister Rizzo to meet his old friend Mister Lombardi in the Bar at The Peninsula at four PM sharp."

Even though Vincent Rizzo was supposedly retired, he still employed a secretary within his law firm.

After an hour, Mario had called the secretary back. "Hi. It's Lombardi. Can you confirm that Vincent is meeting me tomorrow?"

"Yes he is, Mister Lombardi."

"I'm sorry to ask you this, but I must be getting old and senile. Can you please tell me if I told him to pick his favorite restaurant or to meet me at a bar of his choice?"

"His favorite restaurant is Mama's Kitchen, but no you asked him to meet you at four PM in the bar at the Peninsula."

"Thank you."

Mario drove into the downtown area in order to make sure no one on Vincent's payroll was going to get there before him.

Don't need an ambush.

He was early. Mario proceeded to check out the expansive lobby where no one was loitering or looked suspicious.

Next, he went to the bar that was still closed.

Spotting a gift shop, he entered to ensure no one was hiding in there.

The clerk was pleasant but ignored him. The only shopper was a woman in her thirties with a young girl in tow. They purchased two colorful umbrellas with flowers on them.

She's hoping to tell her daughter that today's rain means spring is coming... good luck.

After browsing for a few minutes, he left satisfied.

Mario went back to the lobby since that was where the entrance to the bar was and walked over to the concierge's desk where he took a local newspaper then selected a comfy leather chair.

It had a view of both the main entrance as well as the door to the bar.

He scanned the headlines for thirty minutes.

The world is still insane.

He returned the newspaper and sat silently with one eye on the closed door until he saw it open.

At five minutes to four, he saw a barman dressed in a black vest, black pants and white shirt open the heavy wooden door to the bar.

Mario walked in and scanned the room. Other than the neon lit bar, the room was as dimly lit as he remembered it.

I'm the first one here.

He chose a table in a back corner that had a clear view of the entrance.

With the dim lighting, this feels like a place to take a woman.

As he waited for someone to take his order, he noticed that no background music had started.

A waiter appeared.

Mario's first thought was to order rum. He'd grown to like

the different rums he'd had on St Kitts, especially the local moonshine rum produced by the guys who ran homemade stills up on the mountain.

Vincent likes scotch.

"I'd like to order an unopened bottle of Johnny Walker Black with two ice-free glasses.

Vincent likes his scotch neat.

The waiter said, "Right away sir."

"Oh, and could you please turn on your background music."

"Yes sir."

A moment after the waiter went behind the bar, what sounded like a Miles Davis tune crept through the hidden speakers.

Music will make it harder on anyone trying to eavesdrop.

The waiter brought the Johnny Walker and two glasses.

Ten minutes later, Vincent entered.

Seeing Mario, Vincent stood tall and walked towards the corner table.

He's dressed exactly like a wealthy lawyer.

Without addressing Mario, Vincent waved the waiter over. "Replace this bottle."

68

The waiter knew who Vincent was and didn't question him. Instead, he took the bottle and bowed as he left.

I wonder if Vincent knows how clichéd he looks wearing his pinky ring?

Mario played his part and kept silent. He knew to show his characteristic obedience to the Rizzos.

Vincent watched the waiter as he left.

They were both quiet as if each were stalling for time.

Mario saw the demon that Vincent was. Too slick and tainted to be anything else. He imagined what Vincent's head would look like after he'd taken it to a taxidermist.

Finally, the waiter appeared with the new bottle. "May I pour, Mister Rizzo?"

"Now you may."

The waiter cracked open the bottle and poured two fingers into both ice-free glasses.

Bowing, the waiter quickly left.

Vincent sat up straight to demonstrate that he was feeling his superior self. He finally deemed to look at Mario's face. "I understand you were once again your efficient self and took care of the Phoenix business for me."

Mario tried to read his face. "I did what you asked of me. Now, how is Sonia? If you've harmed her, I'll…"

"You'll what?" Vincent's face turned hard. "You know me Mario. I'm a man of my word. Sonia's safe at home."

Mario stared at Vincent.

Vincent spoke first. "Relax, she's as good as new. Why don't you give her a call?"

Mario deliberately took a deep breath, trying to compose himself.

I remember what Tina the Life Coach said.

"Look Vincent, I'm trying to achieve greater fulfillment in my life. So I'm going to show you that I trust you."

Vincent sat poker faced.

"Vincent, will you now show me that you trust me by telling me that you're prepared to leave me alone once and for all?"

Vincent didn't reply. He just glared at Mario as if he'd rather be undergoing an anal probe.

Finally, he articulated what was on his mind. "Look, Mario, I know you're trying to change your life, but a tiger can't change his stripes no more than you can change who you are. Anthony felt betrayed when you told him you wanted to retire. He saw you as a still young man going through an identity crisis for some unknown reason. However, I knew better. I knew it was because your black woman had put a voodoo spell on you."

"You're a racist pig."

A grin blossomed slowly across Vincent's face. "You can try and rationalize your behavior to yourself Mario, but women like Sonia can make a man become self-destructive. Can't you understand that I'm doing an intervention, to help you; can't you see that?"

"No I don't..." Mario stumbled for the right words. "I see you and me as finished... so look Vincent, I don't want to live by constantly looking over my shoulder. What would it cost me to buy my freedom from you once and for all?"

Vincent continued to stare into Mario's eyes. "The question you should be asking yourself is what price did you agree to pay, when you became Mario."

Mario was stunned. "I did not choose to become Mario Clemenza. You and Anthony created me and told me what I had to do. I did it to pay my way, and I think 25 years of payback is enough."

Vincent was an experienced, arrogant attorney and never shied away from arguing. "You knew the price for not going to prison or being electrocuted. We saved your sorry life. As I recall it was a debt you took on gladly. We saved your ass and you thanked us. Told us that you would spend the rest of your life doing whatever we needed to be done. A man who doesn't honor his word is not fit to be trusted or to live. You know that."

Vincent's face morphed into the look of a grandfather trying to reason with a young child. "I don't think you really want to retire full time, Mario. You could make a very nice living doing the odd favor for me."

Mario shook his head.

Vincent leaned in closer to Mario and half whispered. "Until the Statute of Limitations runs out on my deals with Anthony, I may need you to do the odd clean up from time to time. In return, I'll let you live with your friend Sonia. She'll never have to know. Besides, it'll be profitable for you."

I've got over thirty million, why do I need more?

Mario sat further back in his chair. "Spending time in Phoenix only confirmed my desire to be retired."

Vincent shook his head as if to deflect Mario's words. "I can't see you being happy playing tidily winks and waiting to die. Where is the intellectual challenge in that?"

"I discovered that I like playing tidily winks."

Vincent played with his glass then took a long drink. "After all Anthony and I did for you I'm surprised by your lack of respect." Vincent paused.

Vincent looked at his drink. "You know I can't take no for an answer. When an attack dog turns on its owner, it's put down."

He just told me that I do his bidding, or I'm dead.

"Tell me Vincent, with all your billions, why are you still doing deals?"

Vincent bore into Mario's eyes. "Because the Feds aren't letting me retire."

Now I know I can't change his motivation.

Mario had been surprised that the Feds were after Vincent. On the surface, Vincent had been legit for some time. The Rizzo Investments firm was comprised of Vincent, his wife Gina and their daughters: Carla, Nikki and Sarah. They all worked from their own homes. They only worked with Rizzo funds, which he understood were north of ten billion. As he had heard Vincent say many times, "It's about preservation of capital, not aggressive appreciation."

Mario decided to probe further. "How is Frank Moretti doing?"

Since Vincent's going to have me killed, he'll probably tell me the truth.

Vincent took another sip. "I haven't talked to him since Anthony's modest funeral on St Kitts... Francis inherited

Anthony's home there and like you, seems content playing house with his local girlfriend."

Mario now understood that Vincent's disdain extended to Frank. "I didn't know Frank was still there. I thought he might have come back to Chicago."

"You really don't know much about money do you Mario? If Frank leaves St Kitts to return to Chicago he'll get whacked big time with taxes."

Mario watched as Vincent raised his nose slightly.

"Besides, having him on St Kitts makes it easier for me to keep tabs on Frankie."

I wonder who he's paying on St Kitts.

If I can convince Sonia to move to another island with me, I'll probably never run across Frank or Naomi.

"How about AJ, how's he doing?"

Vincent smirked. "I put him into a twenty-four hour rehab facility and he still went missing. Since I couldn't leave Anthony's Wheelchair Foundation without a manager, I put my daughter, Sarah, in charge. If AJ ever shows up clean and is able and willing to take the job, he can still have it."

My built in shit detector tells me that you're lying.

Mario still wondered about the youngest daughter Sarah.

Sarah tried what she thought would be a guaranteed currency hedge. She had used a few billion of Anthony's funds and lost them. Luckily for her, Anthony died before he found out.

I still think Vincent may have had Anthony killed. Maybe Vincent helped AJ do it, then he eliminated AJ?

Mario asked for clarification. "Is AJ dead?"

A partial smile flashed for a microsecond across Vincent's face. "As I said, he went into rehab and disappeared."

Mario nodded ever so slightly. "I don't want vague euphemisms Vincent. AJ probably knows that you and Anthony told me to kill him before Anthony was found dead instead. Can you personally guarantee me that AJ won't pop up in my future?"

Vincent eyes went cold. "If you're asking me if I had him killed, the answer is no. If he's still alive, then he's a wild card that's a threat to me also."

So he's probably dead.

"Can you give me a few months to make up my mind about working for you? I need to find out if Sonia can get over what you've done to her. Once I find that out, I'll let you know."

Vincent stared hard at Mario and said nothing.

With no additional information to be had from Vincent, Mario passed him a slip of paper. "Here's the account I want my money deposited into."

Without looking at it, Vincent picked up the paper and slipped into his shirt pocket. "Will do. But, you didn't need to come all the way to Chicago just to give me that.

"I'm surprised at you Vincent. You must realize the feds are probably all over your electronic communications."

Vincent drained the rest of his drink and laid a hundred dollar bill on the table. "I agree with you Mario. I think you've lost your edge for playing in my world. I don't trust you anymore. You should go back to St Kitts and retire with Sonia."

Sitting in silence, Mario watched Vincent walk out of the bar.

He's either got a contract out on me or will by tonight.

69

ST KITTS

Sonia was still having nightmares from her ordeal.

In each one, she was once again locked away in the windowless room. She was always alone.

All the time she was worried they were going to kill her if Mario didn't come through for them.

While her most recent joy in life had been her time with Mario, her worst was the kidnapping.

It was even more painful to her than her childhood where her father had left his family when Sonia was barely ten.

While her mother worked several jobs to raise her boy and girl, her grandmother had been the one to spend the final years of her life trying to guide them.

Sonia found that going back to her regular routine was helping her adjust. Spending a few hours each day working on her pottery helped take her mind off reality.

She was in her little kitchen making her favorite goat water stew for lunch and dinner. She had already trimmed the fat and gristle from the goat meat and was getting ready to mix the goat, papaya, breadfruit, and dumpling droppers into a tomato-based stew which already had the red wine, onions, turmeric, chutney and ginger added to it.

Off to the side, she had the curry waiting until the very end.

She heard a knock on the door.

Her nerves kicked in and she dropped the dish she was placing onto the counter.

It broke.

She grabbed the large kitchen knife she'd used to trim the goat meat.

She was afraid that whoever was at the door had come back for her.

Another knock.

It was harder this time. "Sonia, you in there girl?"

It's Kwame.

She'd know her younger brother's voice anywhere. She rushed to the door and opened it.

Kwame was surprised as his older sister flung her arms around his neck and squeezed.

Then he remembered that he was irate as hell. "Where you been sista? I've been worried like crazy."

A tear fell from Sonia's eye and she dabbed at it with her apron.

"I was kidnapped."

"What you mean, you was kidnapped?"

"You'd better come inside." As Kwame entered her kitchen Sonia glanced around in case her nosy neighbors were watching her. The women were all married and avoided her.

"Sit little brother."

Kwame grabbed one of the mismatched chairs. "When were you kidnapped?"

"Let me think, probably about fifty days ago. They broke in

here in the middle of the night when I was sleeping. One man crawled on top of me to hold me down while another injected me with some drug."

Kwame was momentarily too stunned to talk. "I, I dropped by twice… I thought you'd gone run off with Mario."

Sonia bobbed her head. "They must have carried me out to a car and taken me by boat to another island. I think it was Nevis."

"Who took you?"

"I don't know."

"What happened to you when you got there?" Kwame's voice finally showed some compassion for his older sister.

"Nothing. They didn't hurt me if that what's you're askin'."

"If they didn't hurt you then did they say why they took you? No one contacted me asking for a ransom. It makes no sense."

Kwame knew that many of his sister's male friends had been abusive to her, which is why she had never married.

He also knew that she felt her current suitor, a man named Mario respected her.

Even though Kwame didn't like Mario, he knew his sister did.

Kwame had tried to warn her off him. "This Mario guy isn't from St Kitts. He's not one of us. He'll break your heart. He's just like his boss, Anthony Rizzo. I've heard stories about them hiring girls for sex parties."

"Look Kwame, there aren't a lot of local men my age who aren't already married and be just looking for a woman on the side. The rest I've already discounted. I'm too old to be chasing men and I'm tired of playing games."

She sat down. "Mario's told me that he wants to settle down with someone. I don't care what he's done in his past."

"I understand sista. I'm just trying to make sure you'll be safe and happy."

Sonia raised her head. "I heard them say they wanted Mario to do something for them."

Kwame furled his eyebrows. "Do what?"

"They didn't tell me." Sonia was getting upset and her voice went higher.

"Have you asked Mario?"

"No I haven't. He's not back yet." Sonia looked away from Kwame.

"Well it wasn't because they wanted him to paint their house now was it. Can you imagine what kind of shit Mario must be into if people would kidnap you just to blackmail him? Kidnapping is a serious business. For your own safety, it's time to dump him."

Sonia looked down at her feet.

Kwame let her know his feelings. "Mario was the security guy for that big honcho, Anthony Rizzo, until he died. Mario had men who worked for him doing most things. What would someone need Mario for? To break into someone's home, to rob them, or what?"

"I've told you before, I don't know."

"And I told you that Mario was bad news for you. If you are still seeing him after this, you need to stop. If you continue to see him, who knows what else may happen to you. You need to find someone else if you don't want to grow old alone."

That remark cut her deeply.

"If it were easy, I would have already. I can't tell my heart who to love and not to love. Mario has restored my faith that a man can be kind. At my age, I'm not looking for fireworks and butterflies."

Kwame knew his sister was normally reserved and sensitive yet he had seen her blossom since being with Mario.

He wanted to tell her that if she'd lose a few pounds she might have better luck. But he bit his tongue. "Look sis, if you gonna stay with him, that be up to you, but who's to say you won't be killed next time someone wants him to do something?"

Sonia exhaled and looked at her brother as if he may be right for once.

"Look Sonia, why don't you come move in with me and Asha for a while. Maybe just until Mario comes back."

Sonia looked defiant. "Thank you little brother but your place is even smaller than mine and no offense but it's no better than a pig pen. Besides, where would I sleep?"

70

CHICAGO, ILLINOIS

Mario decided to stay in the bar and finish his drink. *Vincent is an arrogant ass.*

He thought back to a lesson he'd heard in Graceful Waters Resort where anyone who tried to paint themselves as something above others in the community was quickly shunned.

Marvin had told him the story of a guy who'd started a motorcycle club and was constantly bragging about how much money he had. "Everyone quit the motorcycle group and the poor guy finally received the message. When you get to be our age it's not about having things. We've all been there and done that. No, the answer to happiness is to make the best of what you have today. There is no past and no future."

Marvin said the guy had moved to the more upscale town of Scottsdale where the wealthy had winter residences.

Assholes like Vincent deserve each other.

Mario kept sitting alone. He next recalled how he'd met a man in a Key West bar who had tried to befriend him. After several beers, it turned out that the man had recently found redemption and was trying to save everyone he met from a life of sin and evil.

Mario knew he'd looked scruffy but he didn't realize he looked like he'd been living like a homeless vagrant on a race to the bottom.

"Brother, I have been where you are and I can tell you that if you give yourself to God, he will save your sorry soul."

Mario had tried to brush him aside. "I don't need redemption."

"But everyone needs redemption. We are all guilty of sin and fall short of the glory of God. Christ's redemption has freed us from guilt. Give yourself to Jesus so he may save you as well."

I believe in God. Once I can retire, I'll no longer have to kill.

Mario stared at the guy. "If you know what's good for you, you'll leave me alone."

I'm not looking for redemption; I just want to have normal feelings like everyone else.

The man shook his head and walked away.

Next, Mario recalled how he'd met Sonia.

He'd developed feelings and grown sick of the cold shell he'd built in order to do the things he had to do.

My shell of rejection has protected me all these years but I'm ready to change. I think living in God's Waiting Room has already changed me.

He had already tried to open up and let Sonia know that he had done many bad things. "Being with you makes me want to change for the better."

At first, she'd been reluctant to believe him. "I've heard that bullshit before. People our age don't suddenly change."

"Just give me a chance."

Once when he'd been sitting for two days as he chronicled a mark's life, Mario had read where a hierarchy of needs placed the feeling of belonging just after physiological needs like water and sex.

For twenty-five years he'd felt useful, but he was only a servant who while residing in the bedroom next to Anthony Rizzo, didn't really belong there, he was merely guarding. He didn't belong.

He smirked as he thought. "Sonia and I could easily live in God's Waiting Room."

Mario knew the last step, letting her know exactly who he was and what he had done, would open him up to being judged as a cold blooded monster.

What if she rejects me and thinks I'm unworthy of her love and affection? That's what I liked about the Graceful Waters Resort. I could start fresh and no one would care about who I'd been and what I'd done.

Feeling emboldened, thinking he had paid his dues, Mario couldn't wait any longer to hear Sonia's voice.

He went into the hotel's gift shop, which sold prepaid long distance cards and cheap cell phones.

Mario went back into the bar and saw that no one had entered since he'd left.

Settling into the same seat he'd left, a fresh wave of guilt rolled over him.

The waiter walked over to him.

Mario pulled out a twenty and handed it to him. "I just need some privacy to make a call."

The waiter took the money, nodded and walked out of sight.

Mario punched in her number.

Sonia answered. "Hello."

Tears came to his eyes. He pinched the top of his nose in an attempt to refocus his emotions.

"Hello, is someone there?"

Finally the words came. "Sonia, it's me, Mario. Are you safe?"

Sonia explained all she remembered. She told him about being drugged, the black hood she'd had to wear, the boat ride to another island and being held captive. "Oh Mario, being kept in isolation in that shack, the walls closed in at night and I was often afraid I might be sleeping in my coffin."

Mario pictured her lying alone and being deathly afraid.

"Did they hurt you?"

"I'm okay. They didn't physically hurt me. How about you, are you okay? Are they done with us yet?"

"I'm fine. Baby, I'm sorry you had to go through all that. Do you have any idea who took you?"

Mario was afraid it may have been one of the guards he'd hired to protect Anthony for his birthday party.

With Anthony dead, they would have been looking for their next gig.

Sonia talked about how she didn't get to look at their faces. "However, the walls were thin and I did overhear them talking several times."

"What did you hear?"

"They called each other Dino and Leo."

Mario felt the punch to his gut.

My own family!

He couldn't speak for a moment. Then he said, "Did you hear anything else?"

"One time they mentioned some guy that I gathered they were taking orders from. The name was Alfonzo."

I should have known that Alfonzo was working for Vincent.

Mario tried to shake it off.

Maybe Sonia misheard the name.

"Are you sure it was Alfonzo and not Alonzo or Alberto?"

"No, I'm sure it was Alfonzo."

Is that the way you say thank you for all my years of loyalty, Vincent?

Mario was trying to control his rage. "Tell me once again that they didn't hurt you."

"I'm fine. I've been worried about you. They said that if you didn't do your job they would have to kill both of us. What job and when are you coming back to St Kitts?"

Now, I have more work to do.

"Listen to me Sonia. My job is done but I have a few loose ends that I need to take care off. It shouldn't take more than a few weeks. I'll be with you soon, I promise. I love you. Wait for me."

"Oh Mario, of course I'll wait for you. Do what you have to do to end this and come back to me."

"Love you, Sonia."

"Love you too, Mario."

71

M ario was in disguise. He knew he looked odd and that was the point. He'd gone to a drugstore and purchased a bottle of temporary blue hair dye for his buzz cut. He was also sporting Salvatore's black glasses with the white tape on one side.

He had introduced himself as Brian and was sitting in a travel agency surrounded by posters of places he hoped to visit with Sonia.

Sitting across from him was the sole agent still in the store.

Her travel agency had closed at 5PM. It was now 5:15.

She was raven-haired and in her thirties. Recently divorced she was putting in extra hours. "Let me get this straight. You want me to phone this Fred guy who's a prep chef and tell him that he's won an all expenses paid trip to Bermuda."

"That's correct Susan. The only catch is that he has to agree to leave tomorrow morning."

"Stop right there. There's no way anyone can leave that quickly."

She's not sold yet.

"Trust me Susan. You just tell him that he'll have to come to you here tonight, where you will give him his itinerary including prepaid first class airline tickets and hotel reservations."

He was playing the role of a southern belle with a limp wrist. "In turn, you'll be compensated, by me five thousand dollars in cash, as a bonus for a job well done. Of course that will be in addition to any fees you will make, for doing me this small favor."

"What if he asks me how he won?"

"Tell him the truth. A mysterious *friend* of his wants to share a week of passion with him and is paying his way."

Susan was now intrigued. "How will I be paid?"

She doesn't mind that we're gay.

Brian pursed his lips as he pulled out a brown envelope and slid it across the desk. "Inside is ten thousand dollars. Twenty-five hundred dollars is for you as soon as you make the call and he agrees to take the trip. If you do a good sales job, I'll pay you the other half tomorrow, as soon as my little prep chef is on the plane. Now please make the call."

The travel agent did an excellent job as the prep chef agreed to come to the agency within the hour.

Susan felt like she'd just won. "What about your ticket?"

"I'll catch the next flight after I know that he's on his merry way. That way he can rest up for a full day before I arrive. He's going to need his stamina." Mario winked at her.

Susan blushed.

72

Having successfully pried the prep chef away from his restaurant, Mario was feeling optimistic.

Still, there was no way Mario was going to pay retail for a diamond ring. He was far too practical, especially when he could buy one from a fence for a fraction of the retail price.

Mario had always had a dim view of fences. Especially after he'd found his wife raped and beaten and the police had told him to sit still until they could talk to him.

That's when I noticed that we'd also been robbed. Our new television, my wife's jewelry and my good watch were all gone.

So while the cops drank coffee I snuck out and went to call on a few fences I knew that bought stuff from druggies.

At the second one's place I found my wife's jewelry. I lost it and made the fence tell me who'd sold him the goods. When 1 went back to the streets I found out where the murdering bastard was crashing and beat him to a pulp.

He pulled out the address of the fence his uncle had given him.

Mario knew that a generalist fence always did deals even if they weren't always profitable.

In hot goods, time is money. If a fence can't sell it quickly, he'll dump it before the cops come snooping.

The fence Alfonzo had recommended turned out to specialize in jewelry and small antiques. Being specialized meant his business was somewhat intermittent in order to remain profitable.

Jewelry is always hard to trace.

Mario knew Sonia craved a diamond engagement ring. She had always oohed and awed whenever they had passed a jeweler's shop down where the cruise ships docked on St Kitts.

Personally, he found diamonds and made-up holidays like Valentines Day too romanticized and commercialized.

It's not for me. However, since Sonia lived through Vincent's hell I'm going to get her a nice one.

The jeweler worked out of his house. Mario looked both ways to make sure no one was watching before he rang the bell.

The man who came to the door was Mario's age but was about fifty pounds heavier. "Whatta you want?"

"My uncle said you could get me a diamond below wholesale."

"Who be your uncle?"

"Alfonzo Clemenza."

"Then come on in out of the cold, fool."

Mario had never dealt with an African American fence before. He entered cautiously. He focused his attention on a possible ambush as he followed the jeweler into his home.

"My office in da basement. Follow me. By the way, what you say your name was again?"

"I didn't."

Mario thought of the reason he was here.

Time has passed us by, but it's not too late to just have each other. Perhaps we can find the kind of bond that Marvin and Joan had.

The basement was set up with filing cabinets and work benches. A large table commanded the center of the space. On it was a lamp with a jeweler's glass next to it.

"You say you want a diamond."

"If you can sell me one at a large discount."

The fence knew the routine.

Another cheap skate.

"The problem with diamonds is like anything else, it's all about supply and demand. That's why stores prefer not to buy diamonds back from customers. The retail markup on a diamond and its setting is a hundred to two hundred percent. If a regular client paid fifteen thousand for a ring, the store might only offer them five thousand dollars. Most jewelers don't want to upset a client or undercut the mistaken notion that diamonds go up in value. That's where I come in."

"I'm not after a fifteen thousand dollar diamond for five grand."

"I understand but I don't sell no cheap glass."

"I want a decent diamond at a hot price, I don't want glass."

"The other problem is that today's diamonds all have cold laser inscriptions on them. If you want to avoid all that then, I have an excellent antique round cut one carat diamond that is worth at least fifteen grand that I can let you have for two thousand dollars."

Since he's giving his pitch, his English has improved.

"That's more like it. Let me see it."

The Jeweler went into a file cabinet and pulled out a brown

velvet bag. With a flourish, he opened the bag and selected a brilliant clear diamond. He placed it on a black cloth and then turned on the lamp. "See the facets and how they catch the light. It will make any woman swoon."

Sonia deserves it.

Mario hardened his eyes and stared into the jeweler's eyes. "Is it hot?"

"Look, you now know me and where my family lives. Trust me. You'll never regret buying this stone. It's untraceable."

He's really lost his jive accent.

"Can you put it in a nice setting for me?"

"It'll take me a day or two."

"I'll wait right here while you do it." Mario counted out twenty five hundred dollars and passed it to the jeweler. "The extra is for the setting and the fact I was never here."

The jeweler took a deep breath then exhaled. "I see. Alright then come back in an hour."

"No, I'm waiting right here."

Sonia is obsessed with making money stretch and as a result is frugal. I know she doesn't know how much I'm worth. If she did, I'd be worried she was after my money and not wanting me for the person I hope to become.

Once Mario had fooled Vincent's secretary into divulging that the Rizzo's current favorite restaurant was Mama's Kitchen, Mario had checked it out. That was how he'd known who the chef and prep chef were.

It advertised itself as a virtual gastronomic tour of Tuscany. Since Vincent's tastes in clothing, homes, automobiles and women all ran towards pretentious display, it made sense to Mario that his choice in restaurants would be just as ostentatious.

While Italian in spirit, the menu was in fact more modern. Reviews on social media raved about its excellent and extensive seasonal Italian menu, including magnificently prepared steaks and fish. The décor was in tones of black, whites and grays and boasted rich woods and leathers, all designed to highlight the patrons.

Vincent and Gina are probably regulars.

Mario showed up at Mama's Kitchen in the afternoon an

hour after the staff had reported for duty. "Can I speak to the chef?"

"Wait here."

The chef was a rotund man in his late forties who obviously believed in sampling each dish he made.

Mario was blunt. "I'm Brian and I'm looking for work as a prep chef. Can you use me?"

"Do you have experience?"

"I have and to prove it I'll work for free for the first week."

A smile crossed the chef's face. "This is your lucky day. Late last night my regular prep chef left me a message that he had a family emergency and would be gone for a week. If you can start right now, I'll give you a try. If you're any good you can keep his job."

"I'm ready."

Mario had spent more than enough time around Anthony's own cooks and hanging around restaurant kitchens watching Anthony's food being prepared to ensure his boss wasn't going to be poisoned.

After closely watching the food being prepared, he would then try preparing it on his own.

Anthony had even let him use one of the apartments back on the property on St Kitts so he could have his own kitchen when he wanted it.

Italian cooking had become second nature to him.

I know to limit the size of my own portions.

Vincent Rizzo was a man of habit and arrogance and he believed that taking his wife out to eat several times a week was like dating.

Besides, Vincent will be celebrating his win in getting out of the court case in Phoenix.

Mario knew that Anthony would fly Vincent and Gina along

with their syndicate to his house on St Kitts to celebrate big wins.

With Anthony and most of the syndicate now dead, Mario figured Vincent would still celebrate.

Beside, Gina hates to be domestic and has never turned down celebrating with her husband.

Having worked so closely with both Anthony and his cousin Vincent for twenty-five years, Mario knew all this.

Habits make you an easy target.

Mario was wearing a white apron and chef's hat since he was now the prep chef. He was also wearing Salvatore's black glass frame although he had to frequently clean the steam off the glass.

It was only his third day in the kitchen but he'd already been offered full time employment.

I hope Fred is enjoying the surprise prize vacation he won in Bermuda. Too bad Susan had to die, but I couldn't risk her ever talking to the police.

Mario paid the maitre d' and sommelier a hundred dollars each to let him know when the Rizzos arrived. "Mister Rizzo used to tip me at another restaurant, so I want to give him a special bottle of Italian wine. Hopefully the chef will keep me on if Mister Rizzo says something good about me."

The maitre d' was the first one to let Mario know that the Rizzo party of two had arrived.

Mario peeked out the kitchen portal to see Vincent and Gina seated in the middle of the restaurant where anyone who was interested would see them dressed to the nines.

They both have a kiss my ass arrogance about them.

Vincent should know better than to sit out in the open like that. He's too easy a target.

Vincent was wearing a shiny silk Italian black suit with a white button down shirt flashing a silk Windsor-knotted tie.

Gina was resplendent in a designer little black dress and her trademark diamonds. The necklace was an eye catching Harry Winston sensation that he had seen her wear on special occasions like Anthony's birthday parties.

The perfect packaging to let everyone know that Chicago royalty is slumming with the general population.

Several men came over to the table to gush and shake Vincent's hand.

Mario finally had to look away.

When the maitre d' and sommelier subsequently came into the kitchen, Mario gave the sommelier an expensive bottle of Giacomo Conterno Montifino, Barolo Riserva.

The sommelier smiled and cradled the bottle. "This Barolo is poetry in a bottle. Mister Rizzo will definitely enjoy this. May I tell him who it's from?"

"No, please don't right away. If he really loves it, then come and tell me and I'll come out to his table."

"Si."

He'd already injected the Batrachotoxin into the wine through the foil and cork before he'd come to work. At 10 micrograms/kg, convulsions and death should occur after 8 minutes. Mario figured that at his dosage it would be much faster.

This is the stuff they use to make poison darts.

Mario peered through the small round window into the dining room.

Vincent has gotten soft because he thinks he's invincible. He should have had a bodyguard checking out the restaurant.

Mario felt a cool sensation travel through his body as he

watched the body language of the sommelier. He presented the bottle with a flourish and then uncorked it.

He could see the sommelier asking if Vincent wanted to taste it first, which he never did.

I don't think Vincent's daughters will come looking for me. They have too much money and are too smart to risk it.

Instead the sommelier filled Gina's glass first then Vincent's.

Vincent raised his glass of red wine in the air while looking at his wife.

Gina reciprocated.

A touching final toast to each other.

Vincent sipped the wine in unison with Gina, their eyes locked.

First, they will feel paralyzed then mutely panic as their hearts seize up.

Vincent cocked his head as if he might have noticed something odd with the taste. He put down his glass and looked into his wife's eyes.

She returned the quizzical gaze.

A moment later Gina collapsed face first onto her place setting while her wine glass poured onto the table and then smashed onto the floor.

Vincent tried to attend to his wife but never made it, as he collapsed as well.

Mario had seen enough. He left his cap, hairnet and apron on as he headed for the rear kitchen exit.

He never saw the look of panic on the faces of the sommelier and maitre d'.

Feeling his heart thumping and a new energy flowing through his veins, he was feeling free and renewed.

Before he opened the door to the cold, he grabbed his winter jacket and pulled up the zipper.

Stepping into the alley, he was inside the freshly stolen Honda and gone within sixty seconds.

Welcome to Happy Hour, Vincent!

74

A s he drove away, Mario felt a sense of relief. He tried to balance it against the guilt he had been feeling since he had eliminated the travel agent.

I shouldn't have involved the travel agent or killed her. It would have been smarter to kill Vincent another way. But I can't dwell on it. I need to finish up without involving any more civilians.

Then he started to second-guess himself.

Should I forgive them and try to build a relationship?

With Vincent dealt with, Mario could now focus on repaying his uncle and his sons for their betrayal.

There's no sense in confronting Alfonzo. What's done is done.

I just need closure. For all I know, they are under contract to kill me. In my family, I guess money is thicker than blood.

Mario had a long history of switching up the way he dealt with each victim.

That makes it next to impossible for the police to connect them.

Anthony had seldom needed information from a mark, so Mario could dispatch the individual any way he saw fit.

Unless the kill was also intended to send a message to others.

That was when Mario would disfigure or inflict torture.

Whenever possible, Mario preferred to have kills appear to be suicides or accidental deaths so there would be no need for an investigation. Since he prided himself on trying to make each one unique, each was a challenge.

Those are my favorites.

Mario drove the front wheel drive Honda through the Chicago snow and ice like it was second nature to him.

He recalled a line he'd heard once. "If driving is better in the winter because the potholes are filled with snow, then you must live in Chicago."

He pulled in behind his Malibu.

Mario ditched the Honda by leaving the keys in it.

Before he took off, he turned the Malibu's heater up all the way.

Needing a few items to dispatch his relatives, he went to a local Walmart wearing his Salvatore glasses.

He purchased another box of latex gloves and an inexpensive 50-lumen headlamp.

As he was walking out of the Walmart he noticed a woman with an unruly child trying to sip a coffee in the Starbuck's area. He paused and watched.

The little boy was tired of shopping and was hot in his warm quilted coat. He was letting his mother know all about it.

Mario went into a stall in the men's room where he pulled out a latex glove and slipped it onto his right hand.

Ready, he left the men's room just as the woman was leaving with the now screaming boy.

She left her coffee cup on the table and hustled the boy towards the exit.

Walking casually, Mario passed the table and picked up the paper coffee cup. He dumped the remains of the coffee into a trashcan and placed the cup in his bag.

With the items he wanted, Mario drove to his uncle's house.

It was dark and he knew his uncle would be sound asleep.

He told me how he now has to take sleeping pills or his mind never shuts off.

Still he proceeded with caution. He broke into the basement as quietly as he could after snapping on a pair of gloves and securing the headlamp onto his head.

Inside the basement, it was dark.

Mario knew it was crowded. He had to immediately switch on his headlamp lest he trip. Surveying the contents, he could see nothing had been moved.

Each thing is probably a special memory to him.

Then he spotted the large gun cabinet.

It was as he remembered it, unlocked.

That's not being very safe uncle.

Mario opened the cabinet and found an arsenal of weapons. He examined several before he selected a shotgun and a pistol he felt he might need before he left town.

Forensically, it's a lot harder to prove that you shot a specific shotgun.

When he found the matching ammunition, he left as quietly as he could.

75

Before he had dispatched with Vincent, Mario had already found Leo and Dino's home address.

Since Dino was the oldest, he decided to start with him. Mario had already surveyed Dino's house for a few hours and determined too many people lived inside to make a quiet hit.

He knocked on Dino's front door standing with his hands on his hips as if he'd just gotten off a horse.

A young man opened the door and stood in front of him.

Maybe it's Dino son; maybe it's even his grandson... I'm so out of touch with my own relatives that I have no idea who he is.

The young man didn't speak. He just stood looking at Mario as if he were out of a cartoon.

Ink was crawling up the young man's neck.

Idiot! That's the easiest way to get yourself caught.

"Dino 'round?" Mario drawled as if he had just come out off a ranch in Texas.

"Naw, he ain't here," came the reply.

"Reckon I could catch him down at Luigi's Bar?"

"Maybe later. Right now he's at the plumbing supply store with my uncle," the young man informed him. "I 'spect he'll be home 'bout five or six o'clock."

"Thank you much." Mario bowed his head a couple of inches as if he were wearing a ten-gallon cowboy hat. "Just tell him that Tex stopped by and I'll be seeing him later."

"Whatever." The young man gave his head a quick shake and closed the door.

Back in his Malibu, Mario drove to the plumbing supply store. It was located in a rundown industrial area that looked like it was long past due for demolition.

This is a friggin' cesspool.

Surveying the other buildings it was obvious the store was probably doing better than the neighbor's. They were all closed and were now sporting boarded up windows and graffiti.

I hope there aren't any homeless nearby.

The plumbing store was badly in need of paint and the windows had been painted over from the inside. Still, with its chain link fence, it was the finest building within sight.

Prevents anyone from entering or escaping.

He knew it was merely a cover for washing their money but was amazed they would let the place look so bad.

I'll bet Dino and Leo do small jobs for people.

Want to get rid of your spouse; call Leo.

Has your extramarital affair gone wrong and you need someone eliminated; call Dino

There will always be problems that my uncle's family can fix.

Mario could see that each window had heavy metal bars protecting it. Out of habit, he parked away from any windows on the store.

He got out of his car and scanned the surrounding area.

If anyone is looking, it'll be either a drunk or a drug dealer.

The cold air smelled like sour milk and feces.

The plumbing store had a twelve-foot wire fence around it and its parking lot. It also had several Guard Dog On Premises signs prominently displayed.

Mario swore to himself. It wasn't that he disliked dogs; in fact, he liked them a lot.

He only hated their propensity to bark at intruders in their territory.

He did however hate people who used guard dogs.

I hate hurting a dog.

The only way in was by opening the sliding wide gate to the parking area where two vehicles were sitting.

Talk about discouraging any buyers or shoplifters from wandering in without an appointment.

He checked the lock on the gate. It was open.

They're too lazy to actually click it locked. Dumb shits.

He heard the low growl.

It had a reddish brown coat with a blackened face.

It's a friggin' Pit Bull.

When it saw Mario looking its way, it lowered its head an inch and intensified its growl.

Mario was sure he saw foam appearing on its lips and he knew the dog was ready to attack.

It takes a larger amount of poison to kill a dog than it takes to kill a human. I don't have the time. Besides, if I poison some meat, he may not eat it anyway.

Mario knew from experience that if he shot it with a silencer right behind and under an ear, right where the brain is located, it would die instantly.

But not before it lets out a death yelp.

Knowing what he had to do, Mario took off his jacket and wrapped it around his right forearm to prevent the canine's teeth from breaking his skin.

I hate to do this but I have no choice.

Mario hesitated then reached up with his left hand to remove the lock.

The dog let out a bark and moved in a crouch towards him.

Mario glanced at the rear of the plumbing store but saw no one opening a door.

I can do this.

He slid the gate open and the dog sprang towards him. Mario braced himself while lifting his right forearm.

He felt the dog's fangs grip and crush his teeth as deeply as it could.

Shhhiiittt!

Mario slammed his left forearm onto the back of the dog's thick neck to brace himself. At the same time, he jerked his right arm up as hard as he could.

He felt the dog let go and drop away as soon as his neck snapped.

Now I'm the alpha.

Sorry, buddy.

Mario unwrapped the jacket from his arm and put it back on.

Another minute and I'd be frozen.

He focused on the shop.

There was no movement so he went to the two parked cars and found neither one was locked.

Bad decisions.

Carefully opening each passenger door Mario was able to easily check the registrations in the glove boxes.

Bingo!

Mario considered his options and made his decision.

Luigi's will have too many potential witnesses. I'll hit them now.

Mario returned to his car, found his lock pick, put on a pair of latex gloves and selected the double-barreled shotgun and pistol.

He lifted his jacket and jammed the pistol in his back beneath his belt. It felt good on his spine.

Mario then put the shotgun into his duffel bag and stuffed a few extra shells in his pockets. He noted that the shotgun was an early model that featured a double trigger.

He reentered through the open gate and stepped over the dog.

Casually walking up to the store, he didn't see anyone nearby or looking his way from any doorways.

The sign on the front door said it was closed.

The window in the door had been painted over long ago. He tried the doorknob.

Locked.

No one trusts anyone anymore.

Using his lock pick, he jiggled the mechanism until it opened.

Before entering, he put on latex gloves, unzipped the duffel and picked up the shotgun.

It's payback time.

With his left hand, he opened the door while his right hand he kept the shotgun leveled straight ahead.

He swung the door open with the shotgun barrel then put his right foot inside the store.

No one behind the counter.

Music from a Classic rock station was blasting.

That's why they didn't hear the dog.

"Hello, anybody in here? I need parts to fix my toilet."

Mario heard the music stop then the sound of metal scraping on cement.

"Can't you read the friggin' sign?" Leo appeared from the back holding a gun in front of him. "We're closed."

Mario pulled the right trigger.

What was left of Leo's face was now on the wall.

Knowing Dino would be grabbing a weapon, Mario moved to his left and ducked down.

As he saw Leo's corpse collapse onto the floor, there was a thud, then another sound of a chair being dragged across the cement.

"Dino, it's me, Mario Clemenza, we need to talk."

A long three seconds passed.

"Where's Leo?"

"He's dead. But the good news is that you don't have to die today."

Dino seemed to be taking his time processing what he'd been told. "Why's that."

Mario dropped onto the floor and took a sniper's crouch aiming into the back room.

No target.

Using his elbows, Mario inched closer into the doorway that led into the rear of the store.

He crept closer as he raised his voice. "I just need your promise that you'll leave me and Sonia alone."

Dino didn't respond.

"Come on Dino, we're blood cousins for Christ sake."

No response.

Mario stopped crawling and took aim again anticipating Dino might rush him.

"Look Dino, I know Vincent Rizzo paid you and Leo to kidnap Sonia but Vincent's dead. There doesn't have to be anymore killing."

Still no response.

"Are you still in there Dino?"

"Ya, I'm here, I'm armed and I'm waiting on your sorry ass."

Mario focused.

He thought he could hear Dino's hard breathing.

Mario waited.

In a shaky voice, Dino blurted out his words. "You've killed Vincent Rizzo and now my brother Leo. Why should I trust you?"

Mario smiled and tried to sound as if he were talking to a new friend back at the Graceful Waters Resort. "Come on out here and we'll talk. As soon as we agree to bury the past, I'm leaving Chicago. I'm heading back to Sonia and St Kitts. I don't want any more trouble. Sonia told me that you both treated her well."

"How did she know it was us?"

Idiot.

"Look Dino, all I'm trying to do is retire. Wouldn't you like to retire as well?"

"S-u-r-e."

Mario heard the tension in Dino's voice drop. "Then let's

talk. Cousin to cousin... I'm coming in now, don't shoot me." Mario slithered slowly into the back room.

He saw Dino standing behind a chair, next to a desk and pointing a handgun five feet off the ground towards the doorway.

As Dino lowered his gaze, Mario squeezed the left trigger.

Bam!

It was over.

Mario stood up.

I'm getting too old for this shit!

He walked over to see if Dino might still be alive.

Unfortunately for him, he had a pulse.

He wouldn't want to live looking like that anyway.

Mario reached into his pocket and pulled out two shotgun shells. He opened the shotgun and ejected the spent shells. Then he inserted two more.

Looking at Dino, Mario pulled the right trigger.

That's for kidnapping Sonia.

Mario reached into a pocket and pulled out the crushed Starbuck's coffee cup. He looked at it before he dropped it onto the floor.

Nothing like a planted piece of forensic evidence to lead the cops astray. Two more down, one more to go.

77

PHOENIX, ARIZONA

U.S. Marshal Services Assistant Deputy Brown and Detective Garcia both arrived five minutes early to meet with Arizona's United States Attorney in downtown Phoenix.

They were shown into a meeting room and told to wait for the AUSA.

Five minutes later the door opened and AUSA Johanson entered. She wasn't smiling.

Both law enforcement men stood up.

She waved her hand. "Please sit."

Still standing, AUSA Johanson read from a piece of paper. "Last night in Chicago, Vincent and Gina Rizzo were found dead. They died simultaneously in a restaurant. Since there were no apparent wounds or injection marks found on the bodies, it is believed they may have somehow been poisoned."

Ingrid Johanson lowered the paper. "Well gentlemen, what do you make of that?"

Garcia spoke first. "That doesn't make any sense to me. If

Rizzo was behind the Happy Hour deaths as we've assumed, why were he and his wife killed?"

Brown connected the dots. "Unless... whoever Rizzo contracted to perform the murders decided to also eliminate Rizzo."

Johanson said, "Now why would a hit man do that?"

Garcia played along. "He wouldn't unless he was afraid you still had a strong case against Vincent Rizzo and he was still close to being prosecuted. In which case he may have been afraid Rizzo would give him up to cut a deal."

"I can tell you that the case against Rizzo was about to be dismissed so that may not be the motive." Ingrid Johanson was shaking her head and looked frustrated.

"Maybe it was an unrelated motive." Brown broke his silence. "Perhaps a rival syndicate or sophisticated gang had a need to take him out."

"From what we can tell," Johanson shook her head, "Vincent Rizzo hasn't been as active as he or his cousin had been in the past so I can't see that being the case."

Garcia reacted. "Or maybe Rizzo just stiffed the killer his fee and the killer wanted to send a message."

Brown grimaced as if the rationale was painful. "I don't see it. If the Rizzos were poisoned that's a very different method than he used for the kills in the retirement community."

Johanson looked at Brown. "And what does that tell you Marshal Brown?"

"It reinforces my belief that the killer is a professional. It takes no effort to pull a trigger or plunge a knife. What makes this killer a professional is his ability to do so in a manner that will not link himself to the other crimes."

Garcia's voice betrayed his attitude. "Well, the good news is that Vincent Rizzo's murder is not my case. It belongs to the Chicago PD."

Ingrid Johanson looked at both men. "The Rizzo murder resolves nothing. The case here in Phoenix has been stayed since both the key witness and the defendant are both dead."

She looked directly at Garcia. "The Happy Hour murders case however is still active and you need to resolve it."

She stood up and left.

Garcia looked at Brown. "A long time ago I discovered that a good detective learns to adapt. Failure to solve a crime is not the end of the world. You need to let go and move on to the next case."

78

CHICAGO

As Mario left his cousin's plumbing supply shop, he looked around to see if anyone was watching him.

I don't see anyone.

He listened for the sound of a police siren.

Nothing.

It was cold and he turned up the heater fan in the car. His mind was considering his next move.

Where should I stop? Do I have to take out their wives and children too?

What do I do with Alfonzo? Once he finds out that his boys are dead, my life is over.

He knew he had no choice but to kill his uncle, the only question was how.

Even though he was angry enough, Mario couldn't bring himself to consider looking at his uncle as he bludgeoned him. He didn't yearn for retribution as much as he just wanted to simply eliminate him so he could move on.

What if Alfonzo kept records of some sort that contain some-

thing about me? Perhaps I should just hold a gun to his head while I put a couple of those quit smoking patches on him that I've used before. Just slit the membrane and all the nicotine is released at once killing him mercifully.

That was the thought that resolved his dilemma.

For my uncle I need a more memorable event. One that will send a clear message to any relatives that figure out that I'm still alive.

He decided to blow up and burn the house along with any evidence it might contain.

I'll make it appear that Alfonzo was working on a bomb and must have blown himself up in a senior moment.

Mario settled on a common fertilizer bomb.

It'll make him look like a terrorist. The components are readily available and there shouldn't be much evidence if any left behind.

Mario still knew the area close to his uncle's neighborhood.

He drove to a garden store that was open until 9PM, even at this time of year.

He walked past the Easter displays of lilies and pastel bunny rabbits and purchased a fifty-pound bag of fertilizer. He selected the one with the highest nitrate content and placed it in his trunk.

He liked how the clerk didn't ask any questions or make any comments.

Next, he found an all-night gun shop that sold reloading supplies and he paid cash for a pound of black powder.

The third stop was to a hobby shop that sold him five bucks worth of parts that he could use to rig a cell phone as the bomb's trigger.

The last stop was an all-night super market where he bought more latex gloves, duct tape and a large glass canning jar.

On all the stops, he wore a Cubs baseball cap and his Arizona sunglasses. He also made sure to look down in case there were any security cameras.

He drove back and parked close to the hotel in an almost empty parking lot next to a dumpster.

Leaving the fertilizer in his trunk, Mario carried the rest of his purchases to his room.

Once inside he wasted no time. Putting on a pair of the latex gloves, he carefully placed the gunpowder inside the jar and then screwed on the lid.

Next, he opened up the cell phone and ran wires from the cell phone to the jar and duct taped it together.

He wiped down his room as well as he could.

Peeling out two twenty-dollar bills, he left them for whoever was going to clean his room.

Since there was no telephone or mini bar and having prepaid in cash, there was no need to check out of the room. He checked in his duffel bag where he saw the brown bag holding the silver jewelry he'd bought in Sedona.

That old Indian in Sedona was right about me. I've let go of the past, releasing feelings of anger and injustice. I'm a true warrior.

Mario grabbed his duffel.

He left the room with his contraption as well as all of his possessions and returned to the Malibu.

It took him two trips.

After he looked around and didn't see anyone sitting in another vehicle, he loaded the duct taped jar with its phone into the trunk next to the bag of fertilizer.

Satisfied, he drove to his uncle's house.

The lights were off in all of the homes on the block. It was close to midnight and he assumed everyone was in bed trying to get some sleep before they had to go to work in the morning.

Before he did anything else, he slipped on a pair of latex gloves.

Mario covered his interior lights with a rag and several pieces of duct tape before he opened his door.

As he opened the trunk, he scanned the neighborhood once again while listening for a dog or person that could spot him.

Since all was good, he made two trips.

First, he carried the fertilizer with the shotgun resting on top and placed them beside the rear basement door.

The lock was old and easy to pick. He went inside.

Using the flashlight he'd grabbed from the glove box Mario lugged the fertilizer into the middle of the basement next to an iron gas heater. He placed the shotgun on top along with a pistol he had taken from the basement earlier.

Next, he gently carried the powder filled jar and cell phone in a second trip into the basement.

He placed it all, cap side down, under the fertilizer.

Then he turned on the cell phone.

Why didn't you tell Vincent to find someone else to do his dirty work?

He scrambled out the basement door and walked to his Malibu. He opened the car door and slid in before pulling the rag and duct tape off the interior lights.

He put on his safety belt.

You are my last loose end.

Jamming the car into drive and accelerating, he drove ten long blocks away, just before a highway on ramp, and pulled over to a full stop.

The world is better off without you uncle. What I'm doing is social cleansing... I'll hold no celebration of life for any of you.

He twisted his shoulders and looked back towards his uncle's house. Mario pulled out his last disposable cell phone and dialed the bomb.

He visualized it vibrating.

He heard the blast.

I'll see you in hell uncle!

79

CHICAGO

Vincent's dead. Alfonzo, Dino and Leo are dead.
Mario checked his watch.
12:03 PM

With his business in Chicago over with, Mario didn't want to delay getting out of town.

Glancing at his dash, he realized he was almost out of gas. Two blocks later, he pulled into a gas station and went to the pump. It had a sign saying that all fills must be prepaid with cash – see cashier inside.

He gave the clerk a fifty.

A half mile later, he was able to turn onto an on ramp. The traffic was light given the late hour.

Things are starting to go my way.

He left Chicago behind heading south towards Miami.

He realized that he felt no guilt.

Mario knew he had been placed inside a knot that if undone, might kill him.

I've freed myself.

His greatest strength was his ability to never feel remorse. Mario Clemenza was a professional and the act of killing had always been the easiest part of his job. He left his ghosts behind him in Chicago.

If he had been a crow and it were the summertime, he knew he could make the drive in less than twenty hours. Being April he knew it would take longer so he decided to split it into three segments. As he left Chicago in his rear view mirror, he decided to catch I-65 heading towards Indiana.

Then I'll head to Nashville.

At first, the drive was dull. Large dark empty fields were waiting for spring. The occasional yard lights of farmhouses swept by.

Ahead was a steady stream of red tail-lights.

He tried the radio but the late night DJ was talking to someone about finding aliens in the trees, so he turned it off.

The boredom became brutal so he tried to focus on watching for suicidal deer.

He started thinking of the people he had left behind in Arizona.

I wonder how Marvin will do with his Joan gone. If there's a Heaven, Joan will be waiting for him.

Perhaps the cat will find him. He'll keep it away from the coyotes.

My money. What good is it? What good did it do Anthony? Without someone to share my days with, I'll have no life.

That is the curse of having lived for a few weeks in Graceful Waters Resort. Now I know what life can be like.

Barbara will hire one of the cleaning crews and knowing her, the house I rented will be forensically clean.

He smiled at his choice of words.

Then he hit the traffic.

Who can live in traffic like this every day and night? But hey, even the traffic on St Kitts is becoming a slow go.

He was still invigorated from killing his enemies and continued driving into the night.

He decided he wanted to give his brain a rest and just watched the white lane markers flashing by until he felt like he was being hypnotized.

In an effort to snap out of it, he turned the radio on once again.

Driving through the darkness of the night, he made it into Nashville at seven in the morning. He was exhausted and had a headache, so when he saw a red vacancy sign he pulled into the motel.

He paid the going rate in cash. "Got any aspirin or Ibuprofen back there?"

"It'll cost you two bucks a pill extra."

Mario slapped an extra ten bucks onto the counter. "Give me five of them."

He took the pills and room key and headed directly to the room.

It was a standard room. After his room in Chicago, this one looked good.

Dropping his stuff onto the floor, he dry swallowed two pills.

Since he wasn't on a schedule, he fell onto the bed fully clothed and slept until he woke at two in the afternoon.

He woke up feeling sweaty, itchy and constrained in his clothes.

After he showered, he placed twenty dollars on the dresser and left the key on top.

Within two blocks, he found a House of Pancakes and had breakfast with two cups of black coffee.

Afternoon rush hour shouldn't start until I'm well out of town.

He watched Nashville in his rear view mirror and took I-24 diagonally towards Atlanta.

Driving at the speed limit, he arrived on the outskirts of Atlanta in less than four hours. He found a roadside chain restaurant and stopped for dinner.

I wonder if Detective Garcia knows that Salvatore's left Arizona?

Will he put out a BOLO for Salvatore?

Perhaps I should have saved Cabella's body in a freezer somewhere then burned it in an auto accident?

He drove onto I-75 and headed south. After three hours, he was getting restless so he stopped for the evening in Adel.

Should I fly or take a series of boats to St Kitts once I make Miami? The boats will ensure there's no trail. I need to hold Sonia; I'll fly.

On the third leg, he drove at the speed limit, stopped for lunch and made it into Miami in seven hours. His first stop was a full service car wash. He had them detail the car. "I'll pay you an extra fifty if you'll make the interior sparkle like new."

He watched for two hours through a large window as two Latinos went through the inside of his car with chemicals and rags.

Trying to live by the values I found in Arizona is unrealistic outside of that gated community.

From now on, I'll only whack people who personally screw with me or Sonia.

An announcement came over a speaker that his car was ready.

It looks brand new.

80

H e slid into the fresh smelling Malibu making sure not to touch anything but the seat belt and steering wheel.

Finding a used car dealer, he parked and wiped down the steering wheel and seatbelt before he went inside.

Mario found haggling over the price to be boring. He ended up selling the Malibu for a fifteen hundred dollar loss. As part of the transaction, the dealer drove him to a hotel near the airport.

He checked in then took a cab to the airport to purchase a direct first class ticket to St Kitts.

If I can get on the flight without any problems, I should be good to go.

He took another cab back to the hotel where he decided to find something to replace his duffel bag.

Luckily, the hotel had several small shops catering to travelers. Browsing, he found a small hard cover bag that was approved for the latest airline regulations for carry on and overhead storage. He ditched his duffel bag in a garbage container in the rear of the hotel.

The next morning he got to the airport early. He wandered the airport stopping at each bookshop to browse. At one point, he stopped in at a Starbucks and treated himself to a double shot latte. Someone had left a newspaper behind so he flipped through it searching for a mention of Vincent Rizzo's demise.

There won't be anything about Alfonzo or his sons. The police will figure it was just another local gang thing gone wrong.

There were no mentions of Vincent Rizzo either.

"This is the First Class boarding call for the flight to St Kitts."

Here we go.

Dragging his new bag, he wandered over to the departure gate.

Handing the ticket to the gate agent, he felt relief to be heading home. The first class flight attendant welcomed him aboard with a smile.

He had been assigned the window seat and fell into the plush leather.

I tasted the bliss of unbound friendships in Graceful Waters Resort and I was on the verge of experiencing oneness with nature in my brief visit to Sedona. I feel like I'm on the threshold of a new life where unknown happiness waits for me.

Mario asked the flight attendant for a small pillow and put it against the window. Then he closed his eyes in an attempt to be someplace else.

Vincent, Alfonzo, Dino and Leo won't be able to bother me ever again. Vincent's girls won't want to get revenge. Vincent protected his girls from the truth about him and Anthony. They wouldn't connect me with him and Gina.

He tried his best to ignore his seatmate.

Hopefully AJ is dead or will soon die of an overdose. When you're young like he is, he can survive it. When you're a rich man's son and people are looking out for you, you can get away with it. Now that he's gone underground and he's on his own, only God knows what'll happen to him. If I ever hear about him it won't take much to pay him a little visit.

As for Frank Moretti and his girlfriend Naomi, if I run into them on St Kitts I'll just act as if nothing bad has ever happened between us.

Besides, perhaps I can convince Sonia to go on an extended honeymoon. I think she would like seeing Europe.

After three hours, Mario saw St Kitts through the window. He felt whatever tension was left in his body melt away.

His first thought was considering a drive past Vincent's old estate.

Na, Frank Moretti owns it now and there's nothing there for me anymore.

Realizing he'd severed his ties with his past he started thinking of his future.

Now I can leave the shell I've had to hide within and start my life anew.

I couldn't tell Sonia who I really was but now that I've made my break with Chicago, I can change. Since living in Arizona, I now know how to become a better person. Perhaps I'll take Sonia to Sedona to experience the vortexes with me.

I'm almost home Sonia.

Once the plane's tires touched down, he deplaned and made his way to the St Kitts Customs line.

One of the senior agents recognized him. The agent walked over to him and held out his hand. "Mista Clemenza. I haven't seen you since Mista Rizzo died. My condolences and welcome home sir."

This is a pleasant surprise.

Mario smiled and firmly grabbed the agent's hand and shook it. "Thank you. You have no idea how good it feels to be back here in paradise."

My past is now behind me. It's time to start the rest of my life.

81

ST KITTS

S onia had grown up loving the scent of wild orchids in the air. It was one of the blessings of St Kitts.

The sun was bright and lifted her spirit. She listened to the birds that were making peaceful background music. It was another morning on the island paradise.

Today however, was another empty day Sonia knew she would spend worrying.

She was still recovering from the shock and ordeal of being kidnapped and taken from her home.

Thank you, Lord for not letting them rape or hurt me!

However, she had many lingering questions.

Why would someone have to kidnap me to have Mario do something?

What in hell was so important?

Ever since Mario had called, she had become even more worried.

I don't understand.

They said Mario had to complete a task and then we'd both

be free. It's been days and he hasn't called me back. What in the world is dat man doing?

She looked in the mirror and admired the pearl necklace Mario had given her.

It was da week before he told Anthony Rizzo he wanted to retire. Then he'd come to tell me he had to leave.

Mighty fine necklace, but I'd rather have Mario.

She heard the soft knock at her door.

"Who be at my door?"

There was no answer.

With her nerves still on edge, she picked up her largest kitchen knife and put it behind her back.

Through her curtains, Sonia could see the outline of a man.

Who be that?

With the knife gripped firmly in her right hand, Sonia opened the door with her left and stepped back.

Her eyes went to the array of flowers hiding the intruders face.

She felt joy.

Mario couldn't help himself. He grinned ear to ear as he lowered the flower arrangement. "Sonia, it's me, Mario."

Sonia held out her arms and the knife clattered to the wooden floor.

Mario held the flowers in his outstretched right hand and returned the hug.

Sonia turned the hug into a kiss.

Mario whispered in her ear.

"I love you Sonia."

Mario stopped hugging and took a step backwards. Reaching forward, he pushed the flowers towards Sonia.

She took them and held them against her breasts.

Reaching into his pocket, Mario pulled out the small jewelry box.

I'll give her the silver jewelry later tonight.

Looking into her big brown eyes Mario went down on one knee.

Sonia closed her eyes and blushed.

"You now know that living with me may have its downsides, but all that is about to change as of right now."

Mario watched as Sonia's eyes opened.

"If you'll marry me, we'll never be apart again." Mario flipped open the box to reveal the flawless one carat diamond ring from Chicago.

Her eyes grew wider. "Oh Mario, stand up and hold me."

Mario did as he'd been told.

Holding the flowers in her left hand Sonia held out her right to grab Mario and bring him to her. Then she whispered in his ear. "I love you too, but we gotta talk."

ALSO BY FREDERICK WYSOCKI

- The Start-up
- A Timely Revenge
- Blood Rivals
- No Time For Fools
- The Arabian Client
- The Reluctant Spy
- Happy Hour Murders

If you enjoyed reading about Mario Clemenza, please consider reading his story chronologically in the following novels:

- A Timely Revenge
- The Start-up
- Blood Rivals
- No Time For Fools

If you enjoyed Happy Hour Murders, please consider:

- Posting a review on Amazon.com
- Posting a review on Goodreads.com
- Liking Frederick's Facebook Author Page at www.facebook.com/FrederickWysocki

ACKNOWLEDGMENTS

Denise Wysocki, Marvin Shadman, Kim Quinn, Susan DiGiovanni, Ted Woodrow, David Folsom and John Schoutsen.

A special thank you to Barbara Goldberg who won having her name (only) in this book by being the winning bid at an auction for a good cause. Any resemblance to actual events or locales or persons, living or dead, is entirely coincidental.

A special thank you to Josh Moulin who consulted on this novel. Josh was a deputized Marshal and has worked for the Marshal Services many times.

A special thank you to all of the people who shared their experiences about living in an active adult community.

Made in the USA
San Bernardino, CA
19 January 2018